ALTERED STATE

JULIE PARKER

This is a work of fiction. Names, characters, places, and incidents are products of the author's imagination or are used fictitiously and are not to be construed as real. Any resemblance to actual events, locations, organizations, or persons, living or dead, is entirely coincidental.

World Castle Publishing, LLC
Pensacola, Florida
Copyright © Julie Parker 2021
Paperback ISBN: 9781953271556
eBook ISBN: 9781953271563
First Edition World Castle Publishing, LLC, January 18, 2021
http://www.worldcastlepublishing.com
Licensing Notes
Cover: Karen Fuller
Editor: Maxine Bringenberg

For Connie.
Sister, best friend, champion.

CHAPTER 1

The world felt different when you were invincible.

Matter was intangible to us. Yet we didn't slip beneath the surface of Earth's crust and fall through eternity. Gravity remained our tether.

There were six of us in the team, strangers united by our desire to achieve freedom. Freedom from the needles, the wires, the beds, the steady barrage of doctors and nurses. Freedom from the misery of our lives, from our bodies holding us captive.

This was our first time out.

The facility making all this possible, Tandem, was buried deep inside the mountains surrounding the small town of Tuck. At the top of the highest mountain, the six of us attempted the experimental project Ghost Walk.

For the first time in all my sixteen years, I felt something inconceivable—hope.

Beneath my feet, I experienced the grass. I did not hover over it as I thought I might. Instead, my bare toes took in each feathery strand, our energies intermingling. My fingertips brushed hanging tree leaves. They moved slightly as if shying from my touch or blowing in a gentle wind. The rays of the sun passed through me, my ethereal body banished from the warmth.

Observing my new form, I touched my arms, my belly, and my legs, exploring, not pressing too firmly, or my hand would infringe upon my image, sinking within. Strange, but free. No longer did I feel afraid to breathe, to touch, to move. The others marveled over their new bodies as well, and the world around them. Their smiles were a novelty to me, having rarely laid eyes on them before.

"Casa, look," Benny, the oldest of our six, called to me. At six foot two, he towered over the rest of us. Standing on a rocky slope, he caught my gaze and stepped off, his feet gliding to the rubble below in slow motion. Shoulder length brown curls reaching his broad shoulders swayed, catching a current of motion. I waved at him and peered over the edge of the mountain, the depth of which must have easily measured a thousand feet.

Though Tandem served as a means for our escape, it also served as a holding place for our bodies that remained within. The separation was a small price to pay for this new lease on life. Our team engaged in a new technology. The term Ghost Walk was accurate, as we were seen outwardly as ourselves in what appeared as a holographic image. The image was slightly less transparent than a real hologram, or what I imagined a ghost would look like. My body was light as air. With little effort, I could will myself to lift and hover half a foot or so above the ground. Three scientists watched us, electronic devices in their hands, measuring and calculating our movements, filled with questions and advice.

"Easy does it, Ethan. Not too high, Mason," Anna directed, her bright blue eyes squinting in the sunlight, before asking me, "How do you feel?"

"Amazing," I answered. How do you describe something like this to them, the healthy ones? Walking high atop a mountain would be breathtaking, yet nothing spectacular. They could go where they pleased, move how they wished. They were not bound to their beds, exhausted by the smallest movements.

They let us remain outside another twenty minutes. Then we were corralled into the elevator and whisked deep inside the mountain. We wound through a labyrinth of tunnels before ending up in the lounge. A room made for comfort and relaxation, it hosted a bunch of easy chairs, a few round tables, even a TV. We were invited to sit and talk about our experiences. I was glad we weren't returning to our bodies. Not yet.

We could only hold these images for a few hours at most, for now. We'd tried it before, inside the safety of the complex. They assured us they were working on the technology. Very soon, in days perhaps, we wouldn't have to return at all. Our bodies would be put into stasis until such a time a cure could be had for our ailments. Eventually, Ghost Walk could allow thousands or more people to live their lives free of diseased or crippled bodies.

"We're close," Kade, the lead scientist of Tandem, informed us. He was tall, even more so than Ben. Broader too, with short, wild, dark hair, he attempted to comb into submission. He hadn't shaved in a week. The combination of dark brown eyes and stubble gave him a dangerous, sexy look I admit I admired. He'd starred in many of my daydreams. "Soon, you won't need to return to inertia. That's if you're ready to disengage."

We'd grown used to his shoptalk over the months we'd been there. What he implied seemed easy enough—like putting down the controller to a video game you were losing or setting aside a piece of fat on your dinner plate. Not what it really was—leaving our bodies behind to become ghosts. Really though, what kind of lives were we living? Shackled to a sick shell that served little purpose?

Three females and three males made up our little crew, none of us over twenty years of age. The criteria for the program had been to have an incurable debilitating condition. We all had something going on, but only Ben was critical. His life expectancy had expired six months ago due to inoperable brain cancer, so he was on borrowed time. My condition was cystic fibrosis. Sofia had multiple sclerosis, Aubrey, muscular dystrophy, Mason had spina bifida, and last but not least was Ethan, with Crohn's.

We sat around in the lounge, rear ends half absorbed by couch and chair cushions, elbows sunk into tabletops, and took turns talking about our experiences, the scientists interjecting their take on our progress. Everyone fairly gushed with excitement. It was easy to tell by our huge smiles how thrilling the experience was. Before, for some of us, just getting up to use the bathroom on our own was a big deal.

Afterward, we were directed back to the large room occupied by the machine used to separate us from our bodies. We knew, in these early days of the experiment, time was of the essence. None of us had catapulted back into our bodies yet, but the distinct impression was that although it wouldn't be fatal, it'd be far from pleasant. The machine they used allowed for a smooth transition. It looked like an upright giant test tube, all made of glass. Taking turns, we stepped inside onto a sterile white disk while a beam of light worked its way from our toes upward until it had scanned our entire ghost body. Then we would disappear back into our mortal cages, figuratively speaking. They were in the process of building four more machines. Now that it appeared the trials were a success, they were sure to proceed.

The process for getting us out of our bodies was more

complex. We were required to remain completely still. Dozens of wires were attached to our bodies, then a transportable machine ran down the side of the metal bed where we lay. It had a two-foot-long laser wand attached to it that lit up and moved over the top of our prone forms. They had three of these so far, but since there was only one pod we could transfer into, we had to go one at a time.

The transition back into my body was painless. It took a few moments of confusion before the familiar lack of oxygen, aching limbs, and heavy chest registered in my mind and settled on me again. Going back was hard. Leaving was elation. The first time had been frightening and exhilarating, getting used to the almost-weightlessness, the freedom. We hadn't been allowed out of the control room the first few times. It was large enough to move around without restrictions, as we'd accustomed ourselves to our new forms. A dance-room-like mirror took up half a wall, and we'd viewed our ghostly selves with awe. I'd been especially aware of Kade's eyes in the reflection, gauging what I'd see in them. Of course, he looked at all of us like a teacher would his star students.

At night, when the six of us were settled into our large room, we talked. Aubrey, a cute redhead with striking blue eyes, questioned that since they were able to transfer our consciousness, why not create mechanical bodies and put us into those? It'd be weird, of course, she admitted. But in this age of AIs and robots, perhaps it'd be a more acceptable alternative than being ghosts.

Consciousness transference was a daily discussion heard among the scientists, considering it was the basis of the experiment. We were extracted from our bodies but not downloaded into a computer or relocated to another type of host. Instead, they had apparently stumbled upon the holographic or ghost image in a fluke test done with mice. They'd described the technique to us in the way of dusting for fingerprints, making the invisible visible. The extractor had some sort of technology — far too sophisticated for me to fully understand or relay — that, during the procedure, coated our essence upon extraction. And the science behind it worked — we were visible to the naked eye. Ghost-like, but still viable, still us.

The debate among us late at night — when we needed a distraction from the aches and pains in our bodies that no amount of medication could conquer — was whether it was our consciousness that was extracted, or was it our soul? What was the difference? Was there a difference? Half of us believed there was. I believed consciousness was a part of the mind, a part of the body, whereas the soul was eternal, spiritual, never ceasing. Unlike the mind, which I was convinced would ultimately die when the body died. It was terribly confusing, to say the least.

Putting all the mumbo jumbo aside, I was elated with the experiment. I didn't overly think about the *how* more about the *what*. I was free, which was all that mattered.

Sofia's bed sat right beside mine, which was up against the wall. She struggled into a sitting position, having to lean against a bunch of pillows. The exertion left her visibly drained. "Casa?" Her voice was little more than a whisper since the room had grown quiet.

"Yeah?"

"What do you think is gonna happen to us, after?" Her huge green eyes always glistened as if on the verge of fearful or painful tears. Long blonde hair and a waif-like body gave her the appearance of a child of eleven or twelve, not fifteen.

"After what?"

"After the experiment's over. When our bodies are in stasis, and we're permanent ghosts. Are they gonna keep us here, or will they let us go home?"

"I dunno," I admitted. I hadn't really thought of the next step.

"And if they do let us go, how far can we get from our bodies, since they say we're technically tethered? I'm excited about what they're doing, but at the same time, I don't want to trade one prison for another. I mean, yeah, we'd be free of the pain, but we may be stuck up on these mountains forever. The whole idea is for us to live our lives. I know it won't be the same as other people, but we could still kinda have normal lives."

Normal? We'd be freaks. Phantoms. That part I had thought of.

When we weren't in hospitals, each of us had lived with our families, who were scattered across the country. Another topic of speculation for us was our tethers. If they couldn't stretch farther than the small town of Tuck, which was the closest civilization to this mountain, would our families pack up and move here? It was a lot to ask, especially when most of us had siblings in school and parents with jobs and friends who owned houses where they lived. If we must remain here, and they wouldn't move, what could we do? Where would we live? How would we live? No one wanted to rent an apartment to a teenage ghost. Even if they did, how would we pay for it? With money from a job? Who would hire us?

In preparation for this, my parents had already pulled up stakes and bought an old house on the edge of town. We had been forewarned that the tethers may not stretch. Instead of being forced to make a choice between living here or abandoning the project, my parents had opted to take the plunge. I hadn't been all that attached to my old home or my school or my friends anyhow. Since I'd spent most of my time being homeschooled and living in the hospital, I hadn't formed many attachments.

The look on Sophia's face made me realize how fortunate I was. I had someplace to go, but I couldn't say the same for the rest of them.

"If your parents don't move here, you can come and live with me. I'm sure my parents won't mind." I laughed lightly. "I mean, how much trouble would it be? You won't eat them out of house and home, and you won't hog the bathroom."

Apparently, I'd said the right thing. Sophia smiled at me and laid back down, settling the blanket over herself again. "Thanks, Casa. You're sweet. Good night."

I watched her eyelids grow heavy, and soon she was asleep. All of them were. How I envied them the ability to drift right off, whereas I pondered the fate of the world and everything else that stormed into my head as soon as I lay down.

"Good night," I whispered, though no one was listening.

CHAPTER 2

We all stood together in the Resting Room, a nice name for the place of not-so-final rest for our bodies. It had been nearly two months since we'd gone above and done our first walk outside. Today marked the one-week anniversary of continuously being in our ghostly states.

It felt strange saying goodbye to my body, watching myself being closed up in a tubular glass and metal coffin filling with icy mist. I looked serene, peaceful. A sleeping beauty waiting to be awoken with a kiss from a handsome prince. Who knew how long I'd slumber deep inside the mountain with the others, waiting for a cure? It could be years, decades, centuries. I'd watch time pass, and those I loved would wither and die while I lived on.

Kade told us to relax after the ceremony. Since we'd all been a little forlorn, we retired early for the night. We could sleep, I'd discovered, and dream as well.

The next morning, Mason was seated in the lounge when I wandered in.

"Hey," I said, taking the seat across from him.

"Morning." He smiled at me and resumed staring at the table.

His transparent straw-colored hair was tousled as usual—same as it'd been when his body was put away. Jokingly, one of the first things he'd told us about himself was how he suffered from the bad-haircut syndrome. Light brown eyes, always twinkling with mischief, combined with his crazy hair and freckled face, made him look like a character from a sit-com. Upon first seeing himself in the mirror in ghost form, he'd expressed annoyance at still having freckles. You had to look hard to notice them, but they were there.

His mopey demeanor didn't take a genius to figure out. I knew his problem because I felt the same way. Now that our bodies were stashed, it cemented our new existence. There were no routines to follow. No need to brush our teeth or wash our face, or shower or dress. Life seemed almost aimless, especially when it stretched out endlessly before us. I had to keep reminding myself there'd be more to do in the outside world.

Aubrey and Ben soon entered the lounge. We exchanged good mornings, and they sat down.

"This is messed up," Aubrey said. "It's like I'm not sure what to do. I laid in bed this morning and actually waited for someone to bring me in something to eat and help me to the bathroom."

Ben laughed. "Yeah, I feel the same way. Although it's great not feeling like crap. I can move without pain. There isn't a nurse helping me to do basic shit other people take for granted." The last few months had been particularly difficult for him. Chronic migraines, dizziness, nausea, and vomiting were a daily occurrence. A couple of times, he'd collapsed, and they'd whisked him away on a gurney to the medical wing. We'd all just stared at each other during those instances, wondering if we'd ever see him again.

"That's just it, though," Aubrey said. "There is no basic shit to do. Yeah, I like not feeling bad and relying on nurses, but at the same time, I feel kinda lost."

"I feel that way too," I admitted. "It's a different kind of life. One we'll have to get used to."

"There's also no making out. Falling in love and having kids, and all that other stuff," Aubrey said. "What kind of life are we going to have, other than observers?"

I had no doubt I wasn't the only virgin in the group. "Don't count all that out yet. Look at what Tandem has already accomplished. They didn't plan to just pull us out and leave us to rot. One day there will be cures. And when that happens, we can go back," I reminded her. Aubrey was impetuous, a lot like my little sister, Tess.

"When? In like a million years when everyone we know is dead?" she demanded.

"Relax." Ethan strolled in next with Sofia. "I can hear you whining all the way down the hallway."

"I wasn't whining," Aubrey snapped. She fidgeted with her transparent hands while the pair sat down. It was obvious Aubrey had developed a crush on Ethan. I couldn't tell now, but when she was in her body, she'd blush every time he spoke to her.

Out of all of us, Ethan, in my opinion, was the one who'd suffered the least. He'd been hospitalized for several weeks before entering the program. It'd been his first and only time. To hear him describe it, you'd think he'd had his legs chain-sawed off and been hit by a bus. Diagnosed with Crohn's the year before he turned seventeen, he'd not suffered for years like some of us had. His symptoms had come on hard and fast, forcing him to give up football and other sports he'd excelled in. He was angry most of the time and could be sarcastic to the point of cruelty. I suppose in his mind, his good looks and unfair diagnosis justified the liberties he took with people's feelings. Despite being an ass most of the time, I'd seen him at his most vulnerable. He loved his family ferociously and confessed to missing his dog to the point of having a physical pain in his gut not caused by the disease. So we let a lot of stuff slide.

"I heard what you were talking about," Sophia said. "Aubrey's right. It could take years. Dozens of 'em. Maybe hundreds."

"It might," Mason agreed. "But our bodies won't age in stasis. This is better. We can watch what happens in the world. We don't just wake up and have to try and figure it all out."

"I think we can all agree this is the better scenario," I said, trying to stay positive despite the doubts that kept me staring up at the ceiling at night.

We didn't have food and beverages to serve as a distraction from everyone's deep thoughts, so it was a welcome relief when Kade and Anna strolled in to talk to us. After a few minutes of polite conversation, they got to the point. Kade said the words to change our lives yet again.

"It's time," he stated, gazing at us proudly and with a little sadness. "We knew this day would come, and now it has. Phase two. Time to go out into the great wide world and spread your wings."

A pretty speech followed about experience, freedom, and pain-free existence—we knew what it meant. Elated as I was, I couldn't help but feel a tingle of what I thought to be fear.

They were cutting us loose. Like birds being pushed from the nest, they planned to send us out into the world to fend for ourselves.

"Don't be afraid," Kade said, taking in our worried frowns in a glance. "You'll all be okay. Great, in fact. Trust me."

Looking at his handsome face, I believed in him. Completely. We should have figured the scientists at Tandem would have plans in mind for our futures. Kade and Anna informed us we'd be free to leave in a few days, and provisions had been made.

I was already set since my family lived in Tuck. Mason's parents were in the midst of making the move here. They'd apparently rented a townhouse along the river flowing through town. Anna informed us that a family who owned a bed and breakfast in the center of Tuck had offered Sofia and Ethan rooms with them. They could act as guardians when their parents weren't in town. The B & B had plenty of room for Sofia and Ethan's parents and siblings to stay when they came to visit. It would be a temporary arrangement, hopefully, if the experiment of stretching the tethers was a success. Then, any of us wishing to leave Tuck could if we wanted to.

Ben's dad and Aubrey's mom — both single parents — would be in limbo, having to wait and see how the "Tether Test" played out. Each of them was immersed in their lives elsewhere due to important careers. If things didn't go well with the test, they would face complex planning with their living situations. This test would be a big deal for all of us.

Five days ago, Kade had brought several members of the press into the lounge to meet us. We were big news, apparently. Tandem was eager to show us off and to talk about the experiment's success. Kade had gone before the cameras, explaining Ghost Walk in layman's terms and how Tandem had just been granted generous funds to continue with their ground-breaking work. The press had interviewed each of us, and later, when we watched ourselves on TV, we laughed at our appearances and wondered what the world thought of us.

Immediately after, offers came streaming in from all four

corners of the globe. News stations, talk shows, major newspapers, magazines, even book deals were now on the table for our consideration. And surprisingly, people had come forward from town offering their homes and services in aiding us in our return to the real world. Kade had been adamant that although he didn't mind where we ultimately wound up living, that we avail ourselves to the press and public as much as possible for the sake of the advancement of the experiment.

Of course, we'd agreed. We owed everything to him and Tandem for our new lives. Although things would be crazy for a while, and we'd have to live under a microscope, he was right that the more people saw us, the sooner we'd be accepted.

Soon, the big day arrived.

We were brought together for one last get together in the lounge. We sat with Kade and Anna, having already said our goodbyes to the other scientists. Despite knowing nothing of their personal lives — if such a thing even existed for them considering, as far as we knew, they spent every waking moment in Tandem's facility — the pair had become like family to us over the past months.

"I want you all to know how proud we are," Kade said, smiling at each of us. His gaze seemed to settle on me longer than the others, and I hoped it wasn't my imagination. Leaving him was hardest on me.

"You'll come and visit us?" I asked, hoping I didn't have a dorky desperate look on my face. The others echoed agreement.

"Oh, I intend to make quite a nuisance out of myself," he assured us. "Don't forget, this will also be a learning experience for us all. As you know, Ben and Aubrey offered to test the limits of the tether. We will all be leaving the mountain together. Your parents are arriving shortly and will wait below. Hopefully, soon, we'll be in touch, and I'll be able to tell you there are no limits to where you can go."

"Just think of it," Anna said, twisting a shoulder-length blonde curl around her finger. "One day, Ghost Walk may be used to send people to the moon, or Mars, or to explore the bottom of the ocean. If there is no limit to the tethers, then you could go anywhere—"

"And not have to worry about eating and using the bathroom," Ethan interrupted.

"Or breathing," Sofia said, looking at me.

"What happens if you stretch the tether too far?" I asked, fearing Ben and Aubrey would catapult back into their bodies and find themselves locked in stasis.

"Don't worry. We have a slew of tech on the jet. We can measure readings of the strength of the ghosts. As soon as we see any indication of fading, we'll turn around."

"That's a relief," Mason said. He'd been especially great to watch as a ghost considering the limitations he'd experience with his condition. Though I felt somewhat guilty, like I was abandoning my body by leaving it behind, Mason had exhibited no qualms. "Why should I feel bad?" he'd said during one of our long nightly talks. "I want to live. I felt trapped, boiling over with anger and resentment like my body had betrayed me."

I could relate. We all could.

"Remember," Kade said. "Even in your current forms, you have limitations. You can't vanish at will. You have to move around like an ordinary person would, by walking or taking a vehicle to get places. People are aware of you now. Walls may feel thick, but you can pass through them. It doesn't give you license to be peeping Tom's or to stroll into places when they're not open, like libraries, theaters, or museums. As of right now, you won't set off alarms, but we're working hand-in-hand with other companies who are adapting to this new technology. Soon, buildings could be equipped with electronic filters that could keep you from passing through, or at least sound an alert if you do. Until that time, you need to be respectful of people's privacy and the rules of society."

We nodded our heads.

"Think of yourselves as ambassadors," he continued. "Together, we are ushering in a brave, new world. One with very minor limitations." He laughed at the face Ethan made. "At least, for now."

We piled into a helicopter that took us all to the bottom of the mountain, where a black sedan was waiting among other cars. My mom and dad, and little sister Tess were standing with Sofia, Mason, and Ethan's parents. They all hung back as we six got off the chopper and grouped together to say our goodbyes.

"Good luck, you guys. Don't forget, we'll be waiting for you in Tuck," I reminded Benny and Aubrey. "Hopefully, you'll come back with good news." We came in close together, so our energies intermingled—a ghostly embrace. After many good lucks and farewells, we went over to greet our parents and climb into our separate vehicles.

"Okay, kiddo?" Dad asked me. He knew the team was the only group of friends I'd had for any length of time.

"Yeah, I'm good," I said, smiling. "It's not like we're never gonna see each other again."

"Either way, whether the tethers stretch or not, it'll work out," Dad assured me, always one to see the positive in things.

"Ready to see our new house and your new room?" Mom asked me. "Tess and Dad and I have been working hard all week to have everything unpacked and to make sure your room's all set up." She was smiling but looked anxious like she was unsure of what to do with her arms. I knew she wanted to hug me but couldn't, and maybe now the ramifications of what I'd done were impacting her. It had to be hard for any parent to have a ghost for a kid.

"Can't wait," I assured her. They'd shown me some pictures of the house when they'd come for a visit. It sat on a large lot outside of town and appeared secluded, which was a good thing. I didn't want to have people gawking at me all the time.

Dad opened the trunk and put in my bag. It contained the stuff I'd brought to Tandem, mostly clothing and a few sentimental items from my old life. I wouldn't need the clothes. In our ghostly forms, each of us in the team had worn green scrubs — pajama-like tops and bottoms — the same as doctors wore. It was what our bodies still had on. At first, I wished they had dressed us up in something else, like regular clothes, but they were right when they said that soon we wouldn't care what we wore. Being a ghost, material things didn't register high on the necessity scale.

Tess opened the car door for me and waited for me to get in. She narrowed her gaze. "You won't fall through the seat onto the ground, right?"

"No," I assured her. "I'd have to push myself through. If I just relax, gravity holds me in place."

"Good," she said, and shut the door.

Everyone else climbed into the car. "All set?" Dad asked, peering at Tess and me through the rearview mirror.

"Yep," we confirmed.

The limo with Kade, Ben, and Aubrey pulled away. I knew they were headed to the small airport we'd landed at in the beginning of the trial. Tandem's jet, along with another group of scientists who'd gone down earlier, would be there waiting, ready to take them off to test the tethers. I hoped it was a success, and they would go far. Kade had hinted that he hoped they would be gone for some time, to see the world while they were at it.

We drove down the winding road away from the mountain and then got onto the two-lane highway and drove for about ten minutes to reach Tuck. It took only a few minutes to pass through town. Conversation in the car was minimal. I knew I was difficult to see since it was past sun-down.

"Just another few minutes, and we'll be home," Mom said.

Home. My hands attempted to clench. Anxiety felt strange in ghost mode. There was no pounding heart, sweating pores, or choking breaths. I did feel antsy, though, unsettled, like I was fearful. Of what, I had no clue. Change, I suppose.

We turned onto a narrow street, with only a few far-spaced homes on it, and drove until we reached the very last house. Dad pulled up the long driveway and stopped. I recognized the place from the pictures. It was big and old — two stories plus a full attic. The exterior was a combination of wood siding — painted red — and stone. Dad had described the details that they hadn't taken pictures of, so I knew what to expect. It had a huge kitchen, a living room — called a parlor in the old days — a conservatory, five bedrooms, two bathrooms, a creepy basement that had shelves with preservatives still on them, and an old coal bin. There was a big attic that wasn't creepy, apparently, since a few large windows let in lots of light. He'd mentioned there being other rooms, small in size, that could be used for a variety of things.

Everyone climbed out of the car. Dad opened the door for me since I was unable to manipulate matter. He opened the trunk and retrieved my bag while I got out.

The clear darkening sky overhead was filling with stars. A large moon had started its ascent, lighting up treetops of the surrounding forest that spread out to the sides and back of the house. The house sat on almost an acre of land, and beyond the backyard was hundreds of acres of crown land and a lake.

Being the end of June, the night air seemed mild, but I wasn't entirely certain. I needed visuals to gauge the weather, such as wind blowing the trees, rain, bright sunlight, snow on the ground. Of course, observing what clothing people wore on their bodies was obviously a clue. The scientists had told us we'd most likely imagine feeling the hot sun and the cold snow due to memory. We were more able to "tune in" to temperature than actually feel it.

"Sure you don't want to be set up in the attic?" Tess joked as Mom unlocked the door and waited for us to go in. Tess swatted a mosquito on her neck, and I smirked. I might be a ghost, but at least I wasn't getting eaten alive.

Dad came in carrying my bag. "Do you want to show Casa her room?" he asked Tess.

"Sure," she said, taking my suitcase from him. I followed her to the solid oak staircase curving up to the second level. At the top was a generous landing. A stained-glass window faced a long hall with several doors.

Tess stopped before each one and waited for me to peek inside. "Mom and Dad's room is first." It was a large chamber with a fireplace and three big windows. The bathroom was directly across the hall. It was a good sized room as well, but it wasn't like I was going to spend any time in there.

Next, she showed me two spare rooms across from each other, both a decent size with a pair of windows and queen-sized beds in case we had any guests. Tess's room was next, larger than the spare rooms. I noticed she had it decorated exactly like her old bedroom from our last house. Right at the end of the hallway was my room. The door to the bedroom was open, and there was another narrower door beside it.

"That's the stairway to the attic," Tess explained. "We can look at that whenever."

I did want to see the attic, but I wanted to see my room. It wasn't quite as large as Tess's, but it had a unique shape to it. I drifted through the doorway, Tess on my heels.

"I know mine's bigger, but I thought you'd like this room the best," she said.

She was right. There was a queen-sized bed, dresser, throw rug over the hardwood floor, and a fireplace with an armchair off to the side. Three of my favorite stuffed animals sat side-by-side in the chair, their glassy gazes staring off into space. The word cozy came to mind. I went over to one of the three windows and peered outside, anxious to see the view before it got too dark.

"Can you open them all up, so I can get some fresh air?" I asked her.

Kade had said that in time and with practice, we might be able to do little things, like lift a piece of paper or move something light across a table. I'd have to rely on others to help me with the larger stuff. Tess pushed up the glass casement of each window, exposing the screens. Moments later, a slight breeze brushed through me. After spending most of my life in the house, or the hospital, and then inside of a mountain, I was desperate to feel the air.

Tess put my suitcase on the bed and opened it up. "Do you want me to put your stuff away?"

"Okay, thanks," I said.

It took her a few minutes to hang up my clothes and arrange the other things on the dresser. She closed the case and slid it under the bed. "All set."

She wandered over to the door, and we stared at each other awkwardly. It was weird. We were only two years apart, and we'd always been close, despite spending so much time separated. She had always been full of gossip and plied me with the newest magazines and puzzle books whenever she came to visit me in the hospital. At home, we could lay on my bed and talk for hours about anything and everything.

But something felt different.

I knew I wasn't exactly the sister she was used to. This wasn't my ideal form of being either. But I wasn't sick. I wasn't going to have to endure Mom and Dad watching me with trepidation every few seconds, wondering if and when I was going to need a rest or a trip to the ER.

"I guess I'll help Mom with dinner." She looked embarrassed after she said it, as though she'd said something wrong.

"Okay," I replied and watched her turn and go. I didn't stop her.

I didn't know what to say either.

CHAPTER 3

Dinner was served an hour later. I sat at the table and watched my family pick at their chicken pot pie. Tess had milk to drink, my parents a glass of red wine each. I noticed Mom topping up her glass every time it reached half empty. It was late for them to be eating, almost nine o'clock. Coming to get me had muddled their routine.

"Don't you find this annoying?" Tess asked me, breaking the tension. "Us eating in front of you?"

"Tess—" Mom said.

"No, it's okay." I interrupted what I knew would be a lecture. "It doesn't bother me at all. Really. I'm just happy to be home."

Tess smiled while Mom inspected her plate.

"Tomorrow, we can wander the grounds, and you can see the lake," Dad said. "It's not too far of a walk," he unintentionally added, out of habit, no doubt. Before the experiment, I couldn't walk farther than a block, two at most, before needing to rest.

"I wish I could join you," Mom said. "I have a showing in Devon tomorrow I have to prepare for. I won't be home until about five." Devon was the next town over.

While my family ate, I thought about breathing. I could go through the motions of pulling air into my body. Whether it entered ghostly lungs, I had no idea. I didn't feel a heartbeat in my chest or achy muscles like when I had a body. Urges to drink or go to the bathroom weren't there either. I tried holding my breath and didn't notice any difference. Maybe what Anna had said about us touring the bottom of the ocean wasn't so farfetched. Maybe I could try it out in the lake out back of the house. Dad would probably freak out if I went beneath the water's surface and didn't emerge after a few minutes. That'd best be an experiment to try solo. I wondered if I could climb trees or if my hands would go right through the branches. At Tandem, the team had jumped off the high hills on the mountain, but never over the edge of the actual cliff. It was about as much as we dared with the scientists hovering. They hadn't warned us to not attempt anything radical once we left. I wondered if they'd be liable if anything happened. But what did we have to fear, considering we were nothing more than thick fog, vapor, smoke? The vacuum cleaner, perhaps?

Tomorrow was Sunday. My family had lived in Tuck for about two weeks. I wasn't sure if Tess had made any friends yet. Both my parents were realtors and had been able to secure jobs here, which had been lucky. I didn't know if they'd made any new friends yet either. School was out for Tess for the summer. When September finally rolled around, I wondered if I'd be expected to go to school. How I would hold a pencil or work a computer was anyone's guess.

When dinner finished, Dad went off to work on arranging his home office. He and Mom would share the space, he'd said. But Mom had hinted she'd checked out the small sewing room off the kitchen and thought that might work better for her. They'd had separate offices in our old house — I don't know why Dad thought they'd share one here. Maybe he'd felt guilty since the only actual dedicated office space had a great view and a fireplace.

Tess helped Mom clear the dishes, and I wandered into the kitchen and took a seat at the table where Tess had pulled out a chair for me. They washed and dried while I sat there, watching them work.

"Hey, I just thought of something," Tess informed me, a plate and tea towel in her hand. "You don't have to clean." She stared at me critically for a second. "Although, to be fair, you won't make much of a mess either." I was relieved she didn't say I hadn't been much help before anyway. That much was true. I'd not helped with the dishes or laundry or done any dusting or vacuuming for as long as I could remember. Tess had done all those things, though. I'd never heard her complain. At least not in front of me she hadn't.

"Kade said we may be able to move stuff with practice," I informed her.

"What? Like a poltergeist?" Tess asked.

"Tess—" Mom said, that warning tone in her voice again.

"Yes, just like that," I interrupted. "Mom, it's okay. Don't feel like you have to watch everything you say around me, okay? I want to have as normal a life as possible." I kept my tone even and gentle, not wanting to come off like I was lecturing her.

"Hate to break it to you, but I don't think you can ever expect to live a normal life in your condition, state of being, or whatever you call it," Tess informed me.

Mom looked like she was going to object to Tess's bluntness. I responded before she had the chance.

"Yeah, you're right. But trust me, this is better. I'm not sick, I don't get tired, I can still do stuff, see stuff, go places. Before, I was stuck in bed all the time or having to take it easy. Missing out. Now I can run for miles, climb mountains, do whatever I want."

"Yeah, to an extent," Tess agreed. "There's lots you can't do, but that could change like you said. On the other hand, I bet there's a lot you can do that I can't. The most important thing is that you feel all right."

"How *do* you feel?" Mom asked me.

"Good. It was weird at first, but I'm getting used to it."

"Well, Tess is right," Mom said. "You feeling good is the most important thing."

I got the impression she was trying to convince herself more than me.

We all sat around in the parlor by the fireplace later. Altogether, there were six fireplaces in this house. Dad had told me it was built over a hundred years ago when Tuck had a population of about four hundred people. There'd been no electric heat or running water in it back then. An old hand pump in the kitchen sink was their only source of inside water. The two bathrooms we had were from a made-over closet and small bedroom. They'd had to use an outhouse for years. Over time things were modernized, but the house still had old charm and character. I liked it. I'd liked our other house too, though it had only been about thirty years old when we moved in. I'd noticed the high school on the drive through Tuck. It was older than my last school. Tess would be going into grade ten this year. I would be a senior since I'd kept up with my studies with the help of tutors.

The parlor was cozy, with a big soft couch and a couple of armchairs. Dad had whipped up some Jiffy Pop popcorn, popping it over the fireplace. The smell was tantalizing, making me wish I could eat. I reclined in one of the chairs, conscious of keeping

myself from pushing right through. Tess sat on the couch beside
Dad, stuffing her face with popcorn, while Mom sat in the other
chair with a brandy.

"This is nice. Together with all my girls," Dad said, giving
me a wink. I smiled back at him.

"You guys really lucked out with this house," I said. "It's
amazing."

"I knew you'd love it," Dad said. "Mom wanted to go with
something more modern in town, closer to everything, but this
place happened to come up, and after seeing it, we just couldn't
turn it down."

"Mmm," Mom agreed. "It's about a twenty-minute hike to
town, or a couple of minutes by car, which is still close. Tess can
take the school bus in September."

I wondered if I'd be taking the school bus as well. Now was
not the time to broach that particular subject, however. I guess I'd
know soon enough if I was to be the only ghost in town and at
school. Once Ben and Aubrey returned, we'd know if we'd all be
stuck together in Tuck or if we could spread out over the globe.
On one hand, I would like not being the only one of us here.
Sure, the others were here now, but who knew how long that
would last if the tethers stretched? On the other hand, if there
were no limitations, I could go anywhere in the world. I had to
keep reminding myself this was a good thing. We were pioneers
of new technology capable of freeing the world. We'd just have
to wait for the world to catch up to us. In the meantime, I'd have
to endure the stares, the comments, and the bias that came with
being different.

"Ugh, I don't want to talk about school. I've got two months
of freedom ahead of me. Casa and I can hang out and do stuff,"
Tess said, talking with her mouth full.

At least I'd have someone to hang with. I could also go into town and see what Sofia, Mason, and Ethan were up to. It'd be harder for them, I bet, living right in the center of it all. I'd noticed the only hotel in Tuck overflowing with cars and vans. Probably reporters and TV crews wanting to get the latest ghost gossip. Kade had told us to do our part and make ourselves available, and I intended to. Soon. Maybe in a few days.

Mom yawned and soon had Dad and Tess yawning as well. It didn't appear to be contagious for me. Being comprised mainly of energy, I guess I didn't wear down and feel the need for rest.

"I think I'm going to head up," Mom said. She looked at me. "Honey, I'm so happy you're home with us." Glass in hand, she moved towards the stairs amidst goodnights from us.

Dad, taking his cue, got up next. "Don't stay up too late," he instructed. He bent and kissed Tess on the head. As he went to kiss me, he paused, suddenly remembering. He gave me a goofy look instead. We both laughed.

"You know I love you," he told me.

"I know. Love you too," I replied.

"Aww, and I love you guys," Tess said.

"Yeah, yeah," Dad said. He smiled. "So good to have you home," he said to me.

"Good to be home," I said.

"Okay, goodnight." He headed for the stairs, leaving Tess and me alone.

After I was sure they were both in their room, I looked at my sister. "How long has Mom been hitting the sauce?"

"Oh, you noticed that did you?" she asked with a smirk.

I didn't find it amusing, considering I was no doubt the cause.

"She's not too bad. Never starts before noon. Usually, during dinner. I guess it's been going on for about a year or so."

I'd been at Tandem nearly six months, and before that, I was too wrapped up in my own issues to notice. Tess yawned again and finished off the last of the popcorn.

"I guess I'll go to bed too unless you want to talk," she offered.

That awkward feeling crept up now that we were alone again. I knew she felt it too. She stood and brushed herself off, sending stray pieces of popcorn scattering.

"No, it's okay. We can catch up tomorrow. Should we just let the fire die out on its own?"

Tess glanced at the low flames. "Yeah, it'll be fine. Are you going to sleep? Do you even need to sleep? Can you?"

"I can, but I don't think I need to," I said, getting to my feet. "We do it mostly out of habit and boredom, I suppose."

"Cool. We'll hike around tomorrow. It'll be fun," she said.

I knew she was humoring me. How much fun would hiking in the woods be for a fourteen-year-old?

"Okay, sure," I agreed. "Goodnight."

"Night," she said, and headed off.

I stared into the flames for a few minutes, then decided I might as well see if I could sleep. My bed had been made up. If I wanted to, I could probably sink beneath the blankets. I approached the stairs, feeling melancholy for some reason. I was home. I wasn't sick. I should be thrilled. But something felt off about my being here like it wasn't right, wasn't natural. And eyeing all the wine and liquor bottles sitting at the area they'd set up as a bar, I think I wasn't the only one feeling that way.

CHAPTER 4

Next morning, I awoke to the sun shining on my face, the dazzling light stirring me. I laid still, blinking my eyes, listening to the birdsongs outside my window, taking in the breeze, which carried with it the scents of the woods and lake. Remarkably, I had slept deeply. I'd dreamed as well, similar dreams to the ones from before. I'd been in my body again — limited, cautious, sick — more of a nightmare. The clock at my bedside table read just past eight. Sounds came from below. Dishes clattering, voices speaking. Words were muffled due to the thick walls of the old house.

I lifted out of bed and moved towards the window, the fresh air and the sounds of summer drawing me over. The aromas of fresh cut grass, scented flowers from the gardens, and new growth from the vegetable patch filled the air. Being able to distinguish scents was a bonus, almost making me feel normal. The yard was wide and deep, going back over two hundred feet before it met with the treeline of the forest beyond. The giant oaks dotting the yard were alive with the movement of squirrels and dozens of birds. I felt part of this energy for life.

The noises below grew louder, beckoning me to venture downstairs. A full-length mirror in my room caught my eye as I passed. I stood before it, staring at my reflection. I looked the same, although transparent. My hair was loose and flowed around my shoulders halfway down my back. I'd yet to see if I could put it up or braid it. Tess was always doing something with her hair. Mine was light brown. Hers was dark. Mine was straight, hers alive with curls. We couldn't be more different, both in nature and appearance. I suppose that's why we were so close.

Used to be so close.

Without the need to shower, dress, or use the washroom, I left my bedroom and drifted down the staircase into the kitchen. My family sat around the breakfast table, eating. A chair was pulled out for me, and I sat while everyone said good morning.

"Sorry girls, but I got a call from my coworker, Jack, this morning. He's sick and asked me to take care of his showing. We can go out when I get back later this afternoon, or maybe after dinner," Dad said, drinking back the last of his coffee.

"I'm heading out soon for the open house in Devon," Mom said. "Will you two be okay until we get home? Dad will probably be back before me since he'll be in Tuck." She wore a dark blue business suit and cream-colored blouse that complemented her neatly styled blonde hair that just brushed her shoulders. Her light brown eyes appeared puffy and her complexion slightly florid, despite the heavy makeup she'd applied. Whether she had attempted to cover up signs of age or a hangover, I wasn't sure. Maybe both. She was still an attractive woman being in her mid-forties. Paired with my handsome father, they made a good couple. My father, being tall, broad, blue-eyed, and dark-haired, set off her petite, fair looks. Out of the pair of them, I think Tess and I both took after my dad in the hair and height department, although we were both slender in stature and brown-eyed, which we got from our mom.

"That's okay. Casa and I can go out to the lake by ourselves," Tess suggested.

"I don't know…." Mom said.

"They'll be fine," Dad insisted. "We can do something else later together if you like."

"Yeah, we'll be fine. At least, Casa will be fine. I'll be eaten alive by bugs."

I nodded my head in agreement. "Yeah, don't worry about us."

Not much later, my parents headed out. Dad apologized again, saying this wasn't how he wanted to spend my first full day back. I assured him we'd have plenty of time. I knew he felt bad. Their jobs meant their lives weren't their own, as we'd seen over the years. It must have been difficult for them both to work plus take care of a sick child.

After Tess finished her primping, she and I headed out across the yard.

"I'm glad it's just you and me," she said, walking at my side. We entered the woods and found a winding trail to follow.

"Need some sister time, do you?" I teased, hoping we could put our awkwardness behind us.

"Hanging out with Mom and Dad can be tedious." She let loose a dramatic sigh. Reaching into her pocket, she dug out what I soon realized was a pack of cigarettes. She put one to her lips and lit it up with the lighter she dug out next.

I stared at her in disbelief. "What are you doing?"

She'd stopped walking to light up, and I'd paused to watch her—no wonder she didn't want Mom and Dad around.

"What's it look like?" She spoke with the smoke dangling out of her mouth. "Don't freak out, okay? It helps me to relax."

"Aren't you kind of young to be smoking?" I tried to keep my voice level, not show what I knew to be anger boiling up inside of me. For years I'd struggled to breathe, and here she was destroying her perfectly healthy lungs.

She shrugged. "We all did it back home."

Meaning her and her group of miscreant friends. "I guess I missed the memo."

At least she had the sense to look guilty—not enough to extinguish the cigarette, though. I should have known Tess would do something rebellious. She was at the age. So was I technically, but surviving had been too high on my agenda to bother acting out like a normal teenager.

We started walking again. "Have you made any new friends in town yet?" I asked her.

She swatted a fly on her bare arm and another on her calf. "Last week, I noticed some kids hanging around the pizza shop. Looked like a bunch of townie losers."

With that attitude, she wasn't going to attract many admirers despite her good looks. Her lips were pursed between drags, and her body language revealed her tension. So much for her relaxing smoke.

"How are things? Everything okay?"

She shrugged and took a long drag. "Sure, why?"

"I dunno. Just wondering what you think of all this. You had to leave everything familiar behind because of me. Our house, your school, your friends. I bet no one's even asked what you wanted."

"It's not about me. It's about what's best for you." There wasn't even a hint of bitterness in her tone.

"But it's always about me. What about you? What about

what you want? What you need? Did Mom and Dad even talk to you before they made the decision to come here?" I knew all these questions were redundant, considering the deed was done, but I wanted to know how she felt. If she resented me.

"I'm fine. Besides, whatever I'm going through is nothing compared to...." She gestured at my ghostly form.

We both laughed.

"What about you?" she asked. "Are you okay with being a ghost?"

Was I okay? I thought about it a moment before I answered her. "I suppose. At least right now, I am. Ask me in another ten or twenty years, and I may feel differently."

"Holy shit, I hadn't even thought that far," she admitted. "I mean, what if you're a ghost for say fifty years before they figure out a cure for you? Your body won't age, and I doubt your ghost appearance will change. And then, wham, you just fly back into your body and take up where you left off, still being sixteen. I'll be an old hag by then. Damn, maybe I should put myself on ice too."

She wasn't saying anything I hadn't thought of before. Yeah, things were good now, but if it did take fifty years for them to find a cure, everyone I knew and loved would be old or dead by the time I resumed my life.

"Casa!" Tess yelled. We both froze.

I'd been so wrapped up in my thoughts, I'd strolled right through a tree trunk. "Whoa, that was freaky."

Tess dropped her smoke on the ground and crushed it out with her heel. She lit up another one, staring at me intently all the while. "How'd that feel?"

"Weird." I started forward again, and Tess followed. "Like we shared our energy for a second."

"Trees are alive. Did you hear anything? Sense anything? Did it convey how it feels about being a tree?"

"That's deep, even for you."

"Piss off. Come on, tell me. Did you get any impressions? Like how it feels about people, or having squirrels crawl around on it, or birds building nests in it? Does it hate it? Or does it like the company?" She wasn't going to let this go.

"I dunno. It's not like we had a conversation." By the look on Tess's face, I had to give her something. "If anything, it felt kind of solemn—you know, old and wise. Like the old man on the mountain that gives out advice about life."

"Did it give you any advice?"

"Yeah, it said no matter what you are, if you fall in the forest, you'll make a sound, even if there's no one around to hear it."

"Very funny. Hey, here's the lake," she said.

Good. Just ahead, the trees thinned, and I spotted water. We approached the clearing. The lake's surface was calm, there being only a slight breeze in the air. All around the water's edge, thick trees grew. The only open shoreline appeared to be where we came up to stand. Beneath our feet were huge, smooth flat rocks.

"This is great. It's so calm and peaceful," I said.

Tess sat down on the rock, crushed out her smoke, and began pulling off her shoes and socks to soak her feet in the water. I hovered close to the edge and tested one bare foot in the lake to see if I sunk or floated. When my foot hovered above the water, I stepped out with both feet.

"Hey, cool! You're floating," Tess stated the obvious. "You could probably walk right across the lake without getting wet."

"I'm wondering if I could sink down and see what's at the bottom. Now that'd be cool," I said.

"Do you want to try it? Stay close to the edge, though. What about breathing? Do you need to breathe? And what if you can't get back out? I won't be able to grab you and pull you up." She lit another cigarette. If she kept it up, her lungs would be toast by the time she hit twenty.

All the questions she asked had run through my mind as well.

"I guess there's only one way to find out." I moved out a couple more feet. With the sun shining, I could see beneath the surface. There was a drop-off to about a six-foot depth just ahead of me. Several large boulders and some old tree trunks rested at the bottom. One of the trunks was half in, half out, of the water. If I went under and got stuck, I might be able to use the gravity of the trunk to walk back out of the lake if I needed to. First, I'd have to see if I could will myself to sink.

Tess got to her feet. "I dunno, Casa. What if you get stuck down there? I'd get in some serious shit from Mom and Dad."

I wondered if she worried more about me or getting into trouble? Hopefully, the former.

"See that log? It only goes in about six feet. I'll try walking down it. If I get into trouble, I'll walk back out."

"Sure that'll work?"

I shrugged. "It should." I didn't want to debate it, so I moved over and stepped up on the log. I started walking into the water, putting my arms out for balance. I had to concentrate on staying on the tree trunk as I reached the water so that I didn't float above it. It was difficult but doable.

When my hips were level with the surface, Tess said, "Why don't you try ducking down from there? If you need to breathe, you can just stand back up."

"Okay." I did as she'd instructed and squatted down. Now my shoulders were submerged, and my chin bobbed on the surface. Though I probably didn't need to, I went through the motions of taking a deep breath and dunked my head. I gazed around. It was like looking through those night-vision goggles. Everything had a green tinge to it. *Cool.* I willed myself to just *be* and not worry about taking air into my body. My lungs—if I had them—weren't rebelling. Releasing my tenuous grip on the log, I let myself sink downward. Soon I was standing straight, my feet hovering over the sandy bottom of the lake. Tiny fish swarmed around, poking in and around the boulders. Seaweed rooted in the lake's bottom swayed with the current. Peace settled over me, experiencing life beneath the surface until a big splash sent everything scattering. I heard Tess's muffled voice yelling my name.

"Casa! Casa, are you okay?"

Her legs cut through the water, her hands splashed against the surface. I willed myself to float, and gradually I lifted up. "Here," I called. "I'm here."

"Holy shit. I was just gonna dive in, clothes and all! You were down there a long time. Like over a minute!"

"Sorry, I lost track of time," I said, steering myself fully upright until I was hovering over the water's surface. I moved towards the shore. "That was amazing. I didn't need to come up for air. Little fish were swimming around me and right through me."

She stared at me a moment. "Good, great."

I could see she was still unsettled. Both of us got out of the lake. Tess resumed sitting on the flat rock, feet dangling in the water. She wiped her hands on her shirt and lit up another smoke. I sat down beside her. We were silent for a while.

"Are you gonna tell Mom and Dad about being underwater?" she asked.

"Yeah, I think so. But I'll say I just leaned in and dunked my head, okay? I don't want them freaking out."

"Yeah, good idea."

We sat silent for a long while after that, me thinking about the ramifications of my newfound abilities, Tess thinking about God knew what. She was hard to read, and I didn't want to pry. I'd hoped being alone together, we could talk things out. Despite her acceptance of our new circumstances, I didn't believe she harbored no resentment. Maybe she felt cheated. Cheated out of her old friends and our old home, her old life. Cheated out of having the big sister I was supposed to be. The gap between us stretched even further, despite how close we sat.

CHAPTER 5

That night I couldn't get the thought of the lake out of my mind. Before, I'd been controlled by my need for oxygen. A constant concern, getting enough air into my lungs. Now, I didn't even need to breathe. I could survive beneath the surface of water and how many untold places as well. This technology was incredible, allowing that once thought unattainable to be granted.

Though it did have its flaws.

Despite my immortality and newfound freedom, I couldn't have any type of physical relationships—no hand holding, no kissing, no anything else. I'd never have a boyfriend, get married, or start a family. Not when I couldn't even get close enough to another person without sinking into their physical form. I couldn't even hug my parents. I would remain sixteen indefinitely. Who knew for how long? Say, twenty years from now, if a cure was found and I returned to my body, how would I feel about dating a guy who was physically my own age? Mentally and emotionally, I'd be much older than him. Then again, dating a guy who was in his thirties, especially if I still looked sixteen, would be kind of weird. People would think he was a pervert. He'd probably seem that way to me, too, even if we were intellectual equals. Socially this was so messed up.

My dreams that night were of loneliness, and when I awoke, it was to the excitement of voices.

"Casa! Are you awake?" Mom burst into my bedroom and woke me with her loud voice. Her face glowed with excitement. "Doctor Hunter was on the phone just now, and he said they've made it halfway around the world on the jet. The ghosts are holding strong. He said he believes there'll be no limits to where you can go."

Kade had called? Processing Mom's words, I realized there was now more I could do. No distance limitations, at least not so far. This could open up more avenues for Ghost Walk like Tandem had hoped. The scientists must be buzzing with ideas for the future of the project.

Later that morning, after Mom and Dad left for work, Tess and I watched a press conference on TV. Kade stood with Ben and Aubrey, beaming at the cameras. They were in Hong Kong, and my ghostly cohorts stared at their surroundings in fascination. Most of my attention, however, was riveted on Kade. Handsome as ever. Even more so as the thrill of success radiated around him.

Tess's eyes were glued to the TV. "Damn, isn't that hottie the lead scientist at Tandem? Doctor Kade Hunter, the guy who called Mom?"

A weird shimmer of something rippled through me. Jealousy perhaps. "Yeah, that's him."

Kade was speaking again, and we listened carefully. "We're going to slow things down. Stop and smell the roses," he said with a laugh. He was talking about continuing their journey around the world. "Knowing the technology can stretch the tether long distance opens up a world of possibilities for Ghost Walk, and humanity," Kade continued, echoing what I'd been thinking. "No more will the sick and infirm be tied to a body limiting their capabilities. Until cures can be discovered for so many debilitating conditions, Ghost Walk has proven to be an effective alternative for living a full life."

The woman interviewing the trio moved the microphone towards Ben and Aubrey. "Can you tell us how you feel?"

"Very good," Ben stated. I could see he was trying to play it cool, but at the same time, he was obviously thrilled.

Aubrey was the same. "I feel incredible," she gushed into the microphone.

The sky was the limit now. Not only could this mean new life for the sick and infirm, this technology could catapult Tandem into the future for all kinds of things, space exploration for one. No doubt there'd be talks with NASA about sending Ghost Walkers to Mars, just as the scientists predicted. No need to worry about spacesuits and sustainable crafts. Ghosts couldn't man ships or cameras, but they could give firsthand accounts about things.

"This is so cool," Tess said. "Now you can go anywhere. We could go to Disney Land, or Paris, or Hollywood."

"Yeah, I was just thinking about going a lot farther than that."

The announcer was talking to my friends about how they were enjoying their journey so far and how different their lives were in their present state. We listened intently until they went to commercial.

"What was that you said? You want to go somewhere else?" Tess asked.

"Think about it. We could send a crew of ghosts to Mars or any of the other planets we want to explore."

Her forehead crinkled as she pondered my statement. "You

think you could actually leave the planet?"

"Possibly. Maybe they'll test that theory next," I said.

"That would be cool. Hey, and you know what else?" she asked, warming to the idea. "If they want to check out planets really far away, they could maybe ship the bodies in pods, keeping them on ice, while the ghosts could talk about stuff they see along the way, you know, on voice activated equipment to people back on Earth. If there was any sort of problem, they could jump back into their bodies. Or if they want to colonize somewhere, that'd work too."

I thought about what she said for a minute. The bodies, of course, would have to be healthy, not like the test team. "Actually, that's a good idea. The machines we used to get back inside seemed pretty straight forward—they could probably set them up to work automatically. And what if it was the end of the world or something? They could make a huge ship to carry hundreds, even thousands of bodies in stasis. Then it wouldn't matter how long the journey to a new world was, as long as the ship had enough fuel. After landing, they'd just get back into their bodies and start new lives."

"Yeah, that would be amazing. I'd say they're probably far off from that technology right now, but the way things are progressing, who knows?" Tess said.

"I want to go into town and talk to Sofia, Mason, and Ethan. They'll be so jacked about this."

"Can I go?" Tess asked.

"Yeah, okay. I need someone to ring the doorbells anyway."

We watched the end of the interview and got ready to leave—well, Tess got ready. God only knew why she needed to doll herself up for a walk into town.

We headed out, walking the short distance to Tuck. I had a

vague idea of where to find my friends. Mason was at a townhouse along the river, which was closest, so we went there first. There were two sets of ten units, each facing the other across the water. We stood on a narrow footbridge and pondered both sets.

"Which one is he in?" Tess asked. She'd foregone her smokes since Dad was working in town, and she didn't want to take the chance of being spotted.

I shrugged. "I dunno."

"Hey! You looking for the other ghost?" a young boy hollered at us from a parkette belonging to the townhomes.

"Yes, we are," Tess hollered back.

The boy pointed across the river to the farthest end unit. "There, last one."

"Thanks," we both called out and headed in that direction.

"I hope it's not too early," I said. "What time is it anyway?"

Tess looked at her watch. "It's almost ten-thirty."

"Think he's up?"

"If he even sleeps. You said you don't need to," she reminded me.

"Yeah, good point. His family does, though."

"If I didn't have to sleep, I wouldn't," Tess said.

"Trust me, you would. Being like this isn't as exciting as you think. I can't do much. It's kind of boring actually when everyone else is sleeping. So I sleep."

"Not me. I'd be cruising all over the place," she informed me.

"You wouldn't be able to smoke."

She pondered that fact a few seconds. "Hmm, maybe that would kinda suck."

We climbed up four stairs to the front porch, and Tess rang the doorbell. A few moments later, the door sprung open. A harried looking woman stood there. She stared at us and seemed to register something, the look on her face changing from suspicious to curious.

"Casa, isn't it? From the team?" she said to me.

"Hi, yes." We'd been introduced at Tandem during one of the family visits. "You remember my sister, Tess?"

She nodded. "It's nice to see both of you. Mason will be glad for some company." She moved back to let us in. "Please come inside."

Tess and I thanked her and entered. I noticed how her eyes darted around outside before she shut the door. From what I could see of the townhome, it appeared Mason's family was still in the midst of unpacking. Boxes were everywhere, the place in disarray.

"Please excuse the mess," his mom said. "Things have been crazy since we arrived. We haven't had much time to get things done."

"It doesn't help that I can't do anything," Mason said, coming down the hall from the kitchen area.

His mom smiled at him, fondly. "Don't worry about that," she said.

He shrugged. "It's no different than before."

"It'll get done, honey, once things settle down," she assured him. "Why don't you and your friends go out for a bit? Just try to stay away from—"

"I know," he interrupted. "Let's go." He smiled at Tess and me and indicated the door.

Tess let us outside and swung the door shut. We walked for a bit along the river, avoiding town.

"Did you see Ben and Aubrey and Kade on TV?" I asked him.

"Yeah, good news." He didn't appear all that thrilled.

"Your mom seemed pretty stressed out," Tess observed.

"She and Dad had most of our stuff unpacked. But after Kade called this morning, Mom dragged out the boxes and started packing stuff up again. She and Dad got into a big fight." It clearly upset him, even though he tried to shrug it off.

"What did they fight about?" I asked.

"She wants to leave and go back home. Dad said they couldn't because they signed a lease on the townhouse, plus we already rented out our old house."

"That blows." I didn't know how else to respond. "Who does your mom want you to avoid?"

If he was in solid form, I would have sworn he fumed. "The press. They're crawling all over town. The first night I got home, they were camped out in front of the townhouses. I guess they caught wind of where I was staying. It was probably the same at the B & B for Ethan and Sofia."

"You haven't spoken to them?" I asked.

"No. I couldn't leave the house. There were too many of them. My parents were afraid I'd be mobbed." He smiled tightly. "Not that anything could happen to me, but it could to my family, and they didn't want me facing the press alone. This is the first time I've been out except for hanging in the backyard — if you can call that being out."

"You're a novelty. Things will settle down soon," Tess said, sounding way older than fourteen.

"Doesn't look like anyone's around now," I observed.

Mason shrugged. "It's not that big a deal to me. Mom's mostly the one freaking out about it. Anyway, Kade asked us to make ourselves available, and we all agreed. I mean, what we have to deal with here is nothing compared to what Ben and Aubrey are dealing with, I bet."

"Yeah, they're like celebrities," Tess agreed. "They probably have reporters on their tail at all times, even following the jet."

"They seemed to be handling it okay," Mason stated.

I agreed to an extent. "I think they're caught up in the excitement of the experiment now, and all it means for us. But I expect they're gonna get sick of having no privacy soon enough."

"Kade will watch out for them," Mason said.

"Yes, he will," I agreed.

"That guy Kade is hot," Tess said. "How old is he, anyway?"

Mason smirked. "Mid-thirties, I'd guess."

"Too old for you," I told her, feeling that pang of annoyance again.

We'd been walking down the river, and aside from a few people staring at us, it was relatively quiet.

"How have things been for you?" Mason asked me.

"Good. Haven't had anyone camping out at our place. Yet."

"Hopefully, the excitement will die down soon. Where I'm from, everyone keeps to themselves, you know? We lived on an acre of land and knew our neighbors and stuff, but the nearby city was busy, lots of people. Not a small town like this where everyone knows each other."

"Yeah, it was like that where we're from too," Tess said. "Houses were closer together though, and we knew most of our neighbors, some people in the city too. But not like here."

Mason nodded in agreement. He was no doubt thinking the same thing as me, that most of what we'd seen was the inside of our own homes and hospitals. And most of the people we knew were nurses and doctors and other patients. Being in the public eye was new to us.

"There's the B & B." Mason stopped and pointed at a large old home backing onto the river. "Sofia and Ethan are staying there," he added for Tess's benefit.

From where we stood, we could see a couple of vans parked on either side of the house and a small group of people standing around on the sidewalk.

"Maybe we could sneak in the back door," Tess suggested. "Or I could stay here, and you guys could slip inside through the brick."

"I dunno," I said. Kade's warning about invading privacy sounded in my head.

"It is kind of a public place, being a business," Mason rationalized.

"Yeah, but if we get caught, it'll be all over the news how we can just walk into any place, any time, and everyone'll freak out," I said.

"There is that," Mason agreed.

"Oh, come on," Tess argued. "Where's your sense of adventure? What good is it being ghosts if you can't walk through frigging walls?"

"There is that, too," Mason said. "You up for it?"

I frowned at Tess. When did she become so wild? She looked a little twitchy to me, probably itching for a cigarette. "Okay, fine. But maybe let's just stick our heads in and peek first."

"Okay. Wait here," Mason said to Tess. The back yard between the river and the house had several trees, so we crept from trunk to trunk, keeping an eye on the small crowd.

"So far so good," Mason whispered.

We were only about twenty feet away and decided to make a break for it. It was hard trying to run in ghost form. Kinda like those dreams when you're being chased, and your legs are suddenly awkward, and you forget how to function. Maybe I'd work on that skill next. We made it to the back of the house, keeping away from the windows. I floated up a few inches to glimpse through one, while Mason looked through the one in the back door.

"See anyone?" he hissed.

"No. You?"

"Nope."

I approached him, and we both stared through the window of the back door. "Together?" he asked.

I really didn't want to do this. I looked back to the river and saw Tess. She motioned with her hands as if to say, *get going!* Easy for her. What if we got charged with breaking and entering? Though technically, we weren't breaking in, more like passing through. I didn't think anyone would buy that it was accidental.

"Let's go through the door," Mason said, no doubt seeing the worry on my face. "If anyone sees us, we'll act remorseful and say the press is after us."

"Yeah, that's good," I agreed, feeling slightly better.

"So, together?" he repeated.

"Okay. On three. One. Two. Three."

We both pushed our heads through the door. I closed my eyes, I guess out of habit of protecting them. Before I had a chance to open them, a woman screamed. Loudly.

Mason and I both pulled our heads back out and took off towards Tess, forgetting our cover story. When we heard the back door open, Mason ducked behind a tree. I ran right through one and stopped.

"I know you're out there!" yelled a man's voice.

The door slammed shut a moment later, and still, we remained rooted to our spots. Tess had seen us running and immediately ducked down at the edge of the river, where there was a slight slope. From the house, she wouldn't be visible. *Chicken.*

"Casa!" Mason hissed. "Can you see if anyone's looking out

the windows?"

I had to push my head through the tree and peek. Mason saw what I was doing and did the same. We watched and waited until the coast was clear. Then we hurried the best we could back to Tess.

CHAPTER 6

"That was stupid," I fumed. The three of us hurried back in the direction of the townhomes. "Now, they'll never let us in. Even if we use the front door."

"Do you think they'll tell?" Tess bit her bottom lip, a nervous habit she'd had for years.

"Now you worry about getting in trouble?" I snapped.

"I doubt they'll report us. They're probably just on edge from having the press camped out front," Mason explained.

"I hope you're right," I said.

"What do you want to do now?" Tess asked.

Mason looked back over his shoulder toward the house. "That couple at the B & B are acting guardians for Ethan and Sofia. I'd bet they're not letting them out. They may let them make a statement from the front porch or something, but I doubt they'll let them hang around in town."

"So they're keeping them like prisoners?" Tess demanded. "That blows."

"At least till their parents get here," I assumed.

"Which could be soon considering they can take them home

now," Mason predicted.

"I hope we at least get a chance to say goodbye before they leave," I reflected.

"I have the feeling that after that little stunt, we won't be very welcome there," Mason said.

"So, what do you want to do now?" Tess repeated.

Mason shrugged. "I guess I'll go home. See what my parents have decided."

"You don't think they'll still want to leave, do you?" I asked him.

"I dunno. I know my mom wants to get out of here. She hates small towns."

"What about you? What do you want?" Tess asked.

"I like it here. But it's not like I have much of a say," Mason replied.

"Well, the good thing is we at least all have the choice now," I reminded him.

"Yeah, though I'll feel kinda bad if you're the only one left in Tuck. Your parents sold your old house and got jobs here," he reminded me.

He was right, though I hadn't wanted to face that reality so soon. "Who knows, we may decide we like it here," I said. "Once the press leaves and things quiet down, I should be able to move around without everyone gawking at me all the time."

"Let's hope," Tess said ominously.

I gave her another narrow gaze. Soon we were back at the townhomes, and Mason headed towards his place.

"Nice seeing you again. Both of you," he said, giving us a wave. "Come over any time."

"Thanks. And feel free to come by our place," I offered. Tess had told him the location of our house during our walk.

We decided to head home as well. As soon as we got to our house and went inside, Tess grabbed her smokes and headed out back.

"If you see Mom or Dad, give a holler," she instructed.

I was tempted to let her get caught. Maybe if she got in enough trouble, she'd quit. Mom was a pro at laying guilt trips.

~*~

In the weeks that followed, a lot happened. Not only with the project, but with my personal life as well.

More and more, I noticed how withdrawn Mom was. How she preferred spending time alone in the office, she'd set up for herself, her only company an ever-present bottle of wine. Dad spent a lot of time working, and I got the feeling he was handling his workload along with most of Mom's. He wore his guilt openly and passed most of the time he was at home apologizing to Tess and me.

Tess made some friends in town, and a couple of times, I'd caught her sneaking out at night when Dad was sleeping or busy working, and Mom was too sauced up to notice. I worried about her, and I began to think the speed at which we went through alcohol in this house wasn't all Mom's doing.

As for the team, Mason and I were the only ones left in Tuck—at least, as far as I knew. I'd heard rumors that Ethan and Sofia's parents had gathered them up within days of Kade's announcement and hightailed it back to their own home towns.

We never got the chance to say goodbye.

Mason and I saw each other as often as we could. I felt bad for him, considering his mom had decided to leave and take an apartment back in the city. She came to Tuck on the weekends to visit. He said she slept in the spare room and that his parents barely spoke during her visits. His little brother was only two, and his mom took him when she left. Mason didn't say it, but I think he felt abandoned. His dad had found a job at a construction company driving a cement truck. Bored and lonely, Mason spent most of his days at home by himself or hanging out with me while we discovered the many ways to avoid what remained of the press. He told me he could leave, go with his mom, but he felt obligated to stay with his dad since he'd given up everything to move here. I knew he blamed himself.

Most of the TV crews left town after a big fanfare when Kade, Benny, and Aubrey returned two weeks past. I assumed the last two of our team left shortly after their world trip, considering I had yet to lay eyes on them. Another pair I didn't get to say goodbye to.

And then there was Ghost Walk. Everything began moving fast. Now that tethers weren't an issue, it appeared the world was gung-ho for the technology and couldn't sign up fast enough. A bevy of workers arrived in town soon after the tether team returned. Work on the portal tubes, pods, and extractor equipment was full steam ahead, which would allow more and more people to partake of Tandem's technology.

Kade did a few more press conferences begging patience and assuring the anxious public that Tandem would soon be able to accommodate anyone requiring Ghost Walk technology. He stressed that precedence would be given to those who were the sickest and needed immediate attention. It didn't quell the rumors abounding that people with money were buying their spot on the Ghost Walk express. Tandem profusely denied this. My family hadn't paid for my place in the team, but I knew the project couldn't run for free, and those newly entering had to pay. Insurance covered the majority of the price tag—it was no doubt cheaper to put a body into stasis than to keep doling out for medical expenses. Those who faced financial hardship were promised that no one in need would be turned away.

Presently, instead of the town being chock full of reporters, it was close to bursting with the sick and infirm seeking aid. The hospital spokesperson begged people to be patient as they could no longer offer accommodations. Meanwhile, B & B's, the motel in Tuck, and the ones in Devon, and even private homes, overflowed with hopeful candidates.

Giving in to the pressure of the wealthy, a section of Tandem's vast mountain facility was privately funded for those seeking adventure. However controversial, Kade pledged that this avenue would in no way infringe on or delay the construction of the equipment being created for the sick. Instead, the influx of funds would help to speed up the process.

The tiny airport became a hive of activity, and Tandem's helicopter buzzed steadily up and down the mountain with its wealthy passengers. Soon it became commonplace to see ghostly apparitions jumping off Tuck's mountain peaks and partaking of other dangerous pastimes.

Jealousy abounded. People didn't seem to care which one you were—infirm or adventure seeker. They only cared that they or their loved ones were still awaiting their turn. With all the discourse in town, I'd been advised by Tandem to avoid the area since people seeing me may become hostile, not knowing if I was one of the wealthy playing around or someone who had actually been sick. I hadn't partaken of a lot of screen time with the press, and my face was not as well known as some of the others on the team, so I heeded Kade's warning.

The light of the full moon mesmerized me as I stood staring out my bedroom window. It was Sunday night, and Tess was out. If I'd had the notion, I could have been annoyed, being left out yet again. But after she relayed the negative attitudes running rampant in Tuck, we both decided I'd best stay home. Not that I faced any real danger, being invincible and all. It was more about adding fuel to a fire already blazing hot. Tess didn't want me hanging out with her and her new friends anyway. If that was an unfair assumption on my part, so be it. Being alone a lot with nothing to do had me feeling somewhat petty.

Just before midnight, a creak in the hall alerted me to a presence. I moved to my closed door and pushed my head through to look.

"Holy crap! Don't do that!" Tess hissed, frozen mid step.

Without invitation, she opened my door and came into my room, barely giving me a chance to pull my head free first. She shut the door and went over to stand in front of the fireplace, wringing her hands.

"What's the matter?" I asked, seeing she was clearly agitated.

She dug around in the giant purse slung over her shoulder, and I wondered if she was searching for her cigarettes. She pulled out her phone.

"I'm a little freaked out." She thumbed through her phone a moment and turned it around, holding it up for me to see. "Check it out."

I moved closer to peer at the image of Tess. Her arms were outstretched to snap the picture of a group of young people surrounding her, her friends, no doubt. Town lights and shadowy buildings were the backdrop.

"What? You and your friends engaging in debauchery?" Most of them had a smoke in one hand, a beer bottle in the other.

She made an exasperated sound. "No, not us. Him!" She used her fingers to enlarge the image, zooming in on a figure almost out of frame, not part of the group.

I looked again, leaned in, and stared, sure I was mistaken in what I saw.

"Benny?" I said aloud.

"Yes! Isn't he from your group? The guy who went with Dr. Hunter and that girl on the jet? Isn't he sick?"

I studied the picture. The image definitely looked like Benny. He wasn't translucent. He was in solid form. But how could that be? Had they discovered a cure for his body? A cure for terminal brain cancer?

"I don't get it. How can he be out?" I gasped aloud.

"Does he have a brother, maybe? A twin? That could explain it," Tess asked.

I thought for a moment. "No. He would have said. I would have seen him on family visits."

"Maybe he went into remission?" she theorized.

"He must have."

What other explanation could there be? There was no way he would have been kicked out of the program, not when sending him back to his body would mean a death sentence. He never would have demanded to return either. Unless he was unhinged? They'd warned us it could get to us, being this way. Granted, I'd felt myself becoming a little loopy, adjusting to being vapor. But no, over the months I'd gotten to know him, Benny seemed the most well adjusted of all of us.

"I noticed him as I took the picture. I turned real quick, and he was gone. It was like he was sneaking around, trying to not let anyone see him," Tess said.

"I could imagine him being afraid considering how hostile everyone in town is lately. And if anyone recognized and drew attention to him, the press would be all over him. His face is well known."

"But why all the secrecy? If he's in remission, great. It frees another stasis pod up for someone else to use," Tess reasoned.

"Good point. But then again, yeah, if another pod is freed up, people will be fighting over it. Kade probably told him to keep a low profile for now."

Tess stared at the picture on her phone for a moment as though it would give her the answers. "Yeah, I guess you're right. But why not get his family to pick him up then? Why stay in town?"

"He lives with his dad, who last I heard was working in Alaska. It would be hard for him to drop everything and come pick him up. And Ben is eighteen, legally an adult—he doesn't have to be released to a guardian. Knowing him the way I do, if he has a chance for freedom, he's gonna take it."

"So what should we do?" Tess asked.

"Nothing. Tomorrow I'll get you to call Tandem, and I'll talk to Kade about it," I said. She looked uncertain. "Look, for all we know, it's not even him. Maybe just someone who looks like him. We may be getting all worked up over nothing."

Tess gave her phone one last look then stuffed it back into her purse. "You're right. It probably is just someone else. The alternative is too bizarre." She appeared to relax a bit.

I smiled at her. "It's late. Why don't you go to bed, and we'll figure it out in the morning, okay? Let's not mention it to Mom or Dad either, in case it's nothing."

She smiled back at me. "Okay. Yeah, we'll figure it out tomorrow." She moved to the door and opened it. "Goodnight."

"Goodnight."

She closed the door, and I wandered back over to stare out the window. I waited twenty minutes, staring at the clock at my bedside table, then I pushed myself through my door and headed down the hall to the staircase.

Something was going on, and if I had a belly, I knew it'd be in knots. That had been Benny in that picture. I was sure of it. And another thing was for sure—I wasn't going to wait till morning to figure out what was going on.

CHAPTER 7

I made it out of the house with none the wiser. The night would be dark as pitch if not for the light of a full moon shining down on the surrounding trees. The wind had picked up, and branches swayed, making the dark shadows appear like boney swinging arms. In the distance, I could make out a dim glow over town. It was past midnight—the streets should be clear, people having gone off to find their beds. Movies were the main source of entertainment here, and I knew the last show let out at eleven. If my parents happened to catch Tess wandering in late, she would use the excuse that she'd missed the early show and had to catch the next one. Luckily for her, they never asked for details.

It didn't take me long to make it to the main street. Tess had taken her picture by the fountain set in the little parkette that acted as a street divider. All was quiet. Store windows were black—the only light came from streetlamps and from the shops that had little apartments up top. Even as I watched, some of them blinked off as people went to sleep. I wasn't sure what I hoped to find. Of course, I was seeking Ben. But if he was in hiding, it wasn't like he'd be cruising around in full sight. I moved between shops and buildings, weaving up and down alleyways, searching.

There was no sign of him. The odd straggler roamed about most likely patrons from the only pub in town, which was now closing. I made certain to hide myself if anyone came near.

A half hour or so later, I decided to give up and head home. If Ben had been here, he was long gone. I would have to get Tess to call Tandem in the morning, just as I'd said to her. Although with privacy laws, I didn't know if they would give me any information about Ben, even though I was part of the team.

Just as I reached our driveway, I caught a flash of something moving to the back of the house. It being tall and slim, I knew it wasn't a deer or raccoon. Curious, I headed in that direction. There I noticed someone at the end of the yard just about to enter the line of trees, moving fast. I wanted to call out, but I didn't want to chance waking anyone inside, so I followed.

I didn't catch up until I reached the lake.

"Ben?"

I knew it was him even before he turned around. As he did, I still couldn't believe my eyes. He remained silent, taking in my appearance with a touch of sadness and resolve.

"Are you okay? You look okay." For a guy with critical brain cancer, he looked good. If he could move as fast as he had, then he must be all right.

"They told me I'm well now." He attempted a smile, which I had the feeling was more for my benefit.

"So, you're in remission? That's why they put you back?"

He nodded. "Yes, remission."

I smiled. "That's awesome. Does your dad know?"

He seemed to think about it for a moment. "He does."

His voice sounded strange to me, as though I hadn't heard it thousands of times before. "Is he coming here to be with you?"

He turned so that he could see the lake. "No. I am leaving to be with him."

"In Alaska? It's so cold there." I laughed to try and lighten the tension I sensed in the air. Considering he'd been given a reprieve, I would think he'd be elated. Something was off about him — nothing I could distinctly pinpoint, but something.

He fidgeted with his hands like they were foreign objects, and the way he moved his body in little jerks, he looked to be wearing it like a piece of uncomfortable clothing.

He shrugged.

"Did you come to say goodbye? Have you seen Mason yet?" I hadn't seen Mason in three days — we were overdue for a visit.

Features of his face became a quizzical mask as he appeared to contemplate my question. "No, I haven't seen him." He looked guilty for a moment, then stared at me with a squinty gaze. "Caassaa." He pronounced my name like it was the first time he'd tried it out on his tongue. "Such an unusual name."

Okay? "I told you why my parents named me that. At Tandem the second night we were there."

"Refresh my memory."

The way he stared at me would have given me the shivers if I'd had skin. Alarm bells started ringing in my ghostly head.

"Spanish word for house. My parents went to Spain for their honeymoon, where my mom became pregnant with me. They bought a house as soon as they returned. Remember?" I watched him carefully.

Contemplating me, he smiled. "Yes, of course. Now I remember." His eyes scanned the area, and he suddenly seemed anxious.

"Everything okay?" I remained still, sensing he may flee at any moment.

"I'm...I'm not supposed to be out. Not yet."

"Ah, that explains why Tess saw you sneaking around town. Why aren't you to come out yet?" It took him so long to reply, I supplied him with a plausible answer. "Oh, they probably want to make sure you're adjusting all right. We've been out of our bodies for a while."

That answer seemed to please him. He nodded enthusiastically. "That's it."

"But you craved a taste of freedom, right?"

His eyes bore right into me. "Yes, freedom. It's been a while." He jerked again, as though shaking off his thoughts. "I should go."

"So, you've come to say goodbye?" I asked again.

He glanced in the direction of the house. "Yes."

"Then why did you take off when you saw me?"

"I...was startled, that's all." He suddenly seemed particularly interested in his hands again.

I watched him for a moment. "Yeah, I guess I'd be a little jumpy too if I was on the run from one of the most powerful companies on the planet. And it's not exactly like no one knows your face, you being all over the news recently. So, where's Aubrey?"

"I don't know," he said, fidgeting even more. "I need to go."

"What's the hurry? It looks like you're traveling light. Where are your bags? The stuff you brought to Tandem with you? Do you have any plans on how to make it to Alaska—plane, train, both? Do you have any money?"

"I have been in touch with my dad. We have plans. He is arranging everything." He didn't look to have everything in order to me.

"Is he sending a car for you? Are you headed to the airport?

You know it's crawling with reporters, right? Along with all the hopeful people trying to get a spot on the project. You'll be spotted, and there will be questions. Are you prepared for that?" I badgered.

His hands clenched into fists. "Yes! I know about all of that. I have a plan. I told you, I have a plan."

I held up my see-through hands. "Whoa, don't get upset. I'm just worried about you, is all."

"Yes, well, if the inquisition is over, it's time for me to leave," he snapped.

"Sure, there's just one thing." He walked past me and paused at my words, his back turned to me. "My dad's favorite movie is *Casablanca*, hence the reason for my name. The real reason. So, who the hell are you, and what did you do with my friend?"

Now he did look at me. "Clever girl," he smirked.

"You know what? I have a feeling you jacked that body, somehow, some way, and you're on the run. Unfortunately for you, my little sister happened to snap your picture. You came to get it, didn't you?"

Silence.

"Go anywhere near my house, and I'll scream loud enough to wake the dead. Whoever you are, whatever you are, you're wearing skin, therefore, are no longer invincible."

He went to leave again, and I had no means to stop him except with threats. "I'll tell Kade. He has half the world on stand-by right now and every resource available to mankind. He will hunt you down."

He stopped and slowly turned. His face was a mask of anger. "Kade," he practically spat. "Who do you think put me in here?" He walked right up and pointed a finger at my face. "Stop seeing him as the hero, you little fool. If you had any sense at all, you would leave. Gather up your family and get as far away from here as fast as you can. Don't look back."

So now he was attacking Kade? He had it right. Kade was my hero, my knight. He was the one who had freed me from a dungeon of pain and torture. "Listen, smart guy. That body you stole has terminal brain cancer. How far do you think you're gonna get?"

"No longer. It's perfectly healthy," he assured me.

"Ben is in remission?" I was suddenly furious. "That's why you stole his body? You're one of the sick, aren't you? You saw an opportunity, and you took it. Never mind that you've stolen an innocent person's body. My friend's body. What's the matter? You couldn't take it being a ghost, so you helped yourself to the next available body and fled? You're a coward."

He moved back from me. "You're right about that. I am a coward. It's why I'm running."

I made a grab for his arm as he turned away. I passed right through him. "How far do you think you'll get on foot? As soon as I get back to my house, I'll wake someone to call Tandem. They will be all over you before you reach the next town."

He spun around, and we glared at each other. "You still don't get it. Go ahead, rush to your house, I can't stop you. But before you get someone to make that call, get them to look up Kade Hunter instead. It may surprise you to discover he's not who he makes himself out to be."

"What are you talking about? Kade Hunter is the world's most ingenious scientist."

He sneered. "For the past ten years, maybe. Before that, he was a C average high school dropout who only cared about playing guitar."

"A lot can happen in ten years." I wasn't about to believe

anything he said.

"Ten years ago, Kade Hunter and Anna Durst were hiking in the mountains outside of Tuck. They disappeared for two weeks, then miraculously returned, telling tales about enormous caves. Their families were amazed at the change in their behaviors. Both of them had become focused, incredibly intelligent people. Not long after, they started a scientific foundation built in those very mountains."

"So?" Everyone knew the story of how Kade, with the help of Anna, had come up with the idea for Tandem while hiking in the mountains.

"Ask yourself how a high school dropout suddenly became one of the smartest human beings on Earth."

The way his eyes bore into me looked like he was willing me to find the answer.

"I don't know. Divine intervention?" I snapped.

"Intervention indeed."

I gawked at him. "Are you implying that Kade and Anna aren't the same people they were when they came down from the mountain? That they're someone else, just like you?"

His silence spoke volumes.

"Impossible. The technology is new. I was part of the test group, the first ever to try the experiment."

"Were you?"

I didn't like the way his eyebrow arched when he said that.

"I'm leaving now. I suggest you do the same," he advised.

"I'm not going anywhere. Not while my body is up in that mountaintop," I informed him.

He laughed without feeling. "Your body is already gone. Or soon will be."

What the hell was he talking about? Before I could question

him further, he took off. I was in too much shock to follow him. Everything in me screamed, *No!* We had spent six months with those scientists—I knew them. I knew Kade. He was kind and compassionate and dedicated to us, to the program, to helping people. So was Anna. There was no way they were the manipulative body snatchers that paranoid jerk tried to paint them as. He was lying. Stalling, no doubt. Trying to make me doubt Kade so I wouldn't go running to him.

I started moving towards the house, my thoughts whirling like mad. Though I tried to deny what I'd heard, some of it had a ring of truth to it. It would be easy enough to look up Kade Hunter's history, and yes, I may discover that he had, in fact, been a C student and a dropout, but what about the other stuff? It was insane. If Kade and Anna had this technology to Ghost Walk people for ten years, then why wait? Why not introduce it to the world earlier?

Maybe they didn't wait? the little voice inside my transparent head whispered. Maybe there'd been others.

At the house, I contemplated my dilemma as I pushed through the door and went upstairs. Outside of Tess's bedroom, I could make out the sounds of her snoring. I pushed through her door and approached the bed.

"Tess," I hissed.

She rolled over, ignoring me.

"Tess! Wake up."

"What?" She rolled back over and propped herself up on an elbow to stare at me with blurry eyes. "Casa? Whatsa matter?"

"I found him." She stared at me, blankly. "Ben," I clarified.

That got her attention. "Really? How was he?"

"He's fine. But look, I need you to cover for me with Mom and Dad."

"What do you mean? Why?" She rubbed her eyes like a little kid.

I needed her help, but I also needed to protect her. Whoever was inhabiting Ben's body was probably long gone, but I couldn't be sure. "I need to go to Tandem. Now. I have to see Kade."

"Can't we call him? In the morning?" she added pointedly.

"No, it's too important to wait. And listen, if you happen to see Ben anywhere, avoid him."

"Why? What's going on?"

I had to give her something. I knew my little sister. If she felt like she was being left out of the loop, she'd dig and dig until she found her answers. "Ben's in remission."

"That's good. Great. Wait. How do you know for sure? Did you see him?"

"Yes. I wanted some answers, so I went looking for him in town. I didn't see him, but when I got back here, I saw someone sneaking around. He saw me as well and took off. I followed and caught up to him at the lake."

She stared at me, impressed as if she was the only one capable of doing something on the sly. I wasn't sure if I should be insulted or proud.

Then came the barrage of questions. "Why's he sneaking around? What's he doing here? Did he break out of Tandem? Are they searching for him?"

"Keep your voice down!" I hissed.

"Okay, okay. What are you gonna do? Are you gonna rat him out?"

"I don't know yet. First, I need answers, and I can only find them at Tandem."

She narrowed her gaze at me, speculating. "There's something else going on. What aren't you telling me?"

I sighed. "Look, what I tell you has to be kept in strictest confidence, okay?"

She nodded vigorously.

I hoped I was doing the right thing. It needed to be crystal clear to her, though. She had to avoid Ben at all costs. "Ben isn't Ben."

"What?"

"Ben's body is in remission. He's fine. Only he's not fine, 'cause the person in Ben's body is not Ben."

"Holy shit!"

"Shhhh!"

"Holy shit!" she repeated in a whisper.

"Yeah, someone jacked his body. Probably one of those rich sick people up there couldn't handle it being a ghost. They saw the opportunity, and they took it."

"But how? How could someone just steal a body? It doesn't make any sense. I was there when they went over the process with you and Mom and Dad. Someone would have to prepare Ben's body, which may be even more work since your bodies are now in stasis, then help whoever-it-is that's occupying him now to get in there. He couldn't have done it alone."

"I know. That's why I need to go to Tandem. Someone helped him. I need to figure out who," I said.

"Do you think he paid someone to do it? That there's some kind of racket going on? God, what if the real Ben sees himself walking around?"

"That's what I'm thinking. It's why I need to go up there in person. I need to talk to Kade."

"You don't think he has anything to do with it, do you?"

"Absolutely not," I assured her. No way was I about to tell her that Kade may not be Kade either.

"I still don't know why you can't just call. Tandem is a long way up. Calling would be faster. If Kade has any doubts, you could send him the picture I took."

"I can't call up there because I don't know who to trust." Before she could argue, I continued. "You need to delete that picture for your own safety. I warned that thief he'd stolen a body half the world would recognize. Not too bright."

"That's what he was doing here, wasn't it? He knew I took the picture, and he wants to destroy the evidence." She visibly trembled.

"Don't worry, I think I scared him off. I told him I was gonna call Tandem, so he's probably high tailing it out of here. But just in case, be careful."

"That's why he was slinking around. What a snake."

"I know. We can't let him get away with it," I insisted.

She started climbing out of bed. "I'm coming with you."

"What? No! No way. You can't." She stared at me with hurt in her eyes. "Look, I'm sorry, but like you said, Tandem is a long way up. I don't get tired, I can move through walls, I can't get hurt. Besides, I need you to do what you do best—lie to Mom and Dad."

She smiled. "Okay. I see your point. I know you can't be hurt, but be careful anyway. Maybe you should take Mason with you? I'm sure he'll be as pissed as you to hear what's happened to Ben."

Maybe she was right. Two ghost heads were better than one. "Okay, I'll go over there first. It's on the way anyway."

"This is so messed up."

"I know. Go back to bed. Try and get some sleep. Hopefully, Mom and Dad will leave for work before they figure out I'm gone. If not, make something up. Tell them I went to the lake," I suggested.

"And what about this afternoon? Do you think you'll be home by then?" she asked, then gnawed away at her bottom lip.

"Hopefully. I don't know. If not, I'm sure you'll think of something to tell them." She watched as I moved to the door. "Remember, keep your eyes peeled for Ben the imposter. If you see him anywhere near the house, call the cops."

"Do you think he's dangerous?" Her eyes widened in dread.

"Possibly. I do know he doesn't want to be found. Delete that picture." Even as I said it, she reached for her giant purse and began digging for her phone.

"Be careful," she repeated.

"You too." I gave her one last look, then pushed through her door.

CHAPTER 8

Mason was awake when I snuck into his room. I'd had to poke through some doors to find him, but when I did, he was staring out the window.

"Took you long enough," he said.

"You saw me?" I demanded both our voices in low whispers.

"Yeah." He turned around and grinned at my indignation.

"You could have helped me out a little. Yours was the last bedroom I checked. Someone could have seen me."

"At this hour? Besides, my dad's dead to the world and my mom and brother aren't here."

"Oh yeah, tomorrow's Monday."

"She and Jack left after dinner." Jack was his little brother. The tone of his voice told me things still weren't good between his parents.

"Listen, there's been a disturbing turn of events," I began.

"Sounds foreboding." He wiggled his fingers around before his face.

"Be serious. This is heavy stuff."

He moved away from the window and sat on the end of his

bed. "Have a seat." He gestured to a chair pulled out from a desk beside where I stood. "What's up?"

I sat down. "It has to do with Ben."

The look on his face became concerned. "Is he okay? I haven't heard anything since he and Aubrey returned with Kade. I figured he'd left town."

"First, the good news. It seems Ben is in remission."

"Wow, really? That's awesome."

"Now for the bad news. Ben's body has someone else in it." I watched his face for a reaction. It took him a moment to process my announcement.

"What?"

"Another ghost has taken possession of Ben's body."

He looked alarmed. "What kind of ghost? Like from a haunted house?"

"No. One of Tandem's Ghost Walkers got into him. You've seen the assembly line going up and down the mountain."

"How can that even happen?"

"That's what I intend to find out. I'm going to Tandem—right now. I want you to come with me."

He sat there for a moment, stunned. "How do you know this? Did you see him?"

I nodded. "Tess was in town tonight and took a group selfie with her friends. Ben was in the background. She came home and showed it to me, so I went searching for him."

"And you found him," Mason finished.

"He found me, actually. Well, in a way. He was at my house. When he saw me, he took off. I caught up to him at the lake."

"What was he doing there? How would he even know where you live? And why would he expose himself? He had to have known you'd figure out he wasn't Ben."

"He saw Tess take the picture. She'd tried to find him afterward but had no luck. She wasn't even sure it was him. He could have easily asked around and found out where we live — there aren't many ghosts around. It was the picture he was after, not me," I told him.

"Holy shit."

"When I caught up to him at the lake, he knew my name. Granted, we've all been on the news. Anyway, I had this weird feeling right away, like intuition. He said my name was strange, so I made up a story about my parents having their honeymoon in Spain and getting pregnant with me and coming home and buying a house right away."

"Casa is house in Spanish. But that's not how you got your name," Mason said.

"Yeah, and of course, you and anyone else on the team would know that. But when I told fake Ben the story, he acted like 'oh yeah, I remember.' Dead giveaway."

"Smart."

"Thanks. So, after we talked a bit more, I confronted him with the truth, and he finally admitted he wasn't Ben. I told him I would call Tandem right away, but he said something that really freaked me out." I still couldn't believe it.

"What?" He was right on the edge of the bed now, staring at me intently.

"He said to look up Kade and Anna from ten years ago. He hinted that they aren't who they say they are. That when they were hiking in the mountains, they disappeared for two weeks and re-emerged with completely different personalities. Geniuses. That's when they apparently came up with the idea for Tandem and set up shop in the mountain, creating Ghost Walk. Or at least that's what they told their families." I let that information sink in.

"What does he mean they're not who they say they are? Did you look them up?"

"No. He implied the ghosting ability they created was available a decade ago."

"But we were the first to attempt it," Mason said, clearly confused.

"Exactly. But the way fake Ben suggests it, whoever they are were capable of the feat a decade ago, and their first guinea pigs were the real Kade and Anna."

Mason's ghostly eyes widened. "That's so messed up."

"I've thought about it and figured he made it up so I wouldn't call Kade and rat him out."

Mason looked slightly relieved with that idea. "Yeah, that makes way more sense. He's desperate and was lying. He has to be."

We stared at each other. "But now the uncertainty is sinking in. Isn't it?" I asked him.

He stood up. "We need to go to Tandem."

I rose to stand before him. "That's why I'm here."

We couldn't hitch a ride to the base of the mountain—we had to walk, keeping off the main road and out of sight. It didn't take as long as we thought it might, considering Mason demonstrated a new way to move. He'd been practicing on all those long, dull days he'd spent at home and figured out a way to zoom. Leaning in, body slightly elevated, he was able to propel himself forward. Outside, with the slight wind, moving was even faster once we immersed ourselves in the breeze. I estimated we zoomed along about the same speed as a brisk bicycle ride. We continued up the mountain using the same momentum, cutting our trip time in at least half. Dawn was soon to break as we reached the top of the mountain. We stood before the elevator that we'd used to go back and forth from the depths of the mountain facility to outside.

"We can push through and let ourselves glide to the bottom," Mason suggested.

"Okay, it's not like we'll lose our stomachs in the drop." Rollercoasters had always been out of the question for me. On rare occasions, if we happened to be out driving down some old roads, Dad would zip over a short hill to make Tess and me grip our bellies in delight.

On route, Mason and I briefly discussed our plan. We wanted to give Kade and Anna the benefit of the doubt, but caution ruled us. First, we wanted to poke around a bit, see if we noticed any funny business going on. We pushed through the steel door and drifted below. After working ourselves through the top of the elevator to get inside of it, we poked our heads through the double doors.

"Looks clear," Mason whispered.

"Let's go." Both of us pushed all the way through and began heading down the long corridor. Despite the random light sconces, the passage was dim. I hadn't recalled it being so gloomy and foreboding. In the past, we'd traveled this hall filled with the excitement of experiencing the great outdoors, something too often denied us. Even upon returning, we'd been filled with the euphoria of our adventures and the promise of future freedom.

At the end of the hall, we were faced with a choice of three destinations. The door to the right led to the dormitory and lounge, along with a kitchen and housekeeping area. The door to the left led to the procedure rooms, where they would take us to perform the extraction and integration procedures. Door number three, directly in front of us, was where our bodies were being held in stasis. Of course, there were many more passageways leading off from the three main ones. Some we'd explored, many more we'd been asked not to. Out of respect for the scientists, we'd obeyed their wishes.

"How long do you think we have until they spot us?" I asked.

"We couldn't have triggered any alarms. Hopefully, they don't have people monitoring the cameras too closely. Either way, your guess is as good as mine."

"I'm thinking we check out the procedure rooms. See if anything nefarious is going on."

Mason stood before the doors, neither agreeing nor disagreeing with me.

"What do you think?" I prompted. Time was of the essence.

"You're not gonna like it," he warned.

"What?" The look on his face made me nervous.

"Okay, what if Ben and Aubrey are still here? Bodies *and* ghosts? Or at least, both ghosts and Aubrey's body."

"It's a possibility, I suppose. It's not like anyone told us anything after they returned. So, we check out the dorms then? We'll have to be really careful—who knows how many people they've got in there now." We'd all shared the largest room during the six-month trial, but we'd seen several other rooms, some large, some smaller.

"That's not where I think they'd be if anything weird was going on. Like you say, it's probably crammed full of people and ghosts too. Not a good place to keep someone you're trying to hide something from."

That made sense. "You're right. That whole wing would be a write-off then. So where should we look?"

He gestured to the door in front of us. "I don't know about you, but I kinda want to make sure I'm still in there. The others too."

He meant our bodies. Ben being in remission was a miracle,

but it wasn't impossible. However, the odds of anyone taking the other bodies really didn't seem likely. Last I heard, there was no cure for what we each had going on. Still, it didn't hurt to make sure. Plus, there had been that ominous warning from Fake Ben about my body being gone — or soon would be. Not that I took anything he said seriously, but it didn't hurt to check.

"Okay. There's also a lot of other doors down that way. Ones they were pretty insistent we stay out of," I reminded him.

He nodded. "Right. Let's go."

One at a time, we pushed through the door and headed down another dimly lit hall. First stop was making sure the bodies we'd left behind were still safely tucked away. That door was the very last at the end of the hall.

"It might save some time if we poke our head in every door we pass along the way," I suggested. "You take the right, I'll take the left. If you see anything weird, holler."

"Sounds good."

We got three-quarters of the way down the hall when Mason called out. "Whoa! Casa, check this out."

I pulled my head from the door of what appeared to be a storage room. "What?"

He was standing just a few feet ahead of me, his ghostly hands pressing up against a door. "I can't get through," he said.

I joined him and saw he was attempting to pass his hand through. I put my hand up and tried as well. There was a tingling sensation, which wasn't out of the ordinary, but another feeling as well. Strangely, I felt ill, disjointed, and lightheaded, which was weird. The harder I tried to get through, the worse the feeling became. Then it was like hitting a barrier — I could go no further. I pulled my hand free, and immediately the bad feelings faded.

"That's bizarre," I mused. "Why can't we get through? I

mean, Kade had mentioned they were working with a company to invent forcefields to keep us out of places, but I had no idea they'd done it."

"Yeah, me either."

There was no window set in the door, so we couldn't even peek inside.

"Try to go around it through the surrounding walls," Mason suggested. He took one side, I took the other. Neither of us could push through. Once I moved far enough down the hall, almost to the next door, I was able to pass into the wall. Past the drywall was solid rock. I powered on, forcing myself to move ahead. Angling toward my destination, I felt strange again—disoriented, then dizzy. I had to back out and return to the hallway. I looked over and saw Mason shaking his head.

"I can't get through. I think I got close, but the deeper I got, the worse I felt."

"Same for me," he confessed.

"Let's move on and see if there's more doors rigged like that," I suggested.

We found two more. Upon closer inspection, we noticed a small triangular device at the top of the door frames.

"It looks like it can be removed if someone wants to get in there, but not by anyone like us, obviously," Mason observed. "And it apparently extends way past the door in an arc. For all we know, it could encircle the entire room."

"I wonder if it keeps everyone out or just ghosts? If it's just for ghosts, are they trying to keep them out...or in?" We didn't hear any sounds coming from within the forbidden rooms, so we could only speculate the intentions.

"Let's keep going. There's nothing we can do about it now," Mason suggested.

We were relieved to discover there was no such device on the door leading to our stasis pods. After we pushed through, we soon located our bodies and sighed with relief. All the others from our team were there as well—everyone except Ben.

Mason contemplated another door at the rear of the room we'd never used before. I went over to stand with him. He looked at me then pushed his hand through. When it met with no resistance, his head went through next. Swiftly, he pulled back.

"Holy shit," he exclaimed.

Needing no further urging, I pushed my head through to look. Seeing an enormous cavern, I moved the rest of me through. Mason soon stood at my side. We gazed around in awe at the area before us. It had to be larger than two football fields. The ceiling was at least fifty feet high. Unlike the modernized rooms in Tandem, this cavern appeared to be part of the original cave and tunnel structures inside the mountain. The walls were solid rock, as was the ceiling. The floor, however, was smooth concrete. Like the halls, it was lit with many wall sconces attached to the rock walls. Several completed pods to hold bodies in stasis were set out in rows. There appeared to be hundreds of them or more.

"I know they were expecting a lot of people to enter the program," I said finally. "But isn't this a bit much?"

We wandered deeper into the space, moving towards the pods which were operational, judging by the power cables hooked up to them.

The door we'd moved through suddenly swung open with a bang. Mason and I spun around as Kade entered the room.

"Well, if it isn't my two star students," he said.

It was a good thing ghosts couldn't faint.

CHAPTER 9

"We're sorry," Mason began, inching closer to Kade. "We didn't mean to break in like this."

"Yeah," I agreed, joining him. "We came to see you, actually. We've been looking everywhere."

Kade raised an eyebrow and smiled tightly. "Have you now?"

"Um, yeah." Mason nodded, then gazed around. "This is... quite the set-up."

"It's moving along at a good pace," Kade agreed. He motioned to the door, and we obediently followed him back through. Kade swung the door shut behind us and leaned against it. "You two look very guilty right now." He chuckled.

"It's true what Casa said. We were looking for you. It's important, and we didn't want to speak to anyone else."

"I'm intrigued. So, what's up? You're not experiencing problems, are you?"

We shook our heads.

"Is it all the negativity in town? I've heard things have been pretty tense," Kade said, a fatherly look on his face.

"It's Ben," I blurted out.

"Ben?" Kade asked.

"Yes. We've seen him—in his *body*—both of us. But we haven't talked to him. He looked like he was hiding out," I said, keeping to the story Mason and I had agreed upon.

Kade exhaled loudly. "I was afraid of this. If you two have seen him, others have as well. Though I haven't heard anything yet."

"So, you know? That he's out?" I ventured, watching him closely. Yet I had to admit, my intent gaze wasn't solely about figuring out the truth—it was also that I'd missed him. Had ached to see him again.

"Not much goes on here I don't know about," Kade admitted.

"Is he okay?" Mason asked.

Kade smiled tightly. "I hope so. He's in remission, but I wanted him to stick around long enough to do further tests. At least till his father came. Seems he had other ideas."

"We wanted to make sure you knew, if you didn't," I told him. "But we didn't want to risk calling. That would have involved explaining the situation to other people." Imposter Ben's warnings sounded in my head. As hard as I tried, I couldn't picture Kade being anyone else but him—the Kade I knew. Fake Ben was lying. Kade could never have been anything but this driven, intelligent, beautiful man.

"No, you're right—the less who know about it, the better. I'm glad you came to me. The last thing I want is the public catching wind of this and spinning it to appear as though things at Tandem aren't secure. They are, I assure you. At the same time, no one is a prisoner here, by any means. They might suggest we were being negligent, though, releasing Ben so soon. I'm sure he knows it's best for everyone if he returns. Once he has a taste of freedom, he'll be back."

I had to wonder if he'd discovered that Ben wasn't Ben. If he did, would he tell us? I understood how protective of us and the project he was. I had to believe that if he did know, he wasn't saying anything because he feared we'd panic if we learned the truth. That we'd worry about someone snatching our bodies as well, unlikely as that was. I doubted they'd get far if they did, considering the conditions we had.

"Speaking of no one else becoming involved, we'd best get you two home before anyone notices you're missing," Kade suggested. "I'll have the helicopter take you down, and a car drop you off near your homes. Sound good?"

No. I didn't want to leave him so soon. But what other choice did we have?

Mason and I nodded in agreement.

After making a few calls on his radio, Kade led us up to the surface and got us settled in the chopper. The whirl of the blades blew his dark hair around as he leaned in the door, seeing us off. His masculine scent swirled around me, making my heart skip a beat, stirring up memories of long talks and lazy smiles.

"I appreciate your discretion and how you both came right here to speak to me. I promise you, Ben will be found safe. Everything will be okay."

"No problem," Mason said.

"I'm sure it will." I feasted on Kade's handsome face as long as possible.

He shut the door, and we took off. At the bottom of the hill, we were hurried into a black car with tinted windows. Mason was let out first, half a block from his townhouse.

"I'll see you soon," he said to me.

We didn't get the chance to share our thoughts about what

had happened. The pointed looks he'd given me had me on edge. If anything, it seemed to me he was suspicious, whereas I was reassured. I'd watched Kade as he explained things to us. There had been no hint of deception. I was certain.

The driver let me out at the top of my street. I thanked him and started down the roadway. It was early morning. I could see Mom and Dad's cars parked in the driveway. If I snuck inside and made it up to my room, they'd be none the wiser.

Luck was on my side. I got into my room unobserved just in time for Tess to swing open my door. She flew in, staring at me with a mixed look of relief and expectation.

"How'd it go? Did you make it up there? What happened?" she whispered loudly.

"I'll tell you all about it after they leave," I promised.

"Okay."

She went into the hall, and I followed closely behind. Sounds of my parents making breakfast in the kitchen met us as we ventured down the stairs. I was glad I had a chance to think about what to tell Tess. I was also anxious to hear if she'd seen any sign of Ben. I doubted it, though—everything seemed calm enough.

After my parents left, Tess and I went to sit in the living room. "Okay, spill," she said, staring at me intently.

I figured I'd best tell her the truth. "Mason and I made it inside and saw Kade. We told him we'd both spotted Ben but kept your name out of it. We told him we didn't speak to him— we wanted to gauge his reaction and see if he would tell us."

"And did he?"

"No. He did say Ben was in remission, and he'd left without authorization," I began.

"Casa?"

We heard Mason's voice coming from the direction of the

front door. Tess and I got up and headed that way and saw Mason's head sticking inside.

"I didn't want to barge in," he said. "I saw your parents leave, and I figured the coast was clear."

"Come in," I invited.

He pushed through the door.

"Casa was just telling me about what happened with Kade," Tess told him.

The three of us headed back to the living room and sat down.

"How far did you get?" Mason asked me.

"She said Kade told you guys Ben's in remission and that he left Tandem without them knowing," Tess said. "I guess you couldn't exactly tell Kade you know that Ben isn't Ben since you said you didn't talk to him."

"Yeah. And Kade didn't reveal it either," Mason replied.

"What's with your tone?" I asked him. "All the way back, you were grilling me with your eyes like we barely escaped with our lives."

"I did not," Mason objected.

"You did!" I argued. "You're freaking out because Kade didn't say anything about someone else being in Ben's body. Maybe he doesn't know."

"I'm not freaking out. And he knows all right. He even said nothing goes on there he doesn't know about. Talk about a dead giveaway."

"If he knows, then he's not gonna tell us. He's protecting us! He's afraid we'd think our bodies could be stolen as well," I insisted.

"Bullshit," he snapped.

"Don't fight." Tess stood up and raised her hands, trying to keep the peace. "I'm sorry, Mason, but I'm with Casa on this one.

What she says makes sense. Kade is probably just protecting you guys."

"More like protecting himself," Mason flared. "He's worried the shit will hit the fan, and he's micromanaging. Do you know how much trouble Tandem will be in if this gets out?"

"I'm taking it you didn't say anything about him and Anna having superpower brains and altered personalities after being lost a decade ago?" Tess predicted.

"How could we? Imposter Ben told me that, and we never talked to him, remember?" I reminded her.

She shrugged. "Well, there's nothing you guys can do but wait and hope they find Ben. Once they do, if they didn't know someone else is in his body, they'll soon figure it out."

"Or they'll cover it up," Mason said.

"Why are you so suspicious?" I asked him. "The reason I said he didn't tell us is more credible than you thinking this is all some conspiracy."

"Yeah, and what about that huge room full of stasis pods? Did you tell Tess about that yet?"

"What? No," Tess said, sitting back down and staring at him.

"And there were rooms we couldn't even get into. There was some kind of force field. They'd said they were working on having something like that created, but no way were they close. Now all of a sudden, they have hundreds of pods and force field technology to keep ghosts out...or in."

The way he spun it made it sound bad. But I'd looked into Kade's eyes. If he was hiding things for some nefarious purpose, I would know, wouldn't I?

"We're just gonna have to agree to disagree. If you think about this rationally, you'll see there is no purpose for any cover-up. Tandem has crews working on pods around the clock. You know how nuts people are over this technology. Just take a walk through town, and you'll see. They need to accommodate as many people as possible. And yes, they're allowing some to enjoy the perks of the technology—for a lot of money. Money that's needed to finance more pods for the sick. Kade knew there'd be huge interest in this, and he was prepared. Hence the mega room we saw, which is a natural part of the mountain anyway. And if he possesses the technology of the force field, it's probably new, and after what happened with Ben, it's necessary. He probably didn't mention the force field to the public yet because it might raise security questions. Questions he doesn't want to answer right now, considering—"

"Considering one of the original team member's bodies was stolen," Mason interrupted. He threw his hands up. "Okay, relax. I get what you're trying to say. It doesn't help that I felt things were very off at Tandem. Don't tell me you didn't feel it too."

"Under the circumstances, it's no wonder," I objected. "Anyway, how do we know how it really felt in there? Possibly, I recognized the feeling of unease, but ghost emotions are new to us. We're still figuring it out. We can't really trust what we think we're feeling, and we can't make any conclusions based on it."

Tess stood up. "I need coffee. Way more coffee." She headed off to the kitchen.

Mason watched her leave. "I miss coffee. Hey, did she say anything about Ben showing up after you left?"

"No, she didn't. I guess he left town. He was in an awfully big hurry to do so."

"Yes, I guess so. What kind of freak steals a kid's body? And for what purpose? Was he one of the sick, do you think? He has to be. He'd been a ghost for what, a few days, and couldn't handle it? What I really want to know is how he managed it. Who helped him?"

"Maybe we should have told Kade the truth," I said. "If there's shit like that going down, he needs to know." I saw the look on Mason's face. "If he does know, he's not a part of it! He would be furious."

"I don't know," Mason said. "Like you said, we're just gonna have to agree to disagree."

Tess wandered in with another cup of coffee. "You two still going at it?"

"No," I replied. "We're good. Want to go down to the lake again?"

Everyone agreed, and we headed out. Despite Mason and I putting our differences aside, I felt on edge. What if Kade didn't know about Ben? What if we'd wasted precious time keeping it from him? Kade was searching, but if he knew the truth, he would be more determined to find him. I faced another dilemma, though. If I told him, he'd know that Mason and I had lied to him. And why would we have lied to him, he'd ask? To gauge his reaction? To see if he was in on it or knew about it and was covering it up? That would make for an uncomfortable conversation. And yet, wasn't a little discomfort worth it to make sure? If Kade was unaware he was working with people he couldn't trust, I had to tell him. I had to take the chance. Ben's life was on the line. The life he could be living right now in his body. He was in remission, but for how long? What if Kade couldn't find Ben's body? He could be anywhere right now.

I made up my mind. Tonight, after everyone was asleep, I would return to Tandem and talk to Kade. Tess wouldn't know, and neither would Mason.

CHAPTER 10

By eleven-thirty, everyone was in bed asleep. At least I hoped they were. It wasn't unheard of for Tess to come sneaking into my room to talk late at night.

I'd been right about this ghost-sister thing being an adjustment for her. It'd taken some time—a few weeks, in fact—but we'd overcome most of the weirdness between us. It was nice to have my little sister back. Now, if only my mom could adjust.

Tess had told me and Mason that all had been quiet after I left the house last night. There'd been no sign of Ben. The chances of him showing up tonight were slim to none. He was well on his way by now. Or maybe Kade had caught him? I couldn't risk a phone call to Tandem, just in case. Kade wasn't going to appreciate a second visit from me, especially after I told him what I planned to say. I was going up there anyway. Alone.

I headed out. Not having to stop by Mason's place and explain everything, let me get a good start. If I played my cards right, I'd be home in plenty of time before anyone woke up. Especially if Kade offered his chopper and driver again.

It was still dark by the time I reached the mountaintop. I

wasted no time pushing through the elevator's steel doors and drifting down through the shaft. At the bottom, I stuck my head out and looked around. The coast was clear — I pushed all the way through. The passageway seemed even dimmer and gloomier than it had last night. At about a hundred feet in, I bounced against what seemed to be a barrier. I used my hands to explore the area. The feeling was similar to pushing through the doors with force fields. Everywhere I touched was inaccessible to me. Remembering what had happened to Mason and me when we tried going around the forcefield, I didn't even attempt to detour. On the ground to the right, I noticed a small device, exactly like the ones put over the doorways we couldn't enter. Someone had blocked the hall. Intentionally.

My mind whirled, and I wasn't sure what to do. Should I wait and see if Kade came out to me? Someone in security must have noticed me lurking around by now. There could be a reasonable explanation for this, I assured myself, as I retraced my steps back to the shaft. Security had been stepped up due to the Ben incident. Certainly, it had nothing to do with our visit here last night. Though why they felt it necessary to install a force field for ghosts entering by way of the elevator was anyone's guess. I had a feeling there weren't many instances of ghosts returning here uninvited once they left.

But I could be wrong.

Part of me couldn't help but take this personally. Sure, we'd poked our noses around in places they didn't belong last night, but we'd had a cover story. A pretty good one, I'd thought. Unless Kade had seen through our lies. He'd seen the team and me at our lowest moments. Our very worst. He knew us. Maybe enough to know when we were lying.

Getting back up the elevator shaft took some maneuvering. If

I'd been solid, I could have just pressed the buttons. I could float, but not far. Trying to get any traction was definitely out. The shaft walls were reinforced with steel bands set around every six feet or so. Fluttering my arms gave me the added boost I needed to reach the narrow ledges, gliding up from one to another. It took a while, but soon I was pushing through the double doors at the top.

This had been a futile mission. I felt strangely deflated, failing at my attempt to warn Kade that Ben wasn't Ben. Even if he already knew, it wouldn't have been a total waste of time just to see Kade again. Seeing him yesterday had been bittersweet, like reinjuring an old wound that'd started to heal. Kade had always been so kind to me, indulging my crush with little winks and hand squeezes that meant more to me than him.

I stared around the mountaintop, sure there must be more than one way to get in and out of the facility. We'd only ever used the elevator, but in the event of an emergency, other exits must exist. The only problem was I didn't have all night to search, not if I wanted to make it back in time.

The sudden sound of a helicopter filled the air. Someone was coming up to the top. The helipad was close to the elevator. I had to hide, or I'd be spotted. Just as the glaring light crested the mountain, I made a dive for cover. From behind a thick tree surrounded by brush, I peeked.

The chopper landed, and the blades slowed to a steady pulse. The side door slid open, and a man jumped out. Despite his hair being tossed around, I recognized Kade instantly by his incredible height and slim, muscular physique. I found myself holding my breath if that was even possible. The chopper's blades came to rest, and the pilot exited the craft. After exchanging words with Kade, he headed off towards the elevator. Kade now appeared to be alone. This was my chance. I could tell him what I knew. Mission accomplished. It wouldn't be a waste of a trip now.

Before I had the chance to call out or come forward, I heard a shuffle behind me. My hand, resting on the trunk of the tree, suddenly appeared solid. Glancing down, the rest of me looked solid as well.

"What the h—?"

"Shhh," somebody hissed, cutting off my words.

It took me a moment to realize it wasn't my own form I was seeing, but someone else pressed into me.

"Get out of me," I hissed.

"Wait. Watch," the voice insisted—a male voice.

Annoyed, I turned to look where Kade was standing. He wasn't alone anymore. Someone else had got out of the chopper and stood at his side. It appeared to be a young woman. As I watched, she reached up to caress Kade's cheek. The look of adoration on his face made that feeling of jealousy come alive in me.

"Who is that?" I was suddenly more concerned about the woman's identity than the person invading my ghost.

"Watch," he repeated.

Another person climbed out of the chopper and pulled the door shut behind him. Now three were standing there. I stared closely at the newest person. When he turned, I saw his face and gasped.

"Shhh!"

"That's Ethan. Ethan's body," I whispered.

The three of them moved towards the elevator and soon disappeared within. I shifted backward, freeing my ghost from the intruder.

"Benny!" For half a second, I was happy to see him until I

remembered. "You! Body snatcher. That's why you didn't want me talking to Kade. You were afraid he'd see you. I thought you'd left," I said, crossing my ghostly arms. This guy had major boundary issues.

"I did leave. But I had to come back," he said.

"Feeling guilty? You should."

"I am. Not for the reasons you think." He maneuvered his position to give him a clear sight of the elevator shaft.

"Don't tell me, more conspiracy theories, right?" I made to move towards the elevator. If I hurried, I could reach Kade and tell him Fake Ben was out here. Ben's next words stopped me.

"That was Ethan with Kade. So now, two bodies from the original team are miraculously cured. Convenient, wouldn't you say?"

I spun around to glare at him. "I saw him. And Ethan has Crohn's disease. He'd said he had some good days."

"But mostly bad ones. Bad enough to be in the program. Use your brain. That's not your Ethan, just like I'm not your Ben."

Why was I even listening to him? He was a body-snatching liar. "I don't want to hear this."

"What are you doing up here in the middle of the night? I'll tell you. You have concerns. You tried to get inside and couldn't, right?"

"How do you know that? Were you in there?" I noticed he was shifting from one foot to the other as though he was tired. Being on the run for days would do that. He'd probably not had a decent meal either. Not that I really cared, but that was my friend's body, after all.

"I know what they're capable of," he said.

"Yeah, you seem to know a lot of things." If I sounded sarcastic, so be it.

He appeared flustered. "Are you in the least bit concerned your friend is walking around with someone else inside of him? Make that two of your friends."

"And whose fault is that? The only one I know of for sure is you. There's no doubt in my mind that Ethan is Ethan. If you must know, I came up here again tonight to tell Kade about you."

"Again? You were here before?"

Damn it. "I was here last night too," I admitted.

He leaned to rest against a tree trunk and crossed his arms. "Why didn't you tell Kade about me then?"

Now I felt slightly embarrassed. "I did tell him. I just didn't...." What? Tell Kade everything because I'd let lies get into my head and was beginning to have my doubts?

"You didn't mention me because you wanted to see what Kade had to say first, didn't you?" he guessed.

"Maybe."

"And he didn't say anything, did he? But then you mulled it over and figured he was protecting you or some other idiotic notion and decided to come back and tell him after all?"

"Piss off." I knew I was transparent, but come on. He didn't know me. He didn't know how I'd struggled over not telling Kade the truth.

"Ha! Then you return to find you're locked out. That's why they set the force field up so fast."

"That doesn't mean it was to keep me out," I argued.

"The hell it doesn't! Look, don't get mad at me. I came up here for a reason. Can I show you something?"

I snorted. "I'm not going anywhere with you. You just expect me to trust you?"

"Please." He looked like he was about to collapse.

"Fine. Lead on."

It wasn't like I had anything to fear from him physically. He'd foiled my chance of catching up with Kade anyway. Plus, part of me was the tiniest bit curious. He'd had the chance to leave, and he'd returned. There must have been a reason.

The mountaintop was a mixture of rocks, trees, grass, and brush. Hiking it wasn't easy. Mostly I found it annoying. As it was, Fake Ben led slowly and carefully. Once we were far enough from the elevator shaft, he withdrew something from his back pocket. It appeared flat and circular, and when he touched it, it lit up like a flashlight. We kept going, and after I'd completely lost my bearings, I grew frustrated.

"How much further?"

"Here, we're here." He gestured to a rock peak covered with shrubs, rising about twenty feet or so. We'd passed a few of these mini-hills, which gave the mountain a jagged appearance from a distance. I knew that several worn trails snaked around the area.

Ben climbed the incline, juggling his light from hand to hand, and paused midway up. Approaching him, I waited as he moved some brush aside, revealing a hidden entrance. He stepped inside. I poked my head into the narrow rocky space. It appeared to be a tunnel. In addition to Ben's light, I saw a dim glow ahead in the distance.

"What is this place? Does it lead into Tandem?" I asked, gazing around in wonder. The scientists had never taken us here.

"No, but there is a hidden entrance nearby here," Ben said.

"Well, it's pretty cool, but why are we here?" I needed to get home soon.

He stared at me a moment, as though deciding something. When he turned and headed deeper inside, I followed. The tunnel widened into an alcove. A small fire enclosed by a circle of stones sat in the middle of the floor space. Larger stones were set further back, acting as seats. Ben sank down onto one and reached out his hands towards the heat of the flames.

"You asked if I'd been inside Tandem. I was," he admitted.

"Why'd you risk going in there? You know they're after you," I said, watching him closely. If this was some ploy for sympathy or comradery, I refused to be swayed.

"I had to retrieve something. Something important," he said.

"What?" When he continued to stare at me funny, I grew annoyed. "Are you going to tell me, or are we gonna sit here all night?"

"Me," spoke a voice off to my left, from inside the rock.

As I watched, a Ghost Walker emerged. I stared, not believing my eyes.

"Benny?" I whispered. "Is it you?"

He nodded his ghostly head. "It's me."

I glided toward him until our energies intermingled. "Thank God," I said.

CHAPTER 11

Ben left my side and approached the fire, the crackling flames visible through his image. He gazed at the thief in his body and smiled. "How're you feeling?"

Imposter Ben attempted to smile back, but it appeared more of a grimace. "In need of food and rest. Two things I haven't thought about in a while. Kade is back with the chopper. He didn't see me. He would have seen your friend here if I hadn't shown up."

They were acting like they were on the same team. I stared at Ben, amazed. "You're okay with this? Your body is in remission, and he stole it out from under you."

"He had a chance to explain things to me, Casa. You need to hear him out."

"He took your body and ran."

"He came back."

"I can tell you everything too. Are you willing to listen?" Ben, the imposter, asked.

"Who are you, anyway? What's your name? Your real name?" I snapped.

"You wouldn't be able to pronounce it. Just call me Jett."

Annoyed and confused and not wanting to join them, I attempted to lean against the stone wall. Jett could talk till he was blue in the face. It didn't mean I had to believe him. "Make it quick. I need to be back before sunrise."

Jett's expression was resolute. "I told you earlier, I felt guilty. As you see, I came back and got Ben out. The real Ben."

"Fat lot of good it does him."

"Casa, I was trapped in there. He freed me. They knew what had happened. That my body was being used by someone else. Kade and Anna, all of them."

"They were trying to cover it up." That much I'd resigned myself to.

"Yes, they were covering it up. But not just for the reasons you think," Ben insisted.

I glared at Jett. "This guy will have you believing all kinds of conspiracies. Don't listen to him."

"He had no other reason to come back for me. He said you two talked a couple of nights ago."

"You mean when I caught him at my house, about to break in to steal Tess's phone? She got a picture of him sneaking around town. He's a thief and a liar. Did you ever think he might have broken you out to cover up what he's done? He spins some crazy story, and gets you on his side, gets you to hide away. Without you, how else can Tandem prove what happened? You're the only leverage they had, and you just strolled right out of there after hearing some fairy tale."

Despite my words, Ben seemed unfazed. "You know as well as I do, Tandem would never admit they messed up."

"You being there was the only chance you had at getting your body back. They're the only ones with the resources. They obviously know your body was stolen. Kade has the power to make things right."

"Or to keep everything a secret. I'm telling you, Casa, they are the ones who did this to me," he asserted.

"Then they must have had a reason." I had to believe that.

"They do. And you're not going to like it," Jett said.

"I've seen what's going on in there." Ben looked at Jett. "How much does she know?"

"I told her about Kade and Anna being replaced a decade ago. She doesn't believe me. Although I think she's having doubts, considering she was here last night and didn't tell Kade about me."

"Well, *she* still isn't convinced," I snarked. "You didn't exactly say they'd been replaced. You implied it. Anyway, we were the first ones to try the experiment. They only had one transfer pod and were working with minimal equipment. We could only hold ghost-form a short amount of time as they adjusted things. It took months for us to be able to stay out. Even then, they had to test the tethers."

"They put on a grand show for everyone to see. Got the world to gradually accept the technology. In truth, they've had it all along. All the technology, all the equipment they need," Jett informed me. "Even the force field technology. It's how they kept things hidden from you and the others."

"For what purpose? Why wait ten years? It makes no sense," I practically shouted.

"There was no need to go public yet. The demand wasn't there. But in case such a time arrived, they wanted to be prepared," Jett explained. "So they created cures. Researching and remedying nearly every human ailment experienced on Earth." He stared at me a second. "But now, the time has arrived. It comes down to them wanting bodies."

"Wanting bodies for what?" His theory about the cures was ridiculous and far outweighed by his last statement. I was glad I didn't have a belly, or I might just throw up. He was going to say it was all about money. I knew it. Everything always seemed to boil down to it—money...and power.

Just as Jett opened his mouth, the sounds of rustlings and flashing lights traveled down the length of the tunnel. All of us stared in that direction and soon saw Kade stalk inside. He wasn't alone. Three big guys came in after him, armed, guns pointed at Jett. Without thought, I slid back into the stone, hidden from view. Before I sunk deeper, I heard Jett holler, "Shit, get out of here."

Sound was disproportionate, bouncing around, unclear. I felt dizzy and confused. The stone around me twinkled, and I felt Ben's energy slide up beside me. At least he was safe.

"Keep going," he said. "Outside...head straight...get out... here."

"What?" His words were muffled and jumbled. I caught only snatches. His energy retreated, going back the way we had come. "No. Come back." Unsure of what to do, I went on ahead, pushing towards outside. If I could get out and circle around, I could surprise them. Or at least see what the hell was going on.

At last, I made it out. I rushed back towards the entrance of the tunnel, close enough to see what was happening, but not be detected. Kade was standing outside. One of the goons came next, then I saw Jett come out, hands fastened behind him. Another man emerged, sidestepping, keeping his eyes towards the entrance. He held a device in his hands instead of his gun. Next, to my surprise, was Ben. Though in ghost form, he seemed to be as captured as Jett. A slim pulsing glow of light surrounded him. The man with the device looked to be in control, having ensnared Ben in a lasso-like containment force field.

The last man exited. Kade peered around in the darkness as though sensing my presence.

"Let him go," Jett implored, indicating Ben. "He won't say anything. Not if he wants his body back."

"I won't," agreed Ben.

Their pleas were futile. Even I knew that.

The men regrouped, checked the restraints on their prisoners, exchanged a few words, and headed out. They didn't appear to be moving in the direction of the elevator. Jett had said there was another entrance nearby. I surmised that was their destination. I trailed them to another elevator shaft, embedded in a wall of rock. Following them below wasn't an option. The halls were no doubt rigged like the other one. I'd be discovered and possibly find myself a prisoner as well. Staying silent was hard while Ben and Jett were taken below.

After several minutes of staring at the elevator shaft, I started for home, consoling myself with the fact that now things could be set right. The conspiracies I'd heard rattled around in my thoughts, but I ignored them. Desperate pleas from a desperate guy trying to justify what he'd done. That's all it was.

About to descend over the edge of a steep cliff, I paused, certain I heard my name called out.

"Casa? Casa, wait." It was Kade.

What choice did I have but to hear him out? He'd obviously spotted me. Soon he appeared, his breath puffing, having run to catch up.

"Thanks...for waiting," he said.

Despite basking in his presence, I couldn't help but feel that sting of jealousy again, recalling that woman he'd been with.

Not to mention the fact I didn't know what to believe about him now. Especially the way he'd come into that cave, armed and dangerous. I remained silent, waiting for him to continue. He raised his hands as he approached, perhaps showing me he didn't have one of those ghost trapper devices.

"You must have a lot of questions."

Mostly about who that woman was. I was tempted to ask but didn't.

When I remained silent, he let loose a breath. "You came back."

I wondered how much he thought I knew. "Yeah. We didn't exactly tell you everything last night. But you already know the truth. About Ben."

"I do," he admitted. "God only knows what Jett said to get him to leave with him. We've been out searching."

"With Ethan?" *And some woman? Where'd she come from anyway?*

"You should have come forward if you saw us. I could have explained things then. Ethan is okay, but he's going back into Ghost Walk as we speak. He agreed to come with us to search for Ben. Ben's ghost, not his body. We were hoping they'd be together, actually, considering we knew it was Jett who broke him out. If Ben saw Ethan, we hoped he'd be more inclined to return with us."

As opposed to catching him in a force field net? "I thought Ethan left with his parents after the tether test. Sofia too."

"Sofia left. We picked up Ethan to keep him out of the public eye. Things are a bit chaotic in Tuck right now. His parents will be joining him here soon."

"Okay." Why the delay? It'd been weeks.

As though sensing my questions, he continued. "We'd seen

some improvement in his condition. That's why we all discussed him coming back here for a while."

Sounded plausible.

And yet, Jett's warning rang through me. A decade spent examining cures. It seemed impossible that Tandem's small team had accomplished in a short span of time what had eluded thousands of the world's top researchers for far longer. Yet, I had firsthand experience with the tech advances Kade and Tandem had made. Had they cured Ben? Maybe Ethan as well? Had that been Ethan in his body, or someone else?

"Now that you have Ben and his body, you'll make things right? Pull that imposter out and put Ben back?"

"Of course," he assured me. "I take it you went below, into Tandem, and had some trouble?"

Was that a hint of guilt I saw on his face? "With the force field? The one that wasn't supposed to exist yet?" I watched him carefully.

"We set it up to prevent any unauthorized Ghost Walkers from entering the facility at will. We don't want a repeat of what happened with Jett and Ben. And we can't reveal the technology. Eventually, but not yet."

"How come?"

"It doesn't exactly belong to us. Government scientists created it. They're working with us in the facility. We aided in the development, but technically, it belongs to them, and they're calling the shots," he explained.

"The government? Why would they be involved in this?"

"It's a long story, one I can't really talk about. I will tell you this—they've proposed a possible solution to both our problems. It has to do with the incarcerated."

"Really?" He didn't look to be joking.

"The demand for ghost technology is unprecedented. Something we never dreamed of. We must explore every avenue. Unfortunately, not everyone's on board with Ghost Walking. They want bodies—"

"That's exactly what Jett said! I asked him who he meant, but you guys walked.... Um, I was in the cave," I admitted.

"I know." He smiled, and I melted. "I don't want you to worry about Ben. He's been lied to. I hate to say it, but he's led a sheltered life. He was no doubt easily manipulated by Jett."

"Who *is* Jett?" I asked.

Kade exhaled loudly. "Someone I had trusted. He entered the project, buying his spot. He said he wanted adventure. I'm embarrassed to say he wound up paying off a couple of staff to put him into Ben's body. I fired them immediately. They also locked up Ben in a room with a force field where he couldn't get out. Someone found him, but by that time, Jett was gone."

"Why didn't Jett just return to his own body?"

"He a paraplegic. If he'd been patient, he could have entered the project legitimately. But he didn't want to wait. He also lied about his intentions. That's on me." Kade appeared regretful and hurt.

"It's not your fault people betrayed you," I was quick to assure him.

"Thank you for saying that. I need people around me I can trust."

Is that who that woman was? Again, I couldn't find the words to ask. Not without sounding like a petulant child with a crush.

"Why the incarcerated?" I asked instead, focusing on what Kade had revealed.

"Do you have any idea how much money the state spends on prisoners? Millions, keeping them clothed, fed, sheltered.

Money that could be utilized to help combat poverty, disease, law enforcement, and hundreds of other ways. The force field technology combined with Ghost Walk would not only free up substantial funds but those bodies—instead of rotting away in cells—could be utilized by deserving people."

"But they're criminals," I argued.

"If you had the choice of living your life in a hospital bed or a wheelchair, wouldn't you appreciate the offer of a healthy body? Not everyone is content to live life as a ghost waiting for a cure. You've been a ghost for a few months. You must see you're missing out on things so many take for granted. Simple human interaction, such as touching, hugging, and holding hands."

It was a good thing I couldn't blush.

"Do you understand?" He stared at me expectantly, hopefully. I nodded. "Yes. I do."

"Please, keep this under wraps, okay?"

"Sure, no problem," I agreed.

"Of course, we're still in the trial stages. Jett actually did us a favor in a way. He showed us that transference of a ghost into a body not their own is possible."

"I think you face a lot of obstacles. Those prisoners have rights, and their families might object," I predicted.

"They've assured us no one will be forced into the project. Participation is strictly optional. Of course, they may be willing to offer incentives, such as shorter sentences."

"I think it's a good idea." I was thoughtful for a moment. "You would have to take mental illness into consideration, though. I've seen a lot of people in hospitals over the years. One night, when I was about ten years old, I remember some woman ran down the hall screaming in the kids' ward. She had to be physically restrained. Later, I heard that the police had taken her away to jail. Even back then, it struck me how some people slipped through the cracks and didn't get the help they needed. Everyone focuses on the physical body first, the other problems later." I was tempted to ask if he had magical cures tucked away.

His warm look made my toes curl. "The bodies will get a thorough once-over before they become available. They'll check for physical and psychological conditions first," he assured me.

The way he referred to them as *bodies* bothered me. I suppose from his standpoint, being a scientist, it was an analytical way of approaching a controversial project.

"Sounds like they have it all figured out. I'm sure you'll get the public to see things your way. Or, the government's way, that is." I'd seen him pitch Ghost Walk to the world. Something about him made people want to get on board with what he wanted. I know he had that effect on me.

"I suspect the public won't differentiate the two." He gazed at me, fondly for a moment. "I have to get back."

"Yeah, me too."

"I'm glad I got a chance to explain things to you, Casa. We're not the bad guys Jett would have you believe we are."

"I know you're not," I assured him. "Look at what you've done so far. I know you will go on to do more great things." Did that sound too sappy?

He smiled. "Good night."

"Good night," I said and watched him turn and walk off into the night.

I headed out, trying not to succumb to the empty feeling that gnawed at me whenever I bid farewell to Kade. The fact he'd confided in me made me feel important. He didn't look at me like a kid. He'd sought me out to reassure me he was not a bad guy.

Even Ben had turned against him.

Kade was right. Ben had led a sheltered life. I guess we all had.

My mission for this night had been successful. I felt better knowing Ben and Jett were in Kade's capable hands. I trusted Kade. He would set things right. I would never doubt him again.

CHAPTER 12

September rolled around, and Tess returned to school. Considering the ongoing controversy in town, I wasn't expected to attend. Tess didn't say as much, but I got the feeling she was relieved. It was hard enough being the new kid, never mind worrying about a ghost-sister haunting the school halls.

Several hours of my day were filled with watching pre-programmed instructional videos on my new "studies" laptop. Mom or Dad would set it up for me before they left for work, and I could use voice commands to view the videos. There wasn't a live person on screen, which allowed me to stop and start the programs at my convenience. I was expected to take tests, verbally, though, when a teacher was available since I couldn't hold a pencil or type on a computer. Many days Mason would join me, and we'd work together. Being the same age came in handy.

Kade had been on the news a lot talking about how they'd opened and planned to open more facilities to implement Ghost Walk around the world. Despite broader availability, things remained the same around town. Tuck was still overrun with people wanting to get into the project and causing trouble if or when they were forced to wait or denied.

Not everyone was a candidate. Anyone over the age of sixty was put to the back of the list. Kade explained on televised news conferences that putting your body into stasis late in life posed risks, possibly serious ones. It was not a popular announcement. Many desperate to enter Ghost Walk were of the aging population. There were a couple of riots, small ones, but bad enough to call in the army to keep the peace. Soldiers' presence around town, and the strict implementation of their rigid rules, only seemed to elevate the tension. A curfew was imposed, and by ten at night, Tuck was essentially closed for business. The name Tuck fit perfectly, considering the town was surrounded on three sides by massive mountains. Having just one main road and a few off-the-beaten-paths into town made it easy to cordon off unless you wanted to hike in by foot. The nearest town, Devon, was still miles away, and though it too was becoming overrun, they hadn't yet felt the need to expand the army's presence.

Despite all the problems the technology had brought with it, no one could complain it wasn't worth it. Ghost Walk had put Tuck — an insignificant little town — on the map, making it the hot spot of the world.

Tess and I agreed the biggest attraction Tuck offered was Kade. He was, after all, the brains behind the technology.

He had called me a couple of times, and I'd had to endure Tess or one or both of my parents listening to our conversations on speakerphone. The first time he'd called wanting to speak to me directly was just days after I last saw him. I'm sure it hadn't been an accident he'd waited for a weekday and my parents to be at work. I'd had to tell Tess everything that happened, especially considering the way things had been left with Mason and me arguing over Kade's motives. Tess hadn't been thrilled I'd gone up there a second time. I got the feeling it was more about her being out of the loop than her worrying about my safety.

During that first phone call, Kade had assured me things had been set right. Ben had been returned to his body, as had Jett, and the authorities had quietly escorted Jett away. Ben had also been reunited with his father in Alaska. I'd been put out a little over that fact, leaving me to wonder if Kade had gotten through to Ben. It was a little surprising that Ben hadn't called me himself. Maybe he was embarrassed or annoyed. I didn't know, but I missed him, along with the others from the team.

Tess walked in early from school. She found me staring at the television set, which I'd asked her to switch on before she left for school.

"You're home early," I observed.

"Yeah. I feel like shit. Have you been sitting here all day?" Her bag hit the floor, and she flopped down on the couch.

I sort of had, but I didn't want to admit it. She'd expressed annoyance once over the fact she had to trudge to school every day while I got to hang around the house.

"I've watched most of the required videos for the week, so it's not a big deal if I watch a little TV," I said.

"Lucky you. I had to listen to old Mizz Marble Face drone on about Shakespeare for like ninety minutes."

"English?" I suppressed a chuckle, knowing how she hated that class.

"Has he been on TV again?"

She meant Kade. "Not today. Not yet, at least."

Her attraction to him had cooled somewhat, and I suspected she now had a crush on Mason. Even in ghost form, I had to admit, he was kind of cute. My assessment of the guys on the team wasn't exactly fair when we were together for those six months. We'd all practically been at death's door, so none of us had been at our best. Out of all the guys, Ben, in my opinion, was the cutest. Honestly, I hadn't thought so until Jett had taken over his body, strange as that may sound. Not that I liked Jett, but he'd possessed that bad-boy persona the real Ben lacked. Too bad he was a jerk, a liar, and a thief.

Tess leaned her head back and put a hand to her flushed face. "You're lucky you can't get sick." Her eyes appeared dull, and her skin had a grey tinge to it, except her face, which looked red and sweaty.

"You do look like shit."

"Thanks. I'm not the only one. Must be something going around. A dozen or more kids left early today. Even some of the teachers called in sick."

"I'd offer to make you a cup a tea…," I began.

She rose slowly off the couch as though her bones ached. "No, thanks. Think I'll lie down for a bit."

I watched her wander to the stairs and head up. It was strange seeing her sick. She'd had minor colds or belly upsets over the years, but nothing to bring her down. Usually, it was me who suffered horribly whenever a cold or flu was going around, making me linger in bed for weeks on end.

That night on the news was a segment about the mysterious illness in town. Mom and Dad, and I were gathered around the television.

"I haven't been feeling too great either," Mom admitted. "I was supposed to show a house today, but the couple cancelled because the husband was sick in bed. I was relieved since I have no energy, and everything aches." She had her socks off and was rubbing one of her feet.

"I hate to say it, but I feel it too," Dad said, as if admitting it aloud would make it true. "My back hurts, my arms and legs too, and I'm exhausted. It's strange. I've never felt like this before, even with the flu."

The look of them had me concerned. They'd both gone up to check on Tess as soon as they got in, but instead of preparing dinner as they usually did, they'd curled up with blankets in the living room.

"It's probably from having so many people in town," I theorized. "Someone probably brought a weird plague in with them." I meant it as a joke, but they both nodded in agreement.

Over the next couple of days, Mom and Dad dragged themselves to work, and Tess dragged herself to school. All of them returned home early each day, and after a light meal, went right to bed. I grew more and more concerned, especially seeing the local news on TV. It wasn't encouraging. Every day more and more people came down with the mysterious illness they'd labelled Tuck Fever since here was the only place it seemed to be occurring. No one knew what it was, where it came from, how it spread, or how to cure it. By the end of the week, Tess didn't bother showing up for school anymore.

"Look at that," Dad said with little enthusiasm that evening, pointing at the television screen. "The army is closing off Tuck. All roads are blocked. No one in or out."

"Seriously? That was fast. Maybe it is the plague," I said.

"They can't do that," Mom objected half-heartedly. "I have to work out of town tomorrow."

The announcer was still talking. "…until further notice," he stated, looking grim.

They all retired to bed soon after, leaving me alone to watch the fate of Tuck's citizens. The next day, no one got out of bed. Or the day after that.

Despair and futility filled my ghostly belly. I spent my time reassuring myself my family was still breathing and watching news updates on the television.

Since calling him was out of the question, I decided to head to town and see Mason. He'd not made an appearance all week, which was so unlike him, it had me concerned. We were immune to sickness in our form, but his dad could have it.

The quiet, deserted outskirts of town were a sneak preview of Tuck. The only people I'd seen so far were men and women dressed in fatigues. If they noticed me at all, it was with a brief nod. The grim, determined looks on their faces displayed the onerous task they faced. Large army trucks and Jeeps rumbled down the road. There weren't any civilian vehicles, which I took as a bad sign.

Tuck appeared a ghost town when I entered it. The streets were abandoned, stores and homes locked up tight. Closed signs were prominent in all the storefront windows. The park near Mason's townhome was empty. When I reached his unit, I pushed through the back door. The lights were dim, curtains were drawn, all was silent. Not wanting to wake his dad if he was in bed, I drifted up the stairway to Mason's room. I poked my head through his door and saw the room was vacant. As I stood in the hall, not sure what to do next, I saw him push through another door that must have been to his dad's room. He saw me and smiled.

"Hey." He approached me.

"Sorry to barge in like this." I nodded towards the door he'd just exited. "Is your dad sick?"

"Yeah," he said with a sigh. "Strangest damn thing I've ever seen. It's all over town too."

"My family has it. All of them."

He shook his head in regret and gestured to the stairway. We descended below, and I followed him into the kitchen. Dishes littered the countertop and filled the sink, bits of uneaten food clinging to them.

"Sorry for the mess."

"My place looks the same," I assured him.

He sat down in one of the chairs pulled out from the kitchen table. "I feel so useless. My dad is really sick, and I can't do anything to help him. I wonder if this is how he and my mom felt, you know, watching me when I was sick."

I'd wondered the same thing about my parents. "What do you think is going on?"

He shrugged. "With all the people coming from all over the world, we were bound to get something."

"Yeah, maybe something like the measles, not the bloody plague," I said.

"The plague." He made a sound like a snort. "I haven't seen the news in about three days. My dad shut the television and computer off, not realizing he wouldn't get up again. I went to the hospital. What a waste of time that was."

"Why, what happened?"

A look of annoyance crossed his face. "They're too busy to send anyone out. People were on stretchers in the halls. Every room is full. There's only one ambulance in Tuck, and it was out. Not like they'd send someone to pick up my dad anyway. There's no place to put him."

"Maybe we should go to Tandem. They may be able to help," I suggested, even though I knew talking to him about Tandem and Kade would be futile. Despite telling him about Kade's assurances, he still had his doubts.

"How're we even supposed to get in, now that they have those force fields set up?"

That had been a real sore spot with him. Especially considering they'd set it up the night after we'd gone up there.

"They have security cameras. If we get caught up at a force field, we'll wait till someone comes to us. If Kade sees it's us, he'll come. Especially knowing what's going on."

Mason shook his head. "I dunno, Cas. I had a bad feeling the last time I was there. It felt like they were hiding shit."

"Well, technically, they were. But Kade explained all that. Anyway, you can't trust your gut in this. We don't even have a gut. Not really."

We heard a thud from upstairs, and Mason leapt up.

"My dad probably dropped his water again. I better go see if he needs help. Not that I can do anything." He started for the doorway and paused to glance back at me. "If you want to go up there, be my guest. But I wouldn't hold my breath waiting for their help."

His doubt annoyed me, but I could see how frustrated he was. "I think I'll just go home and check on my family. If I do decide to go, I'll let Kade know that your dad needs help too."

"Whatever this is, I hope it blows over soon. At least nobody's died. Yet."

I headed home with his ominous words rattling around in my head.

That evening I sat perched on the sofa, eyes glued to the latest news when I heard what sounded like a hurricane outside. I pushed through the back door and was amazed to see a helicopter. I watched as the side door slid open and Kade jumped out. He strode over to where I was standing.

"Kade? What are you doing here?" I yelled over the racket of the chopper.

"I've been calling your house for days, and no one's answered," he yelled back.

It was true. I'd heard the ringing, but I couldn't answer it. "Everyone's sick. They've been in bed all week. I'm really worried. I don't know what to do."

I'd thought about going to the hospital for help, despite Mason's experience, but reporters had cautioned it was at maximum capacity and they weren't accepting more patients. It'd almost been at capacity before the plague with all the sick people vying for a spot at Ghost Walk — I could only imagine how they were handling the new influx. A statement had been released advising people to stay home, and if symptoms worsened, to call a special number they had set up. My family was ill, but they'd been coherent and mainly exhausted. Besides a couple of trips to grab water or ginger ale or go to the bathroom, they'd kept to their beds.

A man and a woman exited the chopper next. The man held a duffle bag. They wore surgical gowns, masks, and gloves.

"Hang on," Kade said to me. He went to talk to the pair, and moments later, the three of them joined me.

"This is Kaylyn and John, part of my medical team. They're going to check on your family. I was afraid when I didn't get hold of you that something like this had happened. If they need special attention, I'll make sure they get it." The pair went into the house.

"The hospitals are full," I told him.

"Tandem has a full medical wing with doctors, nurses, equipment, and medicine at our disposal. They will have the best of care," he assured me.

If I could have cried, I just might have. Here was my knight, my hero, riding in to save me again. Not me exactly, but my family.

"Thank you," was all I could say.

"Casa, you're a member of my team. We're practically family, right?" His smile was devastating. He pulled out a mask from his pocket and put it on, then pulled out a pair of gloves and put them on as well.

"Right."

Kaylyn and John returned shortly. John was escorting Tess, having taken hold of her arm. She weakly complained that she couldn't go anywhere in her pajamas and no makeup. Kaylyn had her arm around Mom's waist.

"I'll go back in for the other one," John said as he passed by.

"Casa!" Tess called out with a burst of energy. "You have to come with us."

"Of course she'll come," Kade assured her.

Mom and Tess got settled into the chopper with Kaylyn, and Dad was brought out next. He looked the worst and was leaning heavily on John.

"Casa, sorry baby," Dad slurred.

"It's not your fault you're sick," I assured him, again feeling like I wanted to cry.

Kade was watching me with sympathy. "Are you okay?"

"I will be if they are," I assured him.

John joined us after settling Dad next to Mom. "The back door was unlocked. I found a set of keys on the counter in the kitchen, so I locked it. Everything else is locked up tight." He handed the keys over to Kade and went back to the chopper.

"Okay, we're all set. Anything they need, we'll have. If we don't, I'll send someone back for it," Kade assured me. "Ready to go?"

"I'm ready. Do you think you can help them? Do you know what's wrong?" I asked.

"I've had a team working on it day and night. We believe we know what's going on, but we're hesitant to say anything until we're sure."

"Is there a cure?"

"We're working on it," he repeated.

A wave of something passed through me. Relief, I'm sure. Kade gestured at the chopper, and together we walked toward it.

He would fix this. He would save my family, just like he saved me.

CHAPTER 13

We reached the top of the mountain.

Three additional medical staff stood by, and as we landed, they hurried forward to help. Two trips had to be made in the elevator since Mom and Dad and Tess were each seated in awaiting wheelchairs and descended first. Kade and I waited for the elevator to return while the other two staff got into the chopper.

"Mason's dad!" I said to Kade, frantically remembering. "He's sick. He needs your help too."

"Already on it," Kade assured me, gesturing to the chopper which was lifting off again.

Part of me worried Mason would refuse to accept Kade's help. Even if he relented and allowed them to take his father, he might not join him.

"It'll be all right," Kade said, probably mistaking my frowning face for concern for my family. He removed his mask and gloves and pushed them into his pocket.

I smiled at him, hoping to relay how much I appreciated his aid.

"They'll need to get your family set up in the quarantined area. You can see them later, but right now, I think it's best we let the medical team assess them. You understand?"

I nodded. "Sure, that's fine. You figure it's airborne?"

"Not sure. It appears to be very contagious. That's why we're seeing entire families getting sick. One catches it and brings it home to the others. Just like a cold or flu."

"It wiped out Tuck fast. I guess that's why they closed off the town, to prevent the spread. Do you know how it originated?" There'd been some speculation it could have come from tainted water or food sources. Testing was being done, but nothing had been confirmed.

"No. Not yet. We've been looking for the source. If we can figure it out, maybe we can stop it and prevent it from happening again. It's nothing we've ever seen before," he admitted. "So far, there's been no fatalities. No one has recovered from it yet either."

"Yeah, that's what the news said."

The elevator doors opened, and we stepped inside. I peered up at Kade, and he winked at me reassuringly. My ghost heart flip-flopped.

Once below, we headed down the dim passageway. When we reached the spot that had stopped me before, I slowed down, then stopped. Kade took a few more steps, then paused to stare back at me.

"It's gone," he told me, meaning the force field.

The weird feeling I got when I stepped into a force field wasn't something I wanted to repeat. I crept ahead cautiously, my eyes on Kade. Soon I was standing beside him. He grinned at me, and we continued.

I considered asking him about that woman I'd seen him with. If anything, I'd always thought he was closest to Anna.

But they'd never displayed any romantic feelings towards each other, at least none that I'd seen. At Kade's age, he was bound to have someone in his life. He didn't wear a wedding ring and hadn't mentioned a significant other, but there must be someone. That woman, perhaps? Maybe they'd been together for years. She could have stood by him, competing for his attention while he dedicated his life to Ghost Walk. I wondered if she'd known him before his sudden drastic change of personality if what Jett said was true.

"I don't want you to worry," Kade said.

His words interrupted my thoughts. "About my family." Of course, he meant my family. "I feel so much better knowing they're here."

"I'm glad."

We came to the hallway that led to where our bodies were kept in stasis. The last time Mason and I were down here, there'd been some doors shielded by force fields. As much as I wanted to ask what was behind them, I didn't. When we approached one of the doors, I was surprised. It appeared I may get answers after all. Kade reached up toward the little triangle at the top of the door and hit a switch or a button on it, disabling it, no doubt, before replacing it.

"Do you mind coming with me in here?" he asked.

How could I possibly refuse? "Sure."

He opened the door and stood aside for me to enter. I went in, and he followed after me, pulling the door shut behind him. Before us was another long passageway, brighter than the other one. We went about thirty feet or so when he turned into the first opening on the right. It was a room. There was no door, even though the room was set up like a bedroom with a single bed and a chair.

"Please, sit a moment." Kade gestured to the chair.

I don't know why it mattered to him whether I stood or sat. It didn't make much of a difference to me. Being a ghost, Mason and I had continued to lie in our beds at night and sit in chairs, out of habit or to put others at ease. Maybe it made us feel more normal? Kade knew what we were, knew we didn't need to rest, or eat, or sleep. During our six months here, we'd always sat down when having talks with the staff, ghost-form or not. They instilled in us the need to fit in, to behave like we were still us, despite being different.

So, I sat.

The room was small, reminding me of a servant's bedroom I saw once when Mom and Dad took Tess and me through a historical landmark home years ago. Kade was a big guy, taking up a lot of the space. He stood at the door frame, half in, half out of the room.

"I know you don't need to rest," he began. "But the quarters where you all stayed during the trial period are full. Here you can at least have some privacy."

With no door? "It must have been packed here even before the outbreak, with everyone wanting to get in on the project. I can only guess how many are here now. It's good of Tandem to open its doors and help out during this time."

"Do you mind staying here? I know it's cramped—"

"It's fine. Really. Please, don't worry about me. It's my family that needs your attention," I assured him.

He released a breath. "You're being very cooperative."

I rose to my feet. As I did, he stepped all the way out into the hallway. He stared at me a moment, then smiled. For some reason, it sent a chill through me. Then he reached into his pocket and pulled out one of those little force field devices. Before I could do or say anything, he snapped it into place over the outside of the door frame and switched it on.

"Wait. What are you doing?" I gasped, watching him move further into the hall.

"I'm sorry, Casa. I can't have you wandering around."

It was then when I moved as close as I dared to peer down the passageway, that I noticed several more rooms, all with no doors. The one I could see clearly had a force field over it. Kade turned and walked in the direction we'd come from.

"Kade! What's going on?" I yelled.

The only sound I heard in return was his shoes on the floor as he left.

CHAPTER 14

What possible reason could Kade have for locking me up? Was he worried I'd make a nuisance of myself, get in the way?

An eerie silence surrounded me, making the conspiracies Jett had told me all the louder in my head. I sat down on the bed, facing the doorway. How many others were locked away in here?

They want bodies.

Was it crazy to think that somehow Tandem had created this plague in order to get them?

Now I was getting as paranoid as Jett and Ben. Thinking of those two made me wonder if what Kade had told me was the truth. Had Ben been returned to his body? Or did someone else inhabit it while he was trapped in a room like me? Had it been sold to the highest bidder?

That was nuts.

There had to be a reasonable explanation for this.

Even if they were swapping out bodies, wouldn't they still be at risk for catching the sickness going around? Unless they had a cure. Or were injecting the bodies with some kind of immunity.

I wished I had room to pace.

My thoughts suddenly turned to Mason. Kade had a chopper heading to his place right now. I leapt up and began feeling the walls all the way around the room. The force field had affected the entire space, not allowing me to pass through. *Damn.*

There was no way to get out of there and warn Mason before it was too late for him too. Soon we'd both be trapped in here like rats in a cage.

I sat back down and contemplated my dilemma. After what felt like hours, I heard a shuffling noise in the hall. Moments later, Ben appeared before the doorway.

"Ben!" I jumped up and approached the door. "Am I ever glad to see you! I'm trapped in here."

"I know." The look on his face was grim.

He reached up and switched off the forcefield. I darted out of the room.

"We need to get out of here," he informed me.

Dressed in jeans and a blue T-shirt, he wore a jacket and had a backpack slung over his shoulder. He looked well enough, though a little haggard. At a brisk pace, he strode down the passageway, going in the direction Kade had gone.

"How'd you know I was here?" I asked.

"Time for questions later. Let's get out of here first."

When we reached the end of the hall, Ben opened the door and headed into the other passageway. From there, we soon entered the dim hall leading to the elevator. The sudden blaring sound of an alarm made us both jolt.

"Shit, they're onto us," I yelled over the noise. We broke into a run.

The elevator came into view, spurring us to move even faster. The doors were open but began to close. I ran into something and got bounced back, landing on my ghostly rear.

The force field.

Great.

Noticing I wasn't beside him, Ben stopped, swore, and came back for me. He disabled the device, and we began running again. He had just enough time to shove his arm between the narrow crack of the elevator doors and force them back open.

It took forever to reach the top.

Luckily, when the doors opened, no one stood there waiting for us. We stepped out and strode no more than a dozen feet before we paused to peer around. The helicopter hadn't returned yet, I noticed.

"We've got to m—"

Ben's words were cut off by a man crashing into him with enough force to knock him off his feet. As I reeled back in shock, another man wearing fatigues rushed at the pair. The first man pulled Ben to his feet.

"Leave him alone," I yelled, terrified they'd beat him to death. Ignoring me, both men went at him, punching, shoving, and kicking. All I could do was watch helplessly.

Ben fell to the ground beside his pack, which had slipped off his shoulder the first time he went down. He remained still. Both men backed up, one reaching for handcuffs on his belt, the other pulling out a gun. Ben suddenly pulled his knees up to his chest as he rolled back on his hands. Next, he kicked out his legs and sprung to his feet. In a blur, he spun around and delivered a kick to the head of the man holding the gun. The man fell to the ground, not moving. The man holding the cuffs dropped them and rushed at Ben, punching him in the face. Ben shook his head, momentarily stunned, and brought his left arm up, driving it into the man's gut. When the man doubled over, Ben punched the back of his head. The man fell forward, knocked out.

"Shit! I didn't know you could fight like that," I said, impressed.

He waved off my praise and grabbed his pack. "Let's go."

We jogged towards the trees, the sound of reinforcements arriving behind us. It was a while before the sound of pursuit faded.

Ben dropped to sit on a fallen log, gasping for air, while I paced before him. All I could think about was Mason. Right now, he was probably arriving at Tandem and being locked up. I hadn't seen him brought in when I was in my cell, but they must have gotten to him by now.

I stared at Ben and waited while he rested. "Are you okay now?" I asked, hearing his breath even out.

He nodded. Even in the dark, I could see his bloody lip and a dark bruise forming on his cheek. His ribs must have ached since he held his left side.

"What are you doing here? Kade said you went to Alaska."

"A lie."

"Obviously." I stared at him hard for a moment. "Damn it. You're not Ben. He never switched you back, did he?"

"No."

I glared at him. "Then where is Ben?"

He met my gaze and held it. "Locked up with the others."

"The others? How many are there?" I demanded.

"More than you know."

"Why didn't Kade switch you back? I don't understand it. He said you were returned to your body and the cops took you away."

"Another lie." Wearily, Jett got to his feet. "We have to keep moving." He started walking, but I didn't follow. When he noticed I wasn't with him, he turned around. "What are you waiting for? If you think they'll just give up, think again."

"Kade sent the chopper back for Mason and his dad. His dad's sick. I don't know if Mason will come here, considering he doesn't trust Kade, but I don't think he'll leave his dad. He will let them take him. He has no choice. And really, what could he do to stop them?"

"Nothing," Jett admitted.

"Well, I can't just leave. I have to warn him. Not to mention my family is in there."

"We can't risk going back. We won't make it out again. The alarm was set off. Kade's soldiers are everywhere."

"I know, I know," I snapped, angry at the obvious. Reluctantly I joined him, and we continued moving. "Why did you free me?"

"I figured you'd believe me now. There's a lot you don't know. The last time I tried to fill you in, we were interrupted."

"You said something about them wanting bodies. Kade found me after you and Ben were caught. He gave me a very reasonable explanation, or at least I thought so at the time. I can't believe he lied to me." My ghost heart was breaking.

"Don't feel bad. He's fooled a lot of people," Jett assured me.

Reaching the downward slope of the mountain, we moved slowly. The trail we walked was old and overgrown, one of many winding footpaths that snaked over the mountains.

"Where are we going? We can run and hide, but Kade will eventually find us," I informed him.

"Not if we expose him," Jett said.

"And how are we supposed to do that? The world looks at Kade as their savior. Especially now that the plague is running rampant. Does Tandem have something to do with that?"

"Yes."

I shook my head in wonder and disgust. "How do you know

all of this? And why are you still here? If he never put you back into your own body, why didn't you leave? You obviously had the opportunity."

"I can't run away from this. There's so much more going on than you know."

"Yeah, big government conspiracy, right? Kade told me the government helped develop the force fields and how they were thinking about using prisoners' bodies. Giving them to people who need them so they could save money on health care and the expense of running prisons. I wasn't supposed to say anything, but piss on him and his secrets."

Jett snorted. "I'm surprised he told you that much. Some of it's actually the truth."

"So, this plague, it's been manufactured by the government and Tandem? Why? Is Tuck some sort of test experiment? Do they plan to use it to force reluctant prisoners into giving up their bodies by making them sick?"

"The 'plague,' as you call it, is a test. But Tuck is just the beginning. Soon it will spread worldwide."

"But why? What could they possibly gain by making so many people sick?" I demanded. "They had people lining up to enter Ghost Walk. They didn't need to resort to this."

"It wasn't enough. The plague will sicken about three quarters of the population. Tandem has been readying facilities all over the world to put the sick into stasis."

"Freeing up the bodies? What could they possibly need all those bodies for?" He was unbelievable.

"They don't need them all. Only about a million or so," he said grimly.

"The government and Tandem working together to steal a million bodies? Yeah, that sounds like a plan," I scoffed.

"And stashing the rest of them away for future use," Jett said, making a cold shiver run through me.

"Future use?" A terrible thought struck me. "They could replace important people in strategic positions to run the world. Is that what they're planning? World domination? No one would be the wiser until it was too late. And the bodies they don't use will be too sick to resist." What a completely paranoid thought.

He veered off the trail a quarter of the way down the mountain.

"Where were we going?" He still hadn't answered my question.

"It's better if I just show you," he insisted.

The walking was hard. At least it was on Jett. I found it slightly awkward to move sideways on a slope across the mountain. Finally, he stopped before a vertical rockface with shrubs sticking out at odd angles. Using both hands, he pulled branches away. From his back pocket, he retrieved the palm-sized disk that lit up when he ran his thumb over it. Shining the light inside, he revealed a hidden tunnel. I peered around him and saw it went deep inside the mountain.

"What is this?" I asked.

"It leads to a cavern. There's other entrances, but this is the most inconspicuous."

He went inside and started walking. Curious, I followed.

"How'd you know this was here? Kade said you were in a wheelchair when you went to Tandem. How could you have found this place or that cave you brought me to? Was it before — ?"

"I was never in a wheelchair," he interrupted. "However, my own body was incompatible."

"For what? The lifestyle you craved?" I knew I was being insensitive, but I didn't feel I owed him courtesy. Not when he walked around in my friend's body.

"No. For this planet."

I stopped walking. He turned to face me.

"Casa, let's keep going. You'll understand everything soon," he promised.

Less than a minute later, the tunnel led us to a huge cavern carved out of the bowels of the mountain. The sheer size of it was breathtaking. Jett's light dimmed, and he returned it to his pocket. The space was lit with circular disks, similar to Jett's on a larger scale, attached to the towering walls in intervals.

What held my attention were the pods. Hundreds of them lined up neatly, row upon row. They were shorter, narrower, and black, not white like the ones Mason and I found inside the other cavern. When I approached one and peered inside, I reeled back in shock. I hurried to another pod. It held the same as the first.

Whatever they were...they weren't human.

CHAPTER 15

From the corner of my eye, I saw Jett approach me. My voice seemed unable to work. I stared from the pod to Jett and back again.

"Don't freak out," he begged.

His comment about his body not being compatible with this planet now made sense. The pleasure of ignorance was no longer an option for me. "Is...is that what you are?" I finally stammered.

There was an uneasy pause before he replied. "Yes."

Of all the conspiracies Jett had conjured in my mind, this hadn't been one of them. Kade had added to them as well when he'd admitted to being in league with the government. But this... this was on a whole other level of crazy.

The pod measured about five feet long. A dome of clear glass covered the body like a transparent coffin. The body was like something out of a sci-fi movie, human-like in appearance—a head, torso, and limbs—but frail, long, thin, gangly arms and legs. Skin so thin I could make out blue veins beneath. The head was egg-shaped and largely out of proportion to the body, the eyes large and wide spaced, the mouth small and round with tiny lips, the nose, a slight bump with two little holes. It wore no clothing except a loincloth over its hips. I wasn't sure if it was male or female.

"Eleven of your Earth years ago, our ship crashed into this mountain. It hit on the other side, hidden from the town beneath. Anyone witnessing it would have mistaken it for lightning — there was a raging storm that night. The ghost technology Kade introduced here was something our race created out of necessity. It enabled us to fly our ships using voice command, allowing our bodies to remain in stasis for however long was necessary."

Funny. Tess and I had discussed this same thing, though it didn't feel quite so amusing now.

"The ones whose pods broke open from the crash reclaimed their bodies. They carved out tunnels and expanded this cavern using salvaged technology from the ship. The intact pods holding the bodies of their comrades were moved into the mountain, their lives sustained by that same technology. It took months, and during this time, they knew their failing bodies were incompatible."

Jett's stare was intense, no doubt gauging my reaction. He shoved his hands into his pockets as though he didn't know what to do with them. When he failed to continue, I gave him a brief nod, encouraging him to go on. What he revealed was incredible, but somehow, it all made sense. It couldn't be denied — the evidence before my eyes gave testimony to his tale.

"The gravity on Earth proved too much, slowly crushing them internally. Earth could not sustain them, even with their advanced knowledge and power. So they waited and came up with the plan to take human bodies and integrate themselves into the world, passing themselves off as their human hosts. Kade was the first, then Anna. It worked. The new bodies maintained them while their old ones remained in stasis. Before the original survivors died, they were able to send out a distress signal to their other ships. But even if help arrived, they had nowhere to go. They couldn't go home. Our planet was dead. Everyone who was lucky enough to secure a pod had been put into stasis, and several ships, each containing a thousand bodies, fled, seeking a habitable world. No one else had been successful — only us. And now the others are coming. But they will need bodies."

"Oh, my God." I didn't know how to react.

"You see now why we have to expose Kade and his plans."

"Why? Why would our own government agree to this?" I asked.

"The key players in charge are replacements. The others are simply following orders," Jett replied.

"And more of these are coming?" I motioned at the multitude of pods resting in the vast interior of the cavern.

"Yes."

"When?"

"Soon," he said. "Just over a year ago, we finally received a response transmission. Another ship reached out and began the journey here. They were still far off — we figured we'd have a few years before their arrival. But recently we received another message. That ship was able to reach out to others. More are coming. And they're closer than we thought. Kade had to change the plan. Instead of a slow roll-out, he now must accommodate the many who will arrive."

"It's why they went public with Ghost Walk."

"They did plan to introduce the technology to the world — eventually. Ghost Walk was meant to be our gift to mankind. Receiving that first transmission just hurried things along. Now it's been turned into something malevolent."

Another horrifying thought struck me. "The plague. They created it."

"Yes. Right after the second transmission, they decided they needed to take some drastic steps."

"And then? Once they've arrived, they'll line up and take the bodies. What happens next?" Did I dare to hear his answer?

He stared at me a moment, the internal battle he waged showing on his face. "You have to understand. Not all of us wanted this. Some of us wanted to reveal ourselves once we heard of Kade's plan. We wanted to ask humans for help. But Kade...he and the others — most of the others — thought the risk too great. We were too weak to fight if humans wished to be rid of us. I'm sorry, but all those years, we watched, and we learned everything we could about your species. We knew your fears. Knew how you destroyed things you didn't understand or perceived as a threat."

"Shoot first, ask questions later. Yeah, I get it. But that doesn't give you the right — "

"There is another even larger problem if we are to succeed and expose Kade and the others," Jett disclosed.

"What's that? What could be worse than flocking to our own demise?" I felt like laughing suddenly over the absurdity of it.

"When our ship crashed, its defenses and weapons were mostly destroyed. But the others, their ships will be intact. If they feel they have no other choice than to take this planet by force, they will. Our technology is greater than Earth's. If you had time to prepare, it might give humans a fighting chance. But that's what it would be — a fight. A great, devastating battle possibly waging for years, destroying many lives and unsettling this planet greatly. Kade sold his idea to the others, pitching peace, saying we would still be allowing humans a life here."

"As ghosts," I said.

"Yes."

"What a choice. Face annihilation or life as ghosts, watching our planet being run by alien invaders."

"I have been many people in many places. One thing I've learned about humans is your absolute desire to be free. You would wish to fight if given the chance."

"I agree," I admitted.

"There are those of us, like me, who feel we can reach a compromise. If humans were willing to share their bodies —"

"Are you kidding me? You think people are just going to willingly give up their bodies?"

"In exchange for the technology we can offer! Many diseases on your planet can be cured by us now. Wouldn't you have given up your body for a year or so if you could get it back cured? I've been here long enough to know that many would consider the trade to be worth it."

"I dunno," I argued. "I think most people would have a hard time believing their bodies would be returned when the year's up. What if one or more of you decides they like the skin they're in and doesn't want to give it back? Ever consider that? Even if you have a contract drawn up, who's going to enforce it? You guys will be holding all the cards, and there's no one to stop you if you change your minds."

"I admit there are some drawbacks. It's why we discussed the incarcerated. That idea was mine."

"Trying to sell the idea of taking over inmate's bodies may not sit well with the general population," I predicted.

"Compared to the alternative?" His polite way of reminding me that this was going to happen whether we wanted it or not. "Don't you see? We have to try!" Jett stared at me, willing me to comply.

"No one would believe us."

"We can show them proof. Show them this place." He pulled a cell phone out of his pocket.

"People could watch a video and hear what we're saying, but Tuck is surrounded by the army! No one in or out. Everyone would be afraid to come here anyway since a plague is raging. People would think we're insane. Where are all the ghosts? Your people?" I asked though I feared I knew the answer.

"Integrated. Before you ask, all the human ghosts are here — at least as far as I know. They're confined. Many of them for several years."

The thought horrified me. The team had spent six months in this mountain, unaware of the lurking treachery. Would that be the fate of my parents? My little sister? "You estimate there's a million more coming?"

"Thereabout," Jett answered, the tone of his voice holding a note of fatality.

"There's not enough room here for the pods, human or otherwise."

"The pods containing the bodies of my people will be held on their ships. The human pods will be stored in all of Tandem's facilities around the world — until they're needed."

"Humans will figure it out," I said. *They have to.*

His look was grim. "They'll have no idea until it's too late. They won't even see the ships when they arrive. Kade sent out warnings, so they'll be cloaked and can elude your radar."

Well, I guess we're screwed.

"What are their plans? They won't need all of us. What happens to the others?"

"Obviously, they won't be able to ghost every human. There

are, after all, over seven billion of you. Once enough of my people are assimilated and placed strategically in society, they won't need to hide their motives anymore. Most humans will be left alone, as long as they don't get in the way. The ones who willingly capitulate will probably be rewarded with a relatively short loss of their body and soon returned to a healthy one— if a cure is necessary. Those who defy them will be ghosted or imprisoned, or I hate to say it—eliminated. Failing a smooth takeover, one of the back-up plans is the 'plague,' as you call it. Debilitate humans into capitulation. It's a last resort. And, as you've seen, very effective."

"Can they...destroy ghosts?" If so, there'd be no need to bother with their force fields. Yet, would the bodies remain alive if the ghosts were dead? *What a fascinating and terrible thought.*

Jett shook his head. "Energy can be contained, but even we lack the ability to destroy it. I have no doubt they will be willing to sacrifice bodies to force submission."

I eyed all the pods, an idea forming in my head. "Then pull the plug on them. Kade's in here somewhere. At least unplug him." As much as I wanted to do just that, I wasn't capable, obviously. But I could lead others to this spot—others who would do the deed.

"You're asking me to kill my own kind," Jett said. The way he looked at me should have made me ashamed. Maybe if I searched long enough, I'd find guilt or disgust buried somewhere inside me. But at this moment, faced with the shock and desperation coursing through me, I couldn't conjure anything but this deadly knee-jerk reaction.

"And mine are as good as dead if you don't. Or may as well be." Let that be my justification.

"I'm determined to reach a compromise. You've got to see it's the only way. Even if you destroy these bodies, thousands more are coming. If they can't contact us, they will know something has happened. They will come in guns blazing." He stared at me a moment. "Think about it. How did you feel all those years trapped in your dying body? We have the technology to heal practically every sickness and disability on your planet," he reminded me.

"Then fix your own damn bodies and leave ours alone."

"Don't you think we've tried that? And before you even suggest it, no, we can't integrate with animals, or insects, or robots. The host must be biologically compatible."

"Why can't you stay as ghosts then? You hold the force field technology. Destroy it. That way, you'll be free. Humans can't very well object to your presence then." I was grasping at straws, but I had to try.

"I already suggested that. They won't be satisfied living here that way."

"Yet, they'd subject us to it," I snapped.

"Then help me. Help me tell the world the truth. If we work together, humans and Teratilas, we can figure something out before it's too late."

I snorted. "That's what you're called?" I had to refrain from calling them tarantulas. I shook my head. What was wrong with me? Life as we knew it was about to end, and I was cracking jokes in my head.

"Laugh all you want. You won't find it funny when they get here."

"Yeah, well, piss on you. Why are you helping me? You have nothing to lose here. You're the one with all the power, and all I can do is watch this unfold. Look at me! Or should I say look *through me.* I can't do anything like this. I'm useless."

"Then let's get you back in your body," Jett said.

"What?"

"Your body. It's here."

"It is? Where?" I tampered down my excitement with reality. "It doesn't matter. My body is sick. I couldn't walk across this giant room without an oxygen tank, never mind getting down this mountain."

He smiled and began winding his way around the pods. "That's where you're wrong. You're all fixed up, ready to go." He talked about my body like it was a car returning from the garage.

"They fixed me?"

He nodded, and I followed him. "Good as new. You're lucky I got to you when I did. They were about ready to give you over for reintegration."

The thought of someone else wearing my body annoyed me. I'd spent years resenting it, but it was still mine.

"The world knows you, or at least they'll remember you. They've seen you on the news promoting Ghost Walk. Accepting Ben being in remission is one thing, maybe even seeing Ethan. But seeing you miraculously cured of CF—now that's another thing. They will listen when you talk. You can make people see the truth."

Was he right? Would the world listen to me, realize the truth before it was too late? Infused with hope, I followed Jett towards my body.

CHAPTER 16

My body looked so serene lying there in my pod, hands folded over my chest. Could it be true I was healed? I'd walk, dance, climb, run? All without fear of collapse from lack of oxygen? All the things I'd seen others take for granted, what I'd longed to do, always dreaming, always praying for a miracle?

Jett opened the glass cover of my pod and gently lifted out my body. He placed it on a gurney and wheeled me over beside a transference machine. Simply step in, and I'd be returned.

"What are you waiting for?" Jett smiled at me, and I couldn't contain my excitement.

"I'm really healed? This isn't some trick, right?"

"I know this is hard, but you need to trust me, Casa." His tone was gentle, his stare unwavering as he met my eyes. "Let's get you home."

Good thing ghosts couldn't cry.

With one last gaze at my translucent image, I plunged into the machine. It took only moments, swirling and twirling through space, to return to my body. Once the dense, familiar feeling settled over me, I blinked open my eyes. I lay still for a moment, reacquainting myself with the heaviness of flesh and bone. My arms and legs twitched, filled with pins and needles, like awakening from a long nap. With Jett's aid, I sat up. Cautiously, I took a breath. Then another deeper one. My lungs expanded, and the pain and breathlessness I expected to feel did not come.

"Ready?" Jett asked, watching me.

I nodded, and his arm went around my waist, supporting my weight as my wobbly legs touched the ground. He continued to hold and steady me as he guided my slow, uncertain steps.

"I don't want to rush you, but once Kade discovers I've snagged your pod, he's going to come. He'll know to look here."

I disentangled Jett's arm and took a few steps on my own. "Okay. I'm okay now." I wanted to run. Jump. Cartwheel— though I'd never attempted one before. But now wasn't the time.

"Good. Right there should be fine," he said, pulling the phone from his pocket.

"Can you get a signal in here?" I asked, self-consciously fiddling with my hair.

He peered at the screen. "No. It's solid rock all around. We'll do some pictures and a video with you showing the pods, then upload everything once we get clear." He took several still shots and then nodded. "You know what to say?"

"I...." What could I say to convince the world of imminent danger without sounding crazy?

"And...go!" Jett said.

Blankly, I stared at the tiny green light on his phone. "Ah, hi. My name is Casa Landry. I'm hoping many of you recognize me from the original six who first attempted Ghost Walk. As you know, each of us had a debilitating disease. Mine is cystic fibrosis. Or should I say, mine *was*? I am healed, and I wish I could tell you it's a miracle, but it's not." I signaled to Jett, and he swung the phone around to show himself before turning it back to me.

"That's Ben's body. Also healed. Now you're probably wondering why I'm telling you this, but I have an extremely important message for you...for the world."

Jett made a circling gesture with his hand, indicating I should continue.

"Please, everyone, I need you to listen to me. I need you to tell your friends, your family, anyone and everyone who will listen. Earth is in danger. I want you to see where I am." I gestured around the cavern, and Jett moved the phone, slowly panning right and left and zooming in on one of the alien pods.

"What you're seeing is the inside of Tuck's mountain. A gigantic cavern carved out, using technology far beyond our capabilities. And this...this is an alien. Please! Please don't tune out. I need you to believe what I'm telling you is the truth. I swear to God."

Jett aimed the phone back at me. I took a deep breath and let it out slowly. He nodded and gave me a thumbs up.

"You have been lied to. Tandem is not what you think it is. Kade Hunter is not who you think he is. Ghost Walk is real. But what you don't know is that it's alien technology. Kade Hunter came up this mountain ten years ago and returned a different man. That's because he *is* different. Ghost Walk is not a new invention. It's existed here in Tuck's mountains for over a decade. The first person to use it was Kade. The man you now know as Dr. Kade Hunter is an alien residing in the real Kade Hunter's body."

I took another deep breath, and Jett again panned around the cavern's interior.

"Look at them. All of them, numbering almost a thousand. Each one is inhabiting a body they have stolen. And that's not the worst part. More are coming. Thousands more, maybe a million, arriving on ships we can't see. There is no plague! Not really. It's been manufactured by the aliens. These aliens are called Teratilas. They come from far away. Their planet is dead, and they used Ghost Walk technology to fly their ships, putting their bodies into stasis, seeking a new world. Kade's ship crashed into the back of Tuck's mountain eleven years ago. They've been here ever since. Waiting. Watching. Slowing stealing bodies and integrating themselves into our world. But now, more are on their way. They needed bodies fast to accommodate them."

I stared at Jett and saw a hint of fear and sadness in his eyes.

"Not all of them are bad," I relented. "Some of them are against Kade's plan. There can be a compromise. Their technology can heal human bodies of disease, sickness, and disabilities. Together, we can reach an agreement beneficial to everyone. We can share this planet. But we need to act. We need to stop rushing into Tandem's facilities and putting ourselves into stasis. We need to say *enough*. We know you're here. We know what you're doing. Tandem can stop this plague and heal the sick. We can reach a compromise without bloodshed without war."

Jett was nodding his head in agreement. He made a gesture to wrap it up.

"If we refuse to succumb to fear, we can rise up together... stand together...as one," I said.

He ended the transmission and put his phone away. "Good. That was good."

"Do you think they'll listen? They'll believe me?"

"I don't know. I hope so. At least the seeds of doubt will be planted. We'll have to wait for them to grow," he said.

"Now what?"

He started winding through the pods, heading in the direction of the tunnel we'd entered from. "Let's go."

The sound of many booted feet echoed around the cavern's interior. I needed no further urging. We raced down the tunnel as fast as my bare feet would allow. Ben wore boots, but for some reason, he appeared to be struggling more than me. He emitted loud, gasping breaths and held his ribs.

We slowed as we approached the exit, knowing our steps would have to be measured and careful now. Awkwardly, we exited and moved downward. The decline grew steeper, forcing us to grab hold of shrubs and rocks to aid our descent.

Exhilaration flowed through me. Despite all that had happened, I allowed myself to rejoice in being reunited with my body. To feel. My lungs expanded in my chest, sucking in deep, easy, painless gulps of air. My hands and feet took in each surface I touched, delighting in the variety of textures. Soft wind caressed my face and ruffled my hair.

"We'll find a place to hide," Jett informed me, pausing to rest a moment. Eyeing my hospital attire, he shrugged out of the light jacket he wore and passed it to me.

I put it on while I gazed at our surroundings. It dawned on me there was no light below. Nothing. We must be on the backside of Tuck's mountain. At the base of it, endless miles of forest stretched out, no civilization for God only knew how far.

"We can't go this way," I informed him. "We'll die out there."

He shook his head. "I know. Made that mistake last time. Kade will search the town first. He'll be waiting. Our best bet is to make our way around. He's probably thought of that too, so we'll have to be on guard."

The loud pulsing noise of a helicopter exploded over our heads.

"Shit," I exclaimed.

Instinctively, we both leaped into a short mound of shrubs

and ducked low. A strong beam of light lit up the mountainside, moving methodically, seeking us out.

"Don't move," Jett warned.

Well, duh.

When the chopper moved on, we did a clumsy, sideways jog down the mountain. Three more times, in the course of an hour or so, we had to dive for cover. Luckily, we eluded detection. The chopper finally gave up searching the backside of the mountain and moved upward, either to land or to search the other side. Jett and I lay on our backs, gasping in air.

"I wonder if they got to Mason and his dad. Kade sent the chopper out to get them right before he locked me up," I said.

"Who knows? There's nothing we can do for them right now." He sat up and peered around, as though getting his bearings. "There's a stream around here somewhere. I brought a canteen to carry water in."

"Let's hope it's good to drink." Now that I was in my body again, I would grow thirsty, tired, hungry, and cold. Hopefully, not crampy with the runs from stream water. Maybe being a ghost wasn't so bad.

"It's fine," he assured me. He got up and put out his hand to help me up. That's when he noticed my feet. "Damn, I forgot about shoes or boots." He eyed his, and I thought he might take them off and give them to me like his jacket, but his feet were too big.

"Don't worry about it. My adrenalin's pumping so fast I didn't even notice." Of course, now that I was thinking about it, my feet began to ache.

"I could carry you."

"How gallant, Sir Galahad."

"Who?" He made a half-hearted grab for me, as though he'd

throw me over his shoulder.

"Never mind. Piss off. Let's go," I insisted, eluding him.

He gave up. "If we find the stream, there's a place nearby we can crash."

"Great."

Nothing about this thrilled me now that the euphoria of being back in my body had passed. My family and maybe my friends were trapped in Tandem, in one form or another. Aliens from outer space were going to invade us any moment, checking out our bodies like books in a library. But they weren't planning on returning them.

An ache in my chest almost overcame me. It wasn't a physical pain, more of an emotional one. I'd failed my family, allowing them to be taken in by the enemy, all the while being grateful. What a fool I'd been. I recalled the conversations Tess and I had about all the possibilities for Ghost Walk. We hadn't known it at the time, but what we'd envisioned had already come to pass. The technology would allow for space travel, putting bodies into stasis, and voice commanded ships to travel long distances. Little did we know it'd be aliens using it to seek out and invade our planet.

CHAPTER 17

We found the stream and sat by the water's edge while Jett filled up his canteen. He'd drunk deeply upon arrival, and I watched him carefully for any signs of discomfort. Despite being desperately thirsty, I refrained. Our only light was the stars and moon. We were too afraid to use Jett's flashlight disc, which could pinpoint our location.

Jett pulled out the phone, turned it on, and held it up. "Got a signal."

"Great," I replied, less enthusiastically than I felt. Once the proof hit the Internet, shit was gonna hit the fan. It was a good thing, I assured myself. Knowing was better than burying our heads in the sand, hoping it'd all go away.

"I'm uploading the video and pictures to all social media sites. Hopefully, they'll go viral."

Several minutes later, he put the phone on the ground and stomped it with his boot. He didn't have to tell me he feared them tracking the signal to us.

"Aren't you afraid Kade is going to destroy your body?" The thought abruptly occurred to me. It'd be the easiest way to eliminate the threat—at least one of them.

"No."

"He's gonna want payback for our escape and exposing them like that." Hopefully, he didn't take it out on anyone I knew and loved.

Jett capped the canteen and returned it to his pack. We sat side by side while he contemplated the water for a full minute.

"He's my brother," he revealed.

"What?"

"Kade. Fake Kade. He's my brother. That's why I know he won't kill me."

"Holy crap." What else could I say?

"Yeah, holy crap." He appeared thoughtful. "That time I saw you at Tandem after I'd hidden Ben, I went back to get Kade out—the real Kade Hunter—hoping the chaos I'd created would distract them. I failed, obviously."

"That's when you saw me outside and stopped me from talking to Fake Kade at the helicopter."

"Yeah. I tried again tonight. And failed again. I know his ghost is in the facility, but even I don't know the complete layout down there. He's hidden well. That could have really convinced the world if I'd managed to spring him." He stared at me a moment and smiled. "It wasn't a complete waste, at least."

I gave him a tight smile back. "I hope what we did worked." I thought for a second. "What if they send an airstrike and destroy the mountaintop? Destroy your people in the pods?"

"Highly unlikely, considering the extent of civilians inside Tandem. Besides, remember the second scenario I told you about?" He peered overhead as though jets were already on their way.

"The new arrivals would show up guns blazing. Even now,

if the world takes us seriously and decides to fight, we'll face war. I know what you said about us is right. We'd rather have a fighting chance than go like lambs to the slaughter. I just worry about what will be left. That it'll be for nothing. You guys will still win, and meanwhile, half our planet will be destroyed, and half of us will be dead, and the rest will still wind up as ghosts."

"Are you sorry you know the truth?" he asked.

"No." Sitting, rubbing my feet, made them hurt more. I moved back enough to stretch out my legs and put my toes in the water. "I remember when I was old enough to understand what was wrong with me. The doctors, and even my mom, tried to sugar coat my condition. My dad told me the truth. He sat with me and explained everything. Together we looked up whatever we could find in medical books, online, even chat rooms. We learned together. Cried together. But it made me feel better knowing the truth."

"You're very brave, Casa."

If someone else had said that, I would think they were bullshitting me. Jett's face was serious.

"I'm scared to death," I admitted. "Even more, I think, than when I learned about my condition. The thing that really sucks about being cured is that they didn't do it for me. They did it for someone else. Like, how long am I going to be able to live in this body? This healthy body, which now feels like a curse since it makes aliens want it?"

"I don't know what's going to happen. I only knew I couldn't stand by and watch and do nothing. For ten years, I've been different people. Most of us stay in the same body cause it's kind of a bitch acclimating, but I couldn't. I felt guilty. I'm ashamed to say it didn't stop me from taking one after another. I wanted to experience what it is to be human. To live on a planet that wasn't taking its last breath. It doesn't excuse my actions, but you've got to understand, we were in that ship for almost fifty years, searching for a place to call home. And I know it doesn't give us the right. What Kade and the others are doing is wrong. There's got to be another way. Damned if I know what it is."

I could hear the emotion in his voice. He was afraid, desperate, same as me.

A wolf or coyote suddenly bayed at the moon, making me shiver.

"You said there was shelter nearby?" I got to my feet, my thirst and sore feet forgotten, momentarily replaced by the need for safety. I was no longer invincible.

The nearby cover he'd mentioned was more of an alcove, an indent in a monstrous boulder that must have rolled down the mountain probably a million years ago. The top part of the rock looked sturdy enough but only allowed us about four feet or so of protection beneath. A blanket of crinkly leaves covered a smooth rock floor.

Jett pulled a blanket from his pack and laid it out for us. "It's long enough we can pull the sides over to cover us," he suggested.

We'd be crammed in there together, side by side. *Great.* Either that or the cold forest floor. I crawled in and laid as close to the edge of the rock as possible. Jett got in and laid beside me.

"Have you got enough blanket to cover you?" he asked, pulling his end over, barely covering his body. Instead of answering, I attempted to do the same with mine. When I'd pulled it far as it could go, our fisted hands brushed each other. A fizzle of warmth shot through me. We lay there in uncomfortable silence for a moment.

Needing a distraction, I cleared my throat and coughed. "Um, so, you're an alien. That's freaky."

"Yup."

"I always wondered, you know, looking up at the stars, if there was life out there."

"There is," he said. "Not anywhere close to here, though."

I wiggled around a bit, trying to get more comfortable. "That must have been pretty cool, flying around in outer space."

His shoulder lifted in a shrug. "I guess. Though the circumstances weren't ideal. Being a ghost that long, it's hard."

"I can imagine." I'd only been one for a couple of months — I couldn't see doing it for decades. "Your planet, what was it like?"

"You mean before?"

When I didn't answer right away, he took my silence as a yes.

"It was...nice — kind of like here, with forests and lakes, mountains and cities, deserts. We had two moons, though. And I say forests, but the trees were different in colors and shapes. There were animals too, I guess you could call them. Not as many as here, and different."

"What happened? Why the urgent need to escape?" I turned my head to study the silhouette of his profile. His eyes remained fixed on the rock overhead.

"Things changed — not overnight, but slowly over time. Our planet, Cambrius, was maybe half the size of Earth. It became overpopulated and had trouble sustaining everyone with food, shelter, medicine, stuff like that. Mostly food. We became divided, closing ourselves off according to where we lived, battling with one another. The ones in charge, like Kade, they tried to discover solutions, tried to get us to work together. They started building ships and sending out scouts to look for other planets to inhabit in our own galaxy. There was nothing."

"You said your planet was destroyed," I reminded him.

"The leaders sent out signals, hoping to get a response. Our world was established by a colony who'd fled their dying planet. We knew we weren't the only life in the universe. There wasn't any intelligent life when we settled on Cambrius. Only animal and plant life."

"How convenient," I said drolly.

He ignored my comment. "Unfortunately for us, one of our transmissions was picked up by a race called Srotagillas. Evil, destructive beings."

That got my attention. I rolled on my side and stared at Jett with rapt attention. "What happened?"

He sighed. "We were invaded."

"Imagine that."

"I know." He'd heard the irony in my voice. "It's kind of the same, but not. The Srotagillas are like the Romans of your history. Conquerors of everything in their path. Unlike the Romans, they didn't come to lay down roots. They rape planets, take everything they can, and annihilate it so no one else can have it."

"Shit," I gasped.

"They have no desire for peace, for compromise, for mercy. They can't be reasoned with, they can't be bribed, they're too powerful to be threatened," he continued. "And trust me, we tried everything. Our technology is equal to theirs. The sheer number of them overcame us. They just kept coming and coming, until there was nothing left to fight for."

"So, you fled," I surmised.

He nodded. "As far and as fast as we could."

"How long did you fight them?"

"I guess it'd equate to one Earth year," he said. "One good thing came of it. It brought our world together, united against a common enemy. Just like the alien invasion movies you earthlings are so fond of."

I snorted. "They always turn out that way, but who knows We'd probably dissolve into anarchy. I guess we'll find out."

He turned on his side, so we were face to face. "What happened to us.... I know how it feels to lose your planet to invaders. That' why I can't be a part of it. Granted, we're not without mercy, and we don't plan to destroy Earth. But still, it's wrong."

I stifled a yawn. "Let's get a few hours of sleep. We'll figure it out in the morning."

He nodded. "Goodnight, Casa."

"Goodnight." I rolled onto my other side, presenting him with my back. If I couldn't see him, maybe I could forget he was there. Right now, I wanted to rest. Needed to, if I had to face what the morning would bring.

Whatever that may be.

CHAPTER 18

A cool, damp morning greeted me when I opened my eyes. Without needing to look, I knew I was alone. Jett wasn't around when I crawled out into the overcast, drizzly morning. I stretched, reaching my arms up over my head, hearing my bones crack and pop in protest.

"Jett?" If he heard me, he didn't respond. My legs wobbled, and the sensation of hunger and something else greeted me. *Ah*, I had to pee. It'd been a while since I'd had that urge.

As soon as I'd taken a moment of privacy behind some brush, the sound of chopper blades blasted over the mountaintop. At least they'd waited for me to finish. The forest was dense on this side of the incline. By leaning up against a tree and holding still, I easily eluded detection. I hoped Jett was as lucky.

"Jett! You need to come back," a voice boomed over a megaphone as the chopper took another low swipe past. That was Kade. Well, the alien in Kade's body. Jett's brother. He sounded desperate, and part of me almost felt guilty for causing him distress. Until I remembered all the lies he'd told. And how he'd stolen my family.

"Jett! Please, listen to me. You're in danger. You need to come back."

Give it a rest, lying bastard. I wasn't brave enough to yell in return. I'd just gotten my body back—my *healthy* body. No way was I going to hand it over.

A stumbling in the brush gained my attention.

"Casa!" Jett hollered, coming into view.

He looked like shit.

I grabbed hold of his shirt when he reached me—it was damp with sweat. "Shut up, idiot! Your brother's out there in the chopper. Can't you hear him?"

He looked around, his face lighting up with what appeared to be hope. "Kade? He's here?"

"In the chopper. They just flew past. We'll have to wait...." my sentence broke off as Jett suddenly took off in the direction of the clearing ahead.

I tore after him. "Stop! He'll see you. Damn it, Jett!"

But I was too late.

We burst into the clearing just as the chopper flew by. It spun back around and paused, dangling overhead. I grappled with Jett, trying in vain to catch hold of him and pull him to safety. Both of us a bedraggled, out-of-breath mess, I stared up at the chopper. Jett's hands eluded mine and swung overhead, reaching out to Kade. I slapped his face—hard—finally gaining his attention.

He bent forward, his hands braced on his knees, his chest heaving as he looked at me.

"Casa. I'm sorry. So sorry," he gasped out. Were those tears in his eyes? And fear? So overwhelming I could almost feel it.

"What is wrong with you?" I stared at him in disbelief, shocked by his betrayal, while I backed towards the forest.

He raised his arm. I followed where his finger pointed

upward, his hand trembling.

In the distance, resting like a falcon floating on the wind, was a huge ship. Black, long and wide, jagged and deadly, it looked like a phantom of hell. I froze mid-step. *How the hell did I not see that?*

"We're too late," I gasped. "They're here."

Jett was shaking his head when I finally tore my gaze away and stared at him.

"No. I don't know how. After all this time...."

I itched to slap him again.

"What are you talking about?"

Vaguely in the background, I was aware of Kade's voice, pleading with Jett. Leaves and small branches whipped around us. We braced ourselves against the whirlwind as the chopper lowered and landed nearby. When Jett gained his balance, he ran towards me and grabbed hold of my arm before I had a chance to react.

"Get off!" My attempts to shake him were futile. My feet dragged, and my free arm swung madly as he hauled me towards the chopper. I saw the side door swing open, and Kade jumped out. In seconds I stood before him, glaring defiantly. Jett let go of my arm when I stopped fighting, a wave of cold calm washing over me. I clenched my left fist and smashed it into Jett's face.

Kade grabbed me when I attempted to hit Jett again.

"Traitor! Liar!" I screamed.

Kade shook me, and I stilled, momentarily appeased by the bloody lip Jett sported. He spit blood and wiped his face with the back of his hand.

"Casa, I'm sorry. That ship. Damn it all! It's not ours. I swear it."

What was he talking about? He'd changed sides. That much

was obvious. Kade's grip on my arms tightened, turning my attention back to him.

"It's true, Casa." Over my head, he stared at Jett. The look on his face frightened me. He didn't look angry or triumphant. He looked scared. "They must have intercepted one of the transmissions we sent and followed it here."

"Have you contacted our ships?" Jett asked.

"I've tried. They've gone silent," Kade replied.

"You don't think they...." Jett let his question trail off.

Kade shook his head once. "No. We have to hope not."

"What the hell are you talking about?" I demanded.

They both looked up, their sights fixed on that huge destroyer looming over Tuck.

"It's not one of ours," Kade said to me.

"It's the Srotagillas," Jett said. He stared at his brother, eyes pleading. "What do we do?" He sounded like a child, desperate not to get into trouble. Like he expected Kade to fix everything.

"Come back to Tandem," Kade said. "Both of you." He included me in his gaze.

Jett, the chicken-hearted traitor, scrambled into the chopper before Kade had finished his sentence. Kade, realizing he still restrained me, let go.

"Casa, I'm sorry. For the lies, the deception. It didn't start out that way, believe me."

I glared at him and retreated a step. "Maybe not, but then you put yourselves first, before us, before the humans you've masqueraded as for ten bloody years. You stole my family, my friends." My voice hitched, and I remembered I could cry now. I wouldn't give him the satisfaction.

"I've made a mess of things. Jett was right. It shouldn't have happened this way. We should have compromised," he said.

"You think? And now that your mortal enemy is here—thanks to you—now you're sorry?"

"It's not too late to fix this. We've fought them before—"

"And lost," I interrupted. "Which brought you here. Ironic, is not it? The invaders are back. But you are not the ones to pay this time. We are. You brought these devils to our door."

I itched to punch his face as well. He was pale, haggard. *Good.* I wanted him to suffer too. All his well-made plans were failing rapidly. Unfortunately, Earth now faced two enemies instead of one. I wondered if anyone had taken our broadcast literally. If they didn't before, the ones seeing that monstrosity in the sky must realize now the danger was real. How many were there? Just this one, or were they all over the place? How did Kade plan to fix this? Their only ship was buried in Tuck's mountainside. Their technology was superior to ours, but how much of it did they still possess? Enough to fight off this threat?

"Come back with me to Tandem," Kade begged. "I have a cure for the sickness. I'm planning to send out drones and the chopper over the town to release it. It's airborne. It should take only hours for people to start to recover. Everyone inside Tandem has been treated."

"Did you ghost my family?" I demanded.

"No. Even now, anyone we pulled out that had the sickness is being returned. The others as well—at least the ones we can get to. Some of the ghosts are still out doing daredevil stuff—it's not like I can reach them. The critically ill ones, many of those ghosts, are gone too, but some of them are here. Their bodies have been cured, and they've been returned. We've been briefing them on what's going on."

"You told them what you did? How you deceived them?" I pressed.

"No. They wouldn't—"

"What?" I exploded. "Even now, you lie. You want their help to fight, don't you? You think they won't help if they know what you planned."

"Casa! Please get in!" Jett pleaded from inside the chopper. "There's nothing you can do from here. It's not safe. I've seen what those monsters are capable of. Come back with us. Kade can tell you everything."

The sheer terror on his face convinced me. Grim lipped, I nodded to Kade, and we both climbed into the chopper. He slammed the door shut, and we took off towards Tandem. Conversation over the sound of the blades was impossible. I glared at both of them—the chicken and the snake.

We soon landed on the helipad and made a hasty exit. Two scientists in white lab coats were waiting, each holding a long metal box with gloved hands. They climbed into the chopper after we left it. I figured that was the cure Kade was talking about. How convenient to have it readily available for just such an emergency.

Kade ushered Jett and me to the elevator shaft. His hand on my back would have sent delighted shivers through me in the past. Now it felt like a cattle prod. We descended below, and as soon as the doors opened, he hurried down the passageway. Jett followed along obediently while I hung back, my narrow gaze fixed on them.

How did I know that ship wasn't some trick? A holographic image aimed at the sky? Something to make us come running back with our tails tucked between our legs? If it weren't for Jett's absolute confirmation of danger, I wouldn't have gone so willingly. The fear on his face had been animated. That look alone held an unspoken volume of panic. A shiver did run through me now — one of fear.

At the end of the hall, we continued towards the resting room. Beyond that room was where Mason and I had seen all those stasis pods. Now I knew what they were intended for and why there were so many of them. In the resting room, Kade opened a cupboard door, scrounged around for a moment, then passed me a pair of running shoes. There were a little tight but fit me well enough.

"Everyone's in here," Kade said, nodding in the direction of the human pod arena.

When he reached for the door, intending to open it, I spoke. "Wait. Where's the rest of us?" I gestured at the single pod in the room. Mine was probably still in the alien pod cavern.

Kade stared at me like he was confused for a moment, then it dawned on him. "Ah, yeah, we moved them. The other four are still in the program. None of their ghosts are here. They left town with their families, except for Mason — he's still in Tuck."

That was good to hear — if it was the truth.

"Even Ethan?" I narrowed my gaze, watching him closely for signs of deceit — not that I knew what they'd be. I highly doubted the real Ethan had been in his own body when I'd seen him with Kade at the chopper anyway. No doubt it'd been one of Kade's alien cronies.

"Yes. Even Ethan."

I guess Ben was the only one of us original six he'd kept prisoner. I wondered where he was right now. Trapped in one of those rooms like I'd been? I felt guilty suddenly, trusting that Ben had been the real deal when he'd freed me. I wondered if Kade would be willing to force his own brother out in order to return Ben's body to its rightful owner. I doubted his goodwill gestures would extend that far.

"Where did you move them?" I asked.

"They're safe in with our own stasis pods. I guess you didn't get as good a look around in there as you thought you did," Kade said, only revealing a slight amount of sarcasm.

I didn't give him the satisfaction of blushing. "Maybe I was too excited about getting my own body back."

"You're welcome for that," Kade said.

"You didn't do it for me," I reminded him.

He avoided my glare as he opened the door to the vast arena, and we went through. The vacant pods were still there, pushed off to the sides of the room to accommodate the large group of people milling about. Tables had been set up down the center of the space, upon which sat refreshments. Some chairs had been brought in, and all of them were occupied. The rest stood. I estimated close to two hundred people.

The climate of the room was mixed. Mostly people appeared confused. As soon as they noticed Kade, the room became silent, then everyone started talking at once.

Kade held up his hands for silence. "Please, if everyone will listen, I'll tell you what I know."

"You said they'd been briefed," I reminded him.

"Casa?" Tess rushed forward and embraced me.

"Tess!" I held her arms and looked her over. Besides the dark circles under her eyes, she appeared healthy. "Mom and Dad?"

"They're here," she assured me. "You're in your body! You're not a ghost," Tess said, as though realizing her hands didn't pass through me.

"Casa!" Dad was soon rushing up to me with Mom right behind him. Both of them embraced me next. They looked tired but recovered as well.

"Are you okay? Why are you returned? Are you sick?" Mom

and Dad both pelted me with questions.

"I'm okay! Really. I never had the plague, and my body has been healed of CF. I don't have all the details right now. Just know, I'm fine and healthy," I assured them. The shocked looks on their faces revealed a bevy of emotions; shock, wonder, confusion, and hope. "Kade's trying to make an announcement."

We moved off to the right of Kade, who was still trying to get everyone's attention. Jett stood beside him, staring around at the crowd as though unsure of what to do. He was wearing Ben's body, and perhaps he worried he'd have to act the part. I highly doubted the real Ben was among the crowd. In fact, I didn't see any ghosts. Now that Kade needed human allies, I wondered what he planned on doing with all the human ghosts he had hidden in this mountain. There would be roughly a thousand of them. Putting them all back would be impossible at the moment since their bodies were probably spread out over the globe and occupied by aliens. How much would Fake Kade admit to? If he told the truth, would anyone be willing to help him? If things didn't go as he planned, this could easily get ugly fast. I doubted any of these people would have seen my broadcast exposing the Teratilas' dastardly deeds. In fact, buried as we were in the mountain, none of them even knew an alien invasion had been unfolding for months, never mind the new one happening right now.

The crowd finally quieted enough for Kade to speak. They watched him intently. He gestured for me to join him and Jett. Reluctantly, I did so. My family tagged along and stood at the front of the pack. Kade gave me a long, hard look before he began.

"I have some very disturbing news to share. It will be difficult for you all to accept." Pregnant pause, my mother would have said. "First, some good news. We have discovered a cure for the mysterious sickness, as many of you may have realized. As I speak, the cure is being distributed around Tuck. We can expect to see a significant recovery within hours." Everyone cheered, and Kade accepted the praise with a grim nod. "Now, what I'm about to tell you is quite alarming, I'm afraid." He took a deep breath and closed his eyes for a second or two, as though praying for guidance, before staring back at the crowd. "Right now, over the town of Tuck, and dozens of other locations around the world, there are enemy spaceships manned by hostile aliens intent on invading Earth."

That answered my question about how many there were. The crowd erupted in fear and disbelief. Some of them actually laughed as though it was a joke. It took several moments for Kade to regain their attention.

"Please! Please, everyone! Listen to me. There is more." Silence reigned, except for a few hiccups from some who'd broken into tears. "I am here to admit that we've known this threat existed and was very much a concern. I am here to admit that Ghost Walk is alien technology."

Jett and I exchanged a look. Now I took a deep breath.

Here we go.

CHAPTER 19

Kade spent several minutes regaining control of the crowd. When a lull in the hysterics happened, he dove right in.

"When you leave the mountain, you may hear false rumors about the intention of Ghost Walk," Kade warned. "Please know, this technology was meant for the betterment of human lives. Not only do we have Ghosting technology, but we also have cures. Hundreds of cures for disease, sickness, and paralysis." He put out his hand for me, and reluctantly I took it.

Kade leaned to whisper in my ear. "This is the only way to win this war, Casa. Otherwise, it is the end for all of us."

I swallowed hard and nodded.

"This is Casa Landry, one of the original members of the team of six. And this is Ben Switt. Both are cured and have been returned to their bodies after only a short while," Kade revealed.

"It's a miracle!" someone in the crowd yelled, causing others to erupt in loud speculation again.

"It is not a miracle!" Kade called out. "Many of you among us came to Tandem entering into Ghost Walk, putting your debilitated bodies into stasis. Those of you who did so must now have realized your bodies have been cured." There were several nods of agreement, and others called out they thought they'd felt better or different. In their defense, they had just been returned and then corralled into this room.

"This technology…is alien," Kade repeated.

"What do you mean, alien?" someone yelled. "Where did you get it? Is there something weird going on with my body now? How long have you had it?" others called out. "Is that why aliens are out there now?"

"Please!" Kade raised his hands for quiet. The crowd remained unsettled, speculating among themselves. "I am an alien," he said, his voice loud to be heard. "Please hear me out." The crowd went deadly silent, then erupted again. It took Kade several minutes to regain their attention.

"We came to Earth seeking sanctuary. We are called Teratilas, and we come from many light-years away. Our planet had been invaded, and we fled, seeking out a new planet to call home. For fifty years, we roamed the galaxies, searching. Ghost Walk technology was used onboard our ships, not knowing how long it might take to find a sustainable planet."

"How many of you are there? Why are you healing us? Are those your ships out there? Several called out questions, fear in their voices.

Kade again raised his hands.

"There are roughly one thousand of us. Our only ship crashed into this mountain over a decade ago. Since that time, our technology has been severely compromised, and we've been working with limited and alternate resources. We've been in these mountains inventing cures for as many human ailments as possible to contribute to society. Our strengths have always been in healing, not harming." He had to raise his voice to be heard over another barrage of questions. "Do not be afraid. We are friends of Earth. However, we must take responsibility for the ships you now see in the sky. When we crashed here, those who survived thought we were safe and had no idea our enemy would find us. The enemy I speak of, the ones who destroyed our planet, are Srotagillas. They are a reptilian race—evil and destructive." Another pregnant pause.

"We do have salvaged technology from our ship—superior technology, as you see, like Ghost Walk. And though we are peaceful, our ship was well armed with weaponry in the event of another attack from our enemy. We are willing to share everything we have to help defend your planet. Together we can fight them. You cannot win alone. Nor can we. We must be united," Kade insisted.

"You can't send us out there when an invading army of reptiles is waiting to attack!" a young woman cried out.

Many others joined in to agree with her. Others argued they needed to get home.

"The choice of whether to leave or to stay is yours. Anyone wanting to return home will be escorted. The army remains in Tuck and will continue to keep people safe. Anyone wishing to remain here is welcome to do so. I must warn you, though, the power is on here due to being solely on generators, the Srotagillas have knocked out power to many places on Earth. All commercial means of travel have been suspended. Whether that influences your decision to stay or go, I'll leave that up to you. Now, to another matter. Some misinformation has recently been circulated," Kade continued, looking pointedly at Jett and me. "I admit, we were not forthcoming about who we truly are and what we were doing. We kept our origins secret for our own protection. Humans have a long history of displaying hostility and fear of alien species. Speculation of the intentions of our presence here has been based on misinterpreted facts. Please know, our intentions have been, and always will be, to aid mankind. To live together in peace. Once Ghost Walk technology had been accepted, we were prepared to reveal the truth of who we are and what we can do for humans in exchange for allowing us to remain here among you."

I bit my tongue so hard I was afraid it would fall off. He wasn't about to reveal the price of them being among us — our bodies. He also didn't tell them that another million of them would be arriving. Or that they were responsible for the recent plague. Those who decided to leave may not see our video if the power was out. But it had probably been viewed by thousands and hopefully shared with tens of thousands. The enemy of our enemy wasn't necessarily our friend — we would learn what they were to us in time.

"I must leave you now and confer with my colleagues and world officials about our next steps in dealing with this threat we face. Several of my staff are here — you can relay to them your decision of whether you wish to go or to stay. There are many of you. Please approach them in an orderly manner. They will carry out your wishes as quickly and efficiently as they're able to do so." Kade turned to Jett and me. "Let's go."

"Let me say goodbye to my family." Before he could dissuade me, I hurried over to my parents and Tess. We embraced again. "What do you want to do?" I asked them.

"Is it true, Casa? Are there alien ships out there? Have you seen them?" Mom asked.

I nodded my head. "It's true."

"How much of this did you know?" Dad asked. The tinge of his face had gone gray, and I worried he was going to be sick again. "God. All this time, we'd left you in the hands of aliens."

What could I tell them without freaking them out? "They're not all aliens. Just some of them. I suspected something was going on," I admitted. "I just wasn't sure what. Listen, if you go home and hear anything about them…. I have to confess, what Kade was talking about—the misinformation—it was J…Ben and me. We were snooping around and found the alien stasis pods. They were full of aliens. We assumed some underhanded stuff was going on. We jumped to conclusions. We were right about the aliens, but we were wrong about the other stuff."

"Pods?" Mom said, confused. "Why are they in pods? Kade is walking around with no problem. Why wouldn't the others? He certainly looks human enough."

I shrugged. How could I tell her they were walking around wearing human bodies, thanks to their precious Ghost Walk? "I think they have a problem with our gravity. Or something like that. It probably tires them out, so they have to come out in shifts." If my parents decided to go home, they might hear about the video Jett and I made. They'd know soon enough anyway, along with the rest of the world, what the aliens actually looked like, and what they'd been up to, no matter how Kade sugar coated it.

Tess looked at me hard, knowing I was full of shit but not exactly knowing how much. I begged her with my gaze to go along.

Dad ran a shaky hand through his already bedraggled hair. "God. Aliens."

"This is unbelievable," Mom said. She took hold of my hands and stared at me intently. I got the feeling the tremors I felt flowing through her might be from more than shock and recovering from the sickness. In hindsight, I should have tried to find a way to dump all the liquor bottles before I left home. "Are you sure you're okay, hon?"

"I'm fine, Mom. Despite everything, we have something to be grateful for. I'm healed! Truly healed." My cheerfulness wasn't entirely faked.

"That is a miracle," Dad said, hugging me. "I'm not sure what to do. I think we may be safer here than at home. What do you think, Casa?"

It surprised me he asked my opinion about a decision that could mean life or death. "I need to stay here, for a while at least. Kade will need Ben and me to help convince the world leaders that they can heal the sick. They have the others, but our faces are well known. It'll be the first step in trusting that the Teratilas mean what they say and are on our side."

"That's true," Mom agreed. "But for how long? If we decide to go home, maybe we should wait for you?"

"No. If you want to go, go. I'll be fine, I promise. But if you want to stay here, then stay. I honestly can't say which is the safer choice. I'll talk to Kade. Don't decide yet. I know they have lots of little private rooms people can stay in." *Like the one Kade locked me in*, but I didn't tell them that. "Just see one of the attendants, and they'll set you up. I'll come find you when I know more, okay?"

"Okay, honey," Dad said.

We all gave each other a last hug, and the three of them went off to search for someone to help them. Tess flashed me a narrow gaze over her shoulder. I knew I'd have a lot of explaining to do later. Right now, I was just glad they were safe. At least for the time being. I had no idea if being in this mountain was the safer option to being in Tuck. I did know those reptilians had an axe to grind with the aliens here. And this was their home base.

Jett was waiting at the doorway to the resting room, and I joined him.

"Kade's gone to the control room. He wants us there when he contacts the world leaders."

"Hopefully, they'll buy the bullshit he's selling. This crowd was totally snowed."

"He has to do what he thinks is best right now," Jett reminded me.

I rounded on him in the passageway. "So now you're all team Kade? Just a few hours ago, you thought he was the devil himself. It was your idea to make that video and warn the world about him."

"I know, I know. But things have changed. Trust me, when it comes to facing off against the Srotagillas, you want Kade on your side. If we want to survive this, we'll need him."

I wish I had as much faith in Kade as Jett did. Right now, I only knew that if we succeeded in dealing with the reptilian threat, we'd soon face another one.

CHAPTER 20

The first round of explosions began rocking the mountain in the middle of the night. All hell broke loose. Jett and I met up in the passageway outside our tiny rooms. The dimly lit hall sconces flickered but remained on. Like me, Jett had thrown on his clothes, having just retired a few hours before. I had his jacket with me, not knowing if I'd have need of it.

"Let's get to the control room. Kade will be there." Jett's voice was raised to be heard over the terror-filled civilians rushing from their rooms filling the halls. Getting anywhere would be nearly impossible. A couple of staff members, still half asleep, had their hands full, trying to get everyone to remain calm. Most of the crowd Kade had spoken to yesterday had opted to remain at Tandem, not wanting to risk going out into the open with the reptilian army so close by. My frantic gaze searched in vain for my family. They'd been put together in a larger room containing three beds. When Jett and I traversed this hall last night, I'd been relieved to see no ghosts being held prisoner. Whether Kade had moved them or returned the ones he could to their bodies, I had no idea.

Earlier in the day, Kade reached a tentative union with many of the world leaders agreeing to join forces despite the viral video Jett and I had made. I guess the global power failure had aided his cause, along with the dire warnings he made about the threat we all faced. Kade still had to do some fast talking, and as galling as it was for us, Jett and I had to admit we were wrong in our assumptions about the aliens. How we now stood with them and understood that the aliens were resting in their pods, not wandering around wearing human bodies. Kade and Anna were the exceptions. Kade eloquently explained that when they'd discovered the couple on the mountain ten years ago, they'd been involved in a severe fall. The Teratilas, he maintained, had saved their lives by Ghosting them and healing their broken bodies after putting them in stasis. Kade admitted they'd attempted transference into the bodies, but only because there'd been no other choice. He said that technically without their interference, Kade and Anna would have died anyway. They admitted to hiding the pair's ghosts all these years and keeping their bodies as their own to avoid having to explain their alien presence to the world. Ultimately it had been a choice of survival for their species. Conveniently, the real Kade and Anna were somewhere safe, but not here at Tandem, according to Fake Kade, so they were not available to verify his story. Where this mystery hiding place was, I had no idea, but I had the feeling it was all bullshit.

Now, Jett and I stumbled into the control room amidst another shaking blast from above.

Kade stood grim-faced, staring at the overhead monitor screens, one of which showed the Srotagillas ship over Tuck. The destruction wasn't being rained down on us from there. It came from the swarm of small roach-shaped ships that zoomed out of the larger craft.

"Shit, there's so many of them," Jett said. "We need to shield the mountain."

"The chopper's still out," Kade informed him.

Another blast made us reel sideways. "You have shields? Can you protect the town?" I asked, my eyes glued to the screen displaying the chaos occurring in Tuck now. Tandem obviously had set up monitoring cameras for miles.

"No," Kade informed me. "Our power source is in the mountain. It won't reach as far as the town."

Although the lights were out in Tuck, we could make out what was happening below. The blasts appeared to be fireballs that exploded on impact. They lit up the sky when released, and several had already hit the ground, spreading fires to nearby buildings and homes. We witnessed people, mainly army personnel, scrambling around in the streets, desperate to escape the devastation. The army had several trucks, many with guns attached to the back. They returned fire at the little ships, their arsenal attempting to damage the enemy. The Srotagillas' vessels were too fast for them, and the shots that made contact appeared to bounce right off.

"Damn it, if I'd had an early warning system, we could have been better prepared," Kade swore.

"We have more than enough weapons to hand out. We can give a quick lesson to the humans here," Jett suggested.

"The chopper's been delivering some of our weapons to the army below," Kade informed him. "We should see some improvement in the circumstances shortly."

At least they were doing something to help.

One of the monitors beeped, and the screen flashed to the helipad, showing the return of the chopper.

"Finally," Kade exclaimed. He flicked up two red switches on the control panel that lay spread out before him like the cockpit of a 747. He pushed a blue button next. "Shields up."

The screen now showed a view of the mountain, newly surrounded by a white vibrating line. Several enemy ships continued to rain down their fireballs, only to have them disintegrate on contact.

I couldn't conjure up feelings of relief when almost half of Tuck appeared to be destroyed or on fire.

"Do you plan to fight back? Or is your strategy mainly defense?" Sure, he'd sent weapons to town, but that was like using bug spray on Godzilla. "Don't you have something to throw at the main ship? Blast it to bits?"

"Nothing that wouldn't do severe damage to Earth in the process," Kade informed me.

"There's got to be something we can do," I insisted. What he had up his sleeve was probably similar, or even more powerful, than our nukes.

The screen now displayed the main ship being attacked by the air force. Dozens of our country's best fighter jets blew past it, firing everything they had. When the smoke cleared, the ship remained intact.

Nothing fazed it.

I felt like a giant schmuck nestled there safe in the mountain while the rest of the world was prey to those reptiles.

"Too bad you don't have a way to remotely ghost them," I said, more to myself.

Jett snorted at my idea. "That would be brilliant if we did."

"Mother Ship on the move, sir," one of the many Tandem soldiers in the room relayed.

We watched as the huge ship glided towards the mountain top.

"What are you planning?" Kade asked, eyes fixated on the screen.

The ship halted directly over the highest peak. A bright blue laser light drew down from its belly. Everything began vibrating. Even I knew that was a bad sign.

"Shields weakening, sir," a woman seated in one of the control seats stated.

"Son of a bitch," Jett swore. "They're gonna break through. We don't have enough power." His face went white. I wondered if he was remembering his own planet's demise. "They've got stronger weaponry than I remember."

Well, it *had* been fifty years.

"We need to…evacuate the mountain," Kade finally said.

"What? No. They'll pick us off like fish in a barrel if we leave," I insisted.

"Shields at forty percent, sir."

"Damn it!" Kade picked up a microphone, gripping it so hard his knuckles turned white. "Initiate evacuation protocol," he instructed, his voice sounding over the speakers.

The scrambling of many feet arose beyond the control room doors as everyone rushed to obey his command.

"I have to get to my family," I said, dashing across the room.

Jett was right behind me. "I'll help you find them," he offered.

Not bothering to reply, I ran through the door and bolted down the passageway, heading back towards our rooms. The lights flickered, and the floor trembled—more and more people piled into the passageway, restricting our movement to a quick walk. Staff called out with raised voices, trying to maintain calm, but chaos reigned. Everyone was rushing for the main elevator.

Jett must have seen my look of despair. "There's more than one way out," he reminded me.

"Yeah, and no doubt they'll be waiting for us at every one of them," I predicted grimly.

We came to the main hall and made it over to the doorway through which the passageway would eventually lead to the rooms. This way was practically deserted.

Breaking into a run, we barreled towards the room my parents and Tess had been set-up in. I should have known it'd be empty.

"They're probably headed towards the main elevator like everyone else," Jett predicted.

"We must have missed them in the halls. Let's get out of here."

We ducked when another blast shook, showering us with bits of debris. Jett continued down the hall in the same direction we'd been going instead of back toward the main hall. I wasn't about to call him on it considering he knew this labyrinth better than me.

"Remember the cavern with the pods holding my people?" he asked me.

I supposed that was where we were going. "Yeah, not that I know how to get there. Shit." It just dawned on me — if the pods were destroyed, the alien bodies would be killed. Jett had been adamant, if the body the ghost was tethered to died, the ghost would also die. It didn't matter where in the world his people were and whose body they inhabited — if their real bodies died, they would too.

"What will happen to the human bodies your people occupy if your own bodies are destroyed?" I asked as we rushed along.

"If they're not put into stasis, or reoccupied, they will die within hours," he said. The grim look on his face revealed the worry he felt.

After several twists and turns, we finally entered the huge cavern containing the alien pods. Thankfully, the area appeared intact.

Jett hurried to check the life support systems on several pods. "They're good — for now. We're buried deep here and far off from the main facility. Hopefully, they won't target this area. Though if they send lizards down, they could find it."

"Let's hope that doesn't happen." I gazed around, wondering which of these alien bodies was Jett's. It was strange seeing him in Ben's body, so big and strong, knowing what he really was.

"What's the plan?" I doubted he was thinking to lie low in here waiting things out.

"Come with me."

He wound his way towards the other side of the cavern. I followed him to a barely visible alcove. Inside was a natural rock shelf covered with what appeared to be an array of weapons. Jett chose one for himself and passed another over to me.

"Let me show you how to use it." He gave me a five-minute demonstration on how to fire laser blasts set on a low level against a vacant section of the rock wall. Surprisingly, I mastered the weapon quickly.

"See? Easy," he said. There was a pile of black duffle bags in the corner. Jett tossed one at me and started loading weapons into the one he held. Following his actions, I did the same. We stowed a mini arsenal onto our bodies, using pockets, belts, and straps around our waists, arms, and legs. I felt heavy even before I slung the bag over my shoulder.

"We'll try and meet up with the others. If we're forced to run, at least we can give ourselves a fighting chance."

Run? I could barely walk.

Exiting the alcove, we headed right, and Jett entered a tunnel

I'd not seen before.

"Is this how it went down on your planet?" I asked, hurrying to keep up with him.

"So far, yes. Our planet was smaller but more high-tech. I think they'll continue their display of power, trying to establish superiority. This also gives them the opportunity to see what Earth has weapon-wise. Once they execute their first offense, they'll begin stage two."

"What's stage two?"

"They enjoy killing face to face. Destroying from the main ship and smaller crafts gets old fast for them. I'd expect them to descend by the end of the day." He patted the weapon he'd strapped to his leg. "That's when these'll come in handy."

The smile he flashed died a quick death. This predator was one he'd faced before — and lost. In the short amount of time they'd been here, the reptiles had already done a lot of damage. Things were only gonna get worse.

Now Jett wore a look of grim determination on his face, no doubt matching my own. I suddenly felt exhausted, and the day hadn't even begun.

CHAPTER 21

When we poked our heads out from the mountain tunnel, the only sight to greet us was the tiniest sliver of light as the sun made its ascent. A hush covered the area, or maybe the entire world, as though humanity held its breath…waiting.

Would today be the day? The day spoken of since the beginning of time? End of days? Armageddon? Granted, that black goliath resting in the sky overtop us sure as shit felt like an omen.

A sudden heat infused me. Jett had taken hold of my hand, giving it a squeeze. I squeezed back, then felt a moment of bereavement as he let go.

"Ready?" he asked.

Was I? I nodded once, and we started out.

Being on an incline, our gaits maintained a tilt. It didn't take long to feel a cramp in my hip. Glancing around, I worried we'd come out of the mountain on the wrong side of the shield. But after several paces, I could make out the gleam of bright sunlight glancing off the force field, Jett and me safely inside.

There were scores of frightened men, women, and children

scrambling around the mountaintop—somewhere. I thought for sure we'd hear something; chatter, crying, speculative talk. There was nothing.

We'd headed upward, intending to backtrack towards the main entrance to Tandem by the helipad where the masses had exited the facility. Reaching the top, we glimpsed up over the edge to look around. Above, the black ship emitted a steady blast of laser light, weakening the unstable protective shield. The vibrating outline overhead grew ever thinner. A grim picture of us all frying like pieces of bacon under that laser rushed into my thoughts.

"We don't have long," Jett predicted grimly.

My family was here somewhere. All my attention focused on finding them. We scaled the edge and barreled through the forest, Jett leading the way.

"How far?" I asked.

"Just ahead." He gestured to the right, and we jogged in that direction.

Soon the sound I'd expected to hear greeted my ears. In a thin batch of trees, we came upon them, huddled and afraid. Staff members wearing long white lab coats had them grouped together and were speaking in hushed tones to convey a calm I doubted they felt. Jett and I joined them, my gaze frantically searching until I spotted Mom, Dad, and Tess. Heart in my throat, I moved through the throng to join them.

Dad immediately pulled me into an embrace. I felt Mom's shaking hand stroke my hair as Tess grabbed hold of my hand and squeezed.

"Thank God you're all right." Dad's mouth moved against the top of my head.

I pulled back and stared at them, assuring myself they were

unharmed. In my haste, I'd dropped my duffle bag beside Jett. Now he hefted them both into the center of the gathering and let them fall from his hands with a thump. He motioned for the staff members to come forward.

"You're in charge of handing out weapons," he ordered. They snapped to attention—him being Kade's brother obviously lent weight to his authority. They got right to work, pawing through the bags, assessing the arsenal and doling them out to anxious, unskilled hands.

"Pay attention, everyone," Jett called out. "Staff have been trained on these weapons. These are alien tech but fairly basic in operation. Please listen to the instructions you're given on safe handling. And remember, only engage the enemy if there is no other choice. If you have the opportunity to hide or to run—take it."

"Are they coming down?" came a terrified voice from the group. Heads snapped up to the sky, fearful gazes searching for the enemy.

"From what I understand, if they keep with the same MO they've used on other planets, then count on it. But this time, things will be different. Humans are badass. This is our planet. We'll send those bastards home with their tails between their legs," he said, keeping in the character of Ben.

"They have tails?" another shocked voice asked.

Jett sighed and looked down for a moment. I wasn't sure if he was angry or frustrated with the futility of this escapade. When his head finally rose, I made out the trace of a smile. He turned his face to me and winked.

"Yes, they have tails," he said, then broke into laughter. To my amazement, others began to laugh, as well.

"I think it best if we break into groups," one of the staff

members said, mainly to Jett. "The men should be armed first and head towards town. Women and children can have an armed leader and head down the backside of the mountain range and then off into the forest."

Jett nodded in agreement, and the staff began to guide people into groups.

"A little sexist, isn't it?" I said to Jett. "And what about families? They should stay together. And maybe if a couple has no kids, they could go together towards town."

"I agree," said Jett. The staff member who seemed to be in charge relayed the new instructions. Jett looked at me. "What about you? Where would you like to be? With your family, I'm assuming?"

"You're heading towards town?" I figured he would be.

"No. I'm going back inside," he said, surprising me. "When the shield comes down, all hell's gonna break loose."

"Don't you think Kade knows that? And he's prepared?"

"Maybe. But most of his staff just bailed to take care of the civilians. He'll be down to a skeleton crew of soldiers. If the Srotagillas breach Tandem, it's only a matter of time before they discover the cavern. No matter where I am if that happens, I'm dead. I'd rather have a fighting chance."

I bit back a retort that it wasn't his body he was wearing. Ben should be given a chance to decide what would happen with it.

"I know what you're thinking," Jett said, watching my face. "Ben's in there. And yeah, the decent thing to do is return his body and let him choose his own fate. But logically, me ghosting right now would be suicide. Maybe for both of us. By the time I did the switch, the lizards could be inside. Ben doesn't know his way around the facility like I do, never mind protecting himself with our weapons. And if he does make it out, everyone could be gone, and he'd be on his own."

I had to admit he had a point. Jett would stand a better chance at keeping Ben's body alive than Ben would. And Ben's ghost was indestructible — as long as his body lived.

"What are you thinking?" he asked when I remained silent.

"That if the worst happens in there, I can't let Ben's body die." I stared at my parents and Tess, who were all armed and getting basic training on the weapons. Eyes still on them, I said, "Now how do I convince my family to hide out in the woods and leave me here with you?"

His smile was grim. "They're distracted. We could go right now. But are you sure that's what you want to do?"

As I watched, I saw Dad nod his head to one of the staff, and Mom and Tess hand their weapons over to two men. It appeared Dad was going to lead a group into the woods. I was proud of him, the way he stood tall and brave, even though this was a scenario he'd never conceived he'd be living. I knew he was terrified, not for himself, but for his family. But you'd never know it looking at him now.

Tess met my gaze suddenly. I made a gesture of crossing my arms over my chest before pointing at her and Mom and Dad. Her face registered her shock for a moment as it dawned on her that I was saying goodbye. She repeated the motion to me and mouthed the words, "Be careful." Then she shifted over to obscure my parents' line of view so I could slip away undetected.

"Let's go," I said over the sudden lump in my throat.

"Think they'll leave without you?" Jett asked, already leading us away into the thickness of the trees.

"They'll have no choice."

We moved through the forest in a round-about way towards the elevator, keeping out of sight. Guilt gnawed at me, imagining

my parents' reaction to my desertion. I hoped Tess would get
them out of there quickly, considering the shield was growing
thinner. Knowing Tess, she would tell them Jett and I went on
ahead to scout for trouble and they'd catch up with us in no time.
I'd worry about the consequences later—if there was a later.

Luckily, the area around the elevator was deserted—we
descended with no problem. Below, the walls rumbled and shook
with the force of the alien ship's unrelenting assault. The halls
were dim, lit only by emergency back-up power.

Jett led us through the winding, debris-littered tunnels
towards Command, where we found Kade. His haunted gaze
was fixed unwaveringly at the overhead monitors. The screen
displaying the town was eerily quiet now. Fires still burned, and
I could make out some townsfolk and army personnel scrambling
around through the haze. The assault from the small alien crafts
appeared to have stopped—for now. The scene changed view
as Kade clicked away at the control buttons. It looked to be just
beyond the base of the mountain, outside the safety of the shield.
Dozens of enemy ships hovered like rats waiting for a drawbridge
to come down. Thankfully they appeared to be focused on the
town-side of the mountain, not the forest side.

Kade became aware of our presence. "You came back," he
said to Jett, a hint of surprise and gratitude in his tone.

"I wasn't going to leave you here to face the devils alone,"
Jett said.

Kade's gaze flashed to me. "Casa. Your family—"

"They're above, making their way to the forest," I informed
him.

"Why aren't you with them? It's no longer safe here." Kade
motioned to the overhead screens to emphasize his point.

"She's concerned about her friend. Or I should say, her

friend's body," Jett said wryly, thumping his palm over his heart.

"I deactivated the filters—the ghosts in this building are free," Kade said. "Where they are now is anyone's guess."

That was a relief. Ben and however many others who had been held captive here could now make their way to the surface. How long they'd survive was another matter. Hopefully, the alien guardians inhabiting their bodies lived through this mess.

"I've ordered a full evacuation of all personnel," Kade said. "When you came in, I was setting a timer to disengage the mountain force field. Once it's down, all power will be diverted automatically to shielding the pod cavern."

After he threw a couple more switches on the control panel, Kade began moving towards the exit in a brisk stride. "Let's go. We've got less than ten minutes till the force field collapses."

"Too bad you couldn't annihilate this place once they're inside," I wished aloud. Blowing up Tandem along with the reptiles was a nice thought but would be too risky with humans running for their lives up top and Kade's precious Teratila pods nestled below.

The elevator ride to the surface was terrifying as the shield thinned even more and the unending assault from above caused the cables to creak and the shaft to tremble. When the doors slowly slid open, we jogged towards the trees. I couldn't help but wonder where that woman I'd seen Kade with was now. Probably long gone somewhere safe, considering how adoring he'd been with her.

"Where are we headed?"

My family should have been well on their way to the forest by now. As anxious as I was to join them, the thought of being out here alone was daunting. It could take me a long time to locate them, and I doubted Jett would offer to escort me. The shield would come down at any minute, and the enemy would be crawling all over the mountain in short order, anxious to get into Tandem. In a way, I was hoping that this was their plan, and they'd abandon their attack on Tuck in pursuit of the greater prize—at least long enough to let people get the hell out of town.

"We're regrouping with some staff I sent out during the first evacuation," Kade said. "After that, we'll head for town. We have vehicles at the base of the mountain."

"Things should be clear by the time we get there," Jett assured me, no doubt thinking the same as me, that the enemy would scramble to storm the facility.

My body gave an involuntary shiver—of fear, no doubt, but also something else. Exhilaration perhaps? For the first time in as long as I could remember, I felt alive. Blood coursed through my veins, my heart pounded, my palms sweat, and my breath panted in and out of my chest painlessly. Even if going to Tuck meant joining in the fray, I wanted in. Where this newfound bravery and desire for action and excitement came from, I had no idea. But after spending most of my life living on the sidelines watching, I was anxious to get into the game. My life could end today, or tomorrow, or down the road.

I was tired of being a spectator.

CHAPTER 22

A riot of colors blanketed the ground, the newly shed leaves a vibrant warning that fall had a firm grip, and soon winter would come. Kade kept up a swift pace. "If the facility collapses, the shield over the cavern should have enough power to withstand the blow." It sounded to me like he was stating these facts to reassure himself.

In the event of a collapse, it seemed unlikely the reptiles would attempt to descend into the tunnels. Even more unlikely that they would uncover the pod cavern. There were more than a couple of ways into the facility, however, so I could understand Kade's caution—their precious species was at risk.

Overhead, more of our fighter planes arrived. Several enemy ships deserted their vigil and rose up to meet the threat. Air battles raged. From what I could see, the majority of the explosions were a loss for our side.

It surprised me that Kade risked being out in the open, exposed. He'd be safer hiding in the cavern with the rest of the stiffs. He carried with him a dark green bag slung over his shoulder. Seeing me eyeing it, he said, "It's anti-gravitational tech to dig through the rubble when all this is over."

Ah, that explains it. Someone had to dig out. I guess he didn't fancy being buried alive and missing the action.

Voices ahead gained our attention, and Kade led us in their direction to a group of his staff and some soldiers. As we got closer, I saw Anna and the mysterious woman who'd been with Kade at the chopper. Undoubtedly one of them, I couldn't help but stare at her. The body she wore was a far cry from the one she had stashed in the cavern. For some reason, that thought amused and consoled me. It wasn't like I had feelings for Kade. Not anymore. Every time I looked at him now, all I could picture was his tiny, frail body pointing its finger and stomping its foot.

Anna, noting our arrival, came over to greet us. "I'm so glad you're all right," she said to Kade but included Jett in her gaze. Then her sights turned to me. "Casa! You're here. Why aren't you with your family?" Was that a touch of annoyance I detected in her tone? We'd gotten along well during the trials, but maybe she felt weird knowing I knew the truth about them. Or maybe she didn't want me around since I was probably the only legitimate human-inhabitor in the bunch.

"They're safe, heading for the forest," I informed her. I counted eleven in the group, plus us three. The rest of them moved in, closing in on Kade like adoring fans.

"Janna," Kade said, smiling at the mystery woman. She smiled and reached out greedy hands, pulling him in for an embrace. I smirked a little when Kade gave her a quick squeeze, only to set her aside to address the group.

"The force field will fall momentarily," he informed them. "All power will divert to shielding the pod cavern." They all nodded as if this was known and accepted protocol. "Best case scenario, the facility will fall, thereby making the tunnels impassible and finding the cavern virtually impossible. As far as we know, they don't have the tech we do, and even if they did, they wouldn't know where to look."

"They know they're in there, though," one of the lab techs stated.

Kade shook his head. "They can only assume. They may also think we wouldn't be so bold as to keep our bodies so close."

"Or so stupid," someone mumbled.

"Yeah, and where would you have put them?" another challenged.

"Stop! We can't be fighting amongst ourselves. There isn't time for this," Kade snapped.

"Kade's right," Jett insisted.

Hearing what I can only describe as a static noise, we all raised our heads and saw the force field disappear. The Srotagillas ship, still lasering at full force, struck the mountain. Everything shook, and we had to hold onto each other and grab onto trees to keep steady until things became calm.

"They've seen the shield is down," Jett said, noting they'd stopped their assault.

"Hopefully, they've caused enough damage below that they can't get inside," Kade said.

The detachment in their eyes and voices surprised me when they spoke about the destruction of Tandem, considering the decade it'd been their home and place of untold medical triumphs and dastardly deeds.

The Srotagillas fighters descended on the mountain like a pack of hungry wolves. Earth fighters were right on their tails, more nuisance than threat.

"Let's go," Kade yelled over the noise, causing us to scatter deeper into the depths of the forest. We were on the town-side of the mountain and soon began making our descent. Fanning out, we kept in pairs to present a harder target. But we didn't appear to be the point of interest. Several enemy ships roared over our heads and disappeared atop the mountain.

"They're landing," Jett informed me. "Trying to get inside."

A thought dawned on me. "Hey, when are your ships coming? You said soon, right?" That'd been the reason for the plague — getting prepared for their imminent arrival, time being of the essence.

He teetered a bit on the incline and grabbed a handful of brush before he met my gaze. "I know what you're thinking. That they'll show up and even the odds. But I don't know."

"What don't you know?" The shameful look on Jett's face helped me to puzzle it out. "You're not worried about *if* they're gonna show up. You're afraid if they see the Srotagillas ships, they'll high tail it out of here like chicken shits. I mean, that is what your kind does, isn't it? Run away?" I was being a bitch, but I didn't care. After all of Kade's glorious speeches about us standing together, he knew damn well reinforcement from his kind wouldn't show up unless they could reap the rewards of victory.

"I honestly don't know what they'll do. You heard Kade. We're healers, not fighters. It's true. We're a peaceful race."

"Of chicken shits."

"Fuck off," he snapped, though he didn't deny it. "We did all we could." He waved his arm overhead. "Just like your kind is doing now."

"But you're afraid it'll end the same way." Unfortunately, we didn't have any giant spaceships stashed away equipped to hold enough of us to ensure our species' survival. Although the rest of Jett's race was still out there looking for a place to set down roots. Who knew how long it would take them to find another habitable planet? "Don't you think Earth would be worth the fight to them?"

"It may, or it may not be worth the risk." At least he was honest.

To my left was a cluster of brush and some trees. I worked my way over to them. Jett saw my intention and joined me. He'd thought to add a canteen each to our array of weapons and survival gear, and once in the shelter of the trees, we sat and drank.

I wiped a sleeve across my lips. "I'm not in shape for this," I admitted. What I needed was to sleep — for about a month.

He grunted. "Neither is Ben."

Having spent so much time in bed indisposed didn't exactly have us in fighting form. How were we supposed to take on an army of alien reptiles when climbing down a mountain kicked our butts?

From where we were, we could see some of the others picking their way down. Our destination was town. "Is there a plan? Why are Kade and the others going to Tuck?"

Jett shrugged. "Don't know. The mountain's not an option anymore. Kade's probably hoping we can lead them away from the cavern. We can't risk trying to regain entry through the alternate tunnels — that would be pointless anyway. Hiking down the other side of the mountain might lead the reptiles to the civilians hiding out in the forest. I guess there's not much choice left." He stared at me a moment. "It's not too late if you want to backtrack around and head for the other side, try to catch up with your family."

As tempting as it was, I shook my head. "No, you're right, we could be followed. Enough of their ships landed up there. It's probably swarming with them. And if they can't find a way in, who knows what they'll do next."

"I can't say what it'll be like in town."

This was his way of warning me to be prepared. I'd already seen the chaos and destruction Tuck had endured. I could just imagine what was going on there now. I glared up at the Srotagillas ship.

"Their timing really sucks."

Despite my earlier excitement of adventure, I was pissed but afraid too. I'd just gotten my body back, and it was healthy. Granted, I wasn't in great shape, but I could breathe, run, even just walk, for God's sakes — finally. And being faced with an alien invasion, when it'd been led by Kade (hot alien), had been sort of thrilling for a girl who'd spent most of her time romanticizing adventures after watching endless movies and reading endless books. The Teratilas had seemed manageable, something we'd wrestle with a bit before coming to a peaceful resolution — like hey, they come bearing cures! But then, three seconds after I'd been reunited with my skin and set to dig my heels in for a power struggle, these reptiles swoop in, and shit gets real. Recently, the biggest dilemma I'd thought to face was looking at spending the next fifty years as vapor. What a treat that looked like now.

"Yeah, that it does," Jett agreed. "Ready?" He got up and held out a hand to me. I took it, and he pulled me to my feet. "You sure?"

"I'm sure. Let's go," I said. Overhead, though it was still morning, the sky was darkening with thick black fast-moving clouds. "We better hurry up. The mountain's gonna be a bitch to maneuver around if it rains, which it looks about to do any minute now."

Jett looked up and agreed. We started moving again, quick

as we dared. When the rain began, the moss and rocks grew slick, causing us to do more sliding than walking. Jett helped me down some especially tricky parts, his hand reaching out for me so often he wound up leaving his fingers laced through mine. I couldn't entirely say this was offensive to me. If anything, the strength he lent me filled me with hope and a strange longing I didn't have time to identify. I pictured instead my dad leading the pack of townspeople safely down the mountain and into the forest beyond. There was fresh water and places to shelter, as I'd seen for myself. They'd be okay. I wondered if that's what those reptiles would reduce humanity to while this battle raged on — citizens forced to become survivalists.

The fighting overhead continued. Loud explosions and debris rained down on us, along with nature's deluge. How long would this go on? How long could we fight, and if we fell, how long would it take the Srotagillas to wipe our existence from the planet? Maybe they'd take what they wanted and leave? I thought to ask Jett the fate of his planet if he knew what happened after they left, but he'd made it clear going home wasn't an option. Was there nothing left? No scrap left to begin again? Apparently not. Would that be our fate as well? The rain came down harder, and when I heard rumbles overhead, I didn't know if it was thunder or the battling airships.

CHAPTER 23

It took hours to descend the mountain. Even in ideal circumstances, it would have taken much longer than when I'd been a ghost. Now we had a barrage of crap conditions to deal with. As it was, when we reached the bottom, soaking wet and exhausted, we still had to search for the others.

"Do you know where we're meeting up?" My hair was plastered to my head, and Jett's jacket hung on me like a wet towel. My stomach growled, reminding me I needed to eat.

"Kade keeps a couple of cars at the landing pad and a couple more at the airport." He looked as bad as I felt. "Let me try and get my bearings, and I'll figure out where the cars would be."

He peered through the drizzle the rain had become. The thunder rumbled distantly, and the battle overhead had quieted some time ago. The silence wore on me, making me wonder if anyone from our side was left or if they'd given up and flown for safety. Part of me hoped reinforcements would come, but then I felt guilty since nothing our planes did appeared to make any difference. How many more would have to die in futility? Right now, the reptiles were undoubtedly doing their damnedest to breach Tandem. What they hoped to find there amongst the rubble was beyond me. Maybe they somehow figured out the Teratilas' bodies weren't compatible with Earth and were stashed in the mountain. It'd seemed to be the consensus among Kade and his groupies. I wondered if the transmission Kade sent out to his people had contained any of that pertinent information.

A figure suddenly appeared, hurrying towards us through a clot of fog nestling the base of the mountain. Arms waving, voice calling, it took me a moment to recognize and register they belonged to Tess.

"Is that your sister?" Jett asked.

Not bothering to reply, I rushed forward to meet her.

"Tess! What the hell? Why are you on this side of the mountain? Where are Mom and Dad?"

She stared at me with a wild, somewhat deranged look in her eyes. "Talenfortenash! Take me." She spoke the demand, almost hissing out the words.

"What?" I said, grabbing hold of her arms to keep her still. Her eyes darted everywhere at once as if searching for something. "Tess! Where are Mom and Dad?" I shook her once, and she flashed a hard glare at me, causing me to release her and step back.

"Casa!" I heard Jett's voice behind me and felt him take hold of my arm.

I shook him off. "Something's happened. Look at her." I indicated my sister. "She's on the wrong side of the mountain. They should have been far off into the forest by now. Safe." I looked around, trying to spot my parents or anyone from the group Tess should have been in.

"We...separated. Confusion, with...battle," Tess said, her sweeping gaze as frantic as mine. "Need to...leader. Take me...."

Jett grabbed hold of me again and snatched the weapon strapped to his thigh. He aimed it at Tess. I struggled, but he held fast. "Say that name again." He aimed the question at Tess as well.

She cocked her head as though she couldn't understand his words.

"The name," Jett insisted.

The snarl that suddenly masked Tess's face reminded me of years ago, the time I'd seen her in grade three recess at school. She'd brought her favorite stuffed cat to school, and one of the bigger boys had yanked it from her and tossed it in a mud puddle. She'd worn that face right before she'd slammed her little body into the boy's, twice her size. Despite the difference, she'd brought him down, then proceeded to screech in his face. It'd taken me and two others to drag her off him.

Jett must have realized what she intended when Tess took a step towards us. He raised his weapon and shot a laser bolt right at her chest. She shook for a moment, flopped to the ground, twitched a couple times, then lay still.

"You killed her!" I screamed, yanking free and pummeling him with my fists.

Jett dropped the weapon and grabbed both my arms. "Casa! She's stunned, that's all. I swear."

He let me go, and I dropped down beside her. I lay my head on her chest, heard her heartbeat, and noticed her chest rise and fall with shallow breaths. I pierced Jett with the look of death and snarled, "Son of a bitch! She was hysterical. Something happened, and now we don't know what because she's out cold."

"That's not your sister," he said, eyes darting between the two of us and then scanning our surroundings.

"Are you out of your freaking head?"

He raised his hands. "Keep your voice down! There may be more of them."

I got to my feet and balled up my fists, ready to strike. He still sported the bruise from the last wallop I'd given him.

"Casa, she wants Kade."

"Well, maybe he can help. You sure as shit are good for nothing right now," I spat.

"You're not getting me. She asked for Kade by name. His real name."

"His what? What are you talking about? Of course, she knows his name...." Then I remembered what Jett had said when I'd asked for his name—that I couldn't pronounce it. Why he'd said to call him Jett.

"She said Talenfortenash. That is Kade's real name," Jett clarified. "There's no way she would know that unless she was one of us."

"Or maybe one of them," I whispered, looking up at the spaceship. "How can she talk at all if she's one of them? Shouldn't she be hissing or whatever the hell those reptiles do?"

"It's complicated," Jett said. "When you inhabit someone else's body, you can access some of their stuff, like their skills. Language is technically a skill. Just like knowing how to eat and walk and use the bathroom. It's how I can speak the language of the person I inhabit, but I can't really access their memories."

"Isn't language a memory? I mean, I learned some French in grade four, but I can't really remember it."

He shrugged. "Like I said, it's complicated. Haven't you ever heard about amnesia patients? How they can forget their own name and people they know, but they can still talk."

"Okay, whatever." I'd process it later. "Right now, I'm worried about the rest of them, especially my parents. Like how the hell did this happen at all?"

"Maybe Tess was isolated? Could be why we haven't seen anyone else. She could have gone off on her own for a bit, to pee in the bushes or something."

"Or to sneak off for a smoke. That must have been it. I really hope that's what happened. But how'd she get swapped out? That's your guy's tech. Do the reptiles have it too?"

"No. But they were on Cambrius. We left all sorts of shit behind. Tech they probably stole. It's possible they have ghosting ability."

I looked at Tess. "They must, or else they were able to get into Tandem and figure it out. Do you think they found the pod cavern? You had the equipment in there as well."

"I hope not. I'm not dead yet, so who knows. They may have it on their ship. Maybe once they landed on the mountain, some of them tried to get inside, and others spread out. It's possible Tess was snatched while away from the others and taken to the main ship, then dropped down here in one of their fighter planes. This one seems to be anxious to find Kade."

"How would they even know where to look? They don't know what he looks like now since he's wearing a human body."

"It's why I'm thinking Tess went up to their ship. On our planet, we had a scanner device we used for interrogations mostly. We don't have it here, though—we left it behind. The scanner allows you to access the memories of someone. It displays them for others to watch on a viewer screen. If they put Tess in one of those, they'd see everything—who Kade is now, who you are, your parents."

"Shit. Then they ghost her, put one of them inside her body, fly her back, and land her down here to find Kade. But she—it—still called him that other name, his real name," I said. "She should know he goes by Kade."

"When you first get into a body, it's hard. You saw how distressed she—it—was. Acclimating takes a while. Days sometimes."

"It didn't take me long once I got back inside my body."

He looked at me like I was a dolt. "It was your own body. Not another human's, and not an entirely new species. Anyway, it makes sense it would still be acclimating and say the first thing that popped into its head, which is Kade's real name."

"Yeah, that does make sense. Lucky for us too, or who knows how long till we figured all this out. So, where is Tess then? Her ghost? Is my sister still up there?" I gestured at the ship, a sudden feeling of dread washing over me. "She could be trapped if they have the force field tech as well."

"I hate to say it, but it's most likely she's still up there," he said.

"Well, they're not keeping her. We have to get her back and get that…thing out of her," I insisted. "Oh, God, I should have stayed with them. This wouldn't have happened if—"

"It still would have happened," Jett insisted. "If not her, then someone else. There could be more of them."

"What if they have my parents too?" I was spiraling, all kinds of terrible thoughts coming at me at once. My legs felt weak and shaky, and my head was dizzy.

Jett put his hands on my shoulders and squeezed. "Casa, keep it together."

"I…I don't know what to do. How to fix this." I stared at him, willing him to do something. He looked as freaked out as I did. He couldn't fix it. "Kade. We need Kade. He'll know what to do."

A look of hurt crossed Jett's face, but I didn't care. He was the one who went running for his big brother when these damn aliens first showed up, thinking Kade would fix it.

I stared at Tess, lying there so still, wondering if she was okay. I knew they couldn't harm her ghost—or at least, I prayed they couldn't. If Kade knew one of those things was in her body, what would he do? Would he kill her? Could I take the chance?

"We've got to go back up," I said, making up my mind.

"What? Where?"

"Up to Tandem. The cavern where the ghost tech is. We'll take that thing out of her." He stared at me like I was nuts, and maybe I was. I was making this up as I went along.

"Then what?"

"They think Tess is one of them. So we take the reptile out and put me in. Stash my body in a spare pod." After that, I wasn't sure. I just knew I'd rather it be me wearing my sister's skin instead of one of those things. And wearing Tess around would be safer than being me anyway since they figured she was one of them.

"You're nuts. Besides, we'd still have a ghosted reptile running around telling the other ones where the cavern is. Then we're all dead," Jett reminded me.

"You must have force field tech in the cavern. Or somewhere close by there. Cause despite what Kade said, it's been hours, and I haven't seen one ghost. There had to be what, at least a thousand of them in there? Unless he moved them someplace else long ago. But I doubt it. I have a feeling they're still in there, trapped by a force field."

"I hadn't even thought about that," Jett admitted. "I honestly don't know where he kept them. When he said he released them, I believed him."

"Yeah, well, I don't give your saintly brother much credit. He's not about to have a bunch of disgruntled rogue ghosts

running around the mountain giving away his precious secrets."
I knelt down beside Tess again and checked her vitals. "She's still
out. We're gonna need to carry her."

"All the way back up the mountain? We barely made it
down, now you want us to carry someone up?" He stared at me
in disbelief.

"It's not like we can frigging fly," I reminded him.

As if on cue, a loud hum noise sounded through the fog.
Quick as a flash, Jett bent and picked up Tess in his arms. He
jerked his head towards a thatch of brush, and we hurried to take
cover. He lay Tess down, and we peered through a thin section of
the foliage to see a Srotagillas fighter plane land not twenty yards
away. Jett and I looked at each other.

"Maybe we can fly," he whispered.

CHAPTER 24

We were rewarded soon after when a single Srotagillas climbed out of the ship.

"It's probably looking for Tess," Jett whispered. "Seeing if she had any luck finding Kade, though why they want him is beyond me."

"Maybe cause he's your leader?" If they had scanned Tess like Jett assumed, then it would make perfect sense. Kill the leader of the opposition and cause anarchy. Everyone knows that. "How many do you think that fighter holds?" I asked, nodding at the little spaceship, a plan rapidly forming in my head.

"Not sure. Why?"

"Do you think it'll hold four?"

"Possibly. Why four?" I watched his face while he put it together. "Wait. No. You're not thinking…," he said.

"I am. Let's take him down and steal his plane."

"And then what?"

"Can you fly one of those?" I asked. None of this would work if he couldn't. He was right when he said we'd not make it up the mountain with Tess. Not unless we had days.

"When I said maybe we could fly up the mountain, I was thinking of the chopper, not commandeering an enemy vessel."

"They'd shoot us out of the sky if we had the chopper. Besides, I think it's still parked up top unless Kade risked taking it down. So, can you fly one of those or not?"

He stared at the fighter a moment, assessing. "We had similar small crafts on Cambrius, and I could fly those."

That was all I needed to know. "Let's hope it's not too different. Keep your weapon on stun." Killing the lizard wasn't part of my plan. I rose to my feet and stepped clear of the brush, pulling my weapon from its side holster. "Hey, lizard lips, over here!"

"Casa!" Jett hissed, trying to make a grab for me.

When the reptile turned in my direction, I blasted him. Still perfecting my aim, it took me three tries to hit him. Even then, I only nicked his side. Angered, it raised its arm, displaying what looked to be a weapon strapped to it. It leveled it at me just as Jett leaped out of hiding, raised his gun, and felled the beast with a single shot.

"How about a head's up next time?" he snapped.

"I figured you'd catch on. You only stunned him, right?"

"For now."

"Good," I said. "Let's get him. Bring Tess."

A bunch of colorful swearing from Jett followed as he fetched Tess and carried her to the craft. He laid her down outside and climbed on board the vessel, I assumed, to inspect the instruments.

I stalked over to examine the reptile alien.

Not a pretty sight, though I must admit, magnificent. Even knocked out, it was formidable. I watched closely for any signs of consciousness. The thing must have been about seven feet tall — a huge, greeny-black, muscular specimen. The head looked like it was crafted for a horror movie—wide and thick, covered with a design of raised bumps stretching in a row from just above the eyes, like eyebrows, straight to the back of the head. Another line of bumps began above the eyes and went up and over the scalp. Though its wide, lipless mouth was closed, I could make out canine teeth jutting from either side. The pair of big, almond-shaped eyes were widely set above a slight protrusion with two holes serving as the nose. The neck was thick, the chest massive and decorated with more intricate designs of darker green bumps. The arms and legs were long and sturdy, and its broad hands were tipped with long-fingered claws. The feet were the same, with claw-like toes. It wore no armor, though it appeared thick-skinned enough to not need any. It also wore no clothing, but from the mound over the groin area, I assumed this one to be male. Lying on its back, its hips rose slightly due to its thick tail, which curled out from underneath the body to rest alongside the pair of legs, almost appearing to be a third limb. Strapped to the underside of its arms, from elbows to wrists, were narrow cylinders, I presumed to be weapons. There was a long, deadly-looking blade strapped to one thick thigh. The other thigh had what appeared to be a holstered laser gun attached to it. A strained wheezing noise escaped from its nostrils as it breathed.

I couldn't believe one of those things was in Tess. That it would fit in Tess.

Jett stuck his head out from the side door of the fighter. "I think I can figure it out."

"Good."

He jumped down and came over to my side, glaring at the alien. "Why keep it alive? It's not going to give us any information. Even if it did, we couldn't understand it."

"I have my reasons," I eluded.

Shaking his head in annoyance, Jett lifted Tess up to load her inside. It took both of us several minutes of struggling to carry the reptile onboard and then divest him of his weapons. The fighter was slightly smaller than the chopper, with a back area having enough seating for two. Two seats were set in the cockpit area before a basic looking control panel and a protruding windshield. Jett took the pilot's seat and pushed a button to close the side door.

"This may be a little jumpy," he warned, just before we lifted straight up in the air and swung a hard left. Both of us hollered — my stomach felt like I'd left it behind. There weren't any seatbelts, but the seat molded to my body, gripping it tight like a hug when necessary. In a zig-zag motion, brushing treetops and barely missing jagged rock formations, Jett maneuvered his way up the mountainside. When he finally reached the top, we both breathed a sigh of relief. He zoomed around a bit until nearing what I assumed to be the vicinity of the entrance to the pod cavern. He landed with a few bumps and skidded to a halt. Sensing we had landed, the seat released its grip. I leaped up when I heard Tess mumble a few words.

"Quick, she's waking up. Let's get her out and zap her again," I said.

We got both our captives out of the fighter and zapped one into each of them for good measure.

"Let's leave the alien here for now and just concentrate on Tess," I suggested.

Jett stared at me a moment, a dawning look of comprehension on his face.

"What?" I asked, shuffling my sore feet.

"You plan on taking the alien out of Tess and putting yourself in her body." It wasn't a question. He already knew that much.

"Now we're lugging around this lout," he gestured at the reptile. "And I have a bad feeling I know why."

I shrugged.

He shook his head, incredulously. "Are you out of your mind? I know what you're thinking."

I returned his stare, annoyed. "What am I thinking, smart guy?"

He jerked his arm like an axe at the reptile. "You want to put me into...that. Why?"

So he'd figured it out. It didn't take a genius. "We have a ship. We'll have disguises."

"You think we can just fly up there and rescue Tess?" he demanded.

"I'm not leaving her up there a moment longer than I have to," I vowed.

He turned his back on me and took a few hasty steps before spinning around. "You're crazy. We can't—"

"Why can't we?" I argued. "Look, if you're too bloody chicken to do it, then I'll go in the alien."

"I'm not going into Tess's body," he informed me.

"I'm not asking you to. I'll go by myself."

His jaw dropped open. "You can't."

"I can."

"Will you listen to yourself, Casa? How do you plan to fly the ship?"

"You said yourself you can access the skills of the host after transferring in," I reminded him.

He clamped his lips shut so tight the edges of his mouth turned white. After a full minute of seething, he finally sighed. "Fine. I'll go into the damn lizard."

I nodded and turned away, not allowing him to see the smug

smile on my face.

We covered the fighter ship and the reptile in brush and then set out with Tess to find the tunnel entrance. All was blissfully silent except for the thunder overhead, which had crept close again, along with the rain.

Tess dragged between us, a dead weight, causing us to keep a slow pace. How we were going to manage with the alien between us, I had no clue.

"It's not far," Jett said, his hushed tone attempting to be encouraging.

He was going too slow for my liking. I knew he was being cautious, ever wary of the reptile army, but my fear for Tess and my parents drove me on.

"Casa. Slow down. We'll make it there. We'll do everything we can for her, okay? But you need to pace yourself. We've been going on just hours of sleep, and barely any food."

Last night we'd gone back and scavenged what we could from that spread laid out for the civilians in the human pod arena before retiring to our rooms. There hadn't been much left.

Fear, exhaustion, and discomfort suddenly overwhelmed me. "I can't lose her. My little sister." My voice hitched, making me gulp down the lump in my throat. Crying wouldn't fix this. I had to keep focused on my plan.

"I know how you feel, Casa. I've lost people too. Not only family but an entire world. But we'll fix—"

"Don't talk to me about loss. Don't you dare," I interrupted, glaring at him around Tess's body. "Tess is more to me than just my little sister. She's my best friend. For years she was my only friend." I saw he was about to talk again, but I cut him off. "And you say we'll fix this? All I can even hope to fix right now is saving Tess. Even then, nothing will be the same again."

"You don't know that," he dared to say.

"Where do you get off? Yeah, your planet was invaded—well, so is mine. Why? Cause you dolts brought them here. Led them straight to us. Before the invasion, how were things for you on your planet? Tell me, Jett, how was your life? Did you spend days, weeks, months in your bed, too weak to walk without carting an oxygen tank around to breathe? Could you walk, run, dance? I couldn't. Were you ever so desperate that you would willingly ghost yourself? The closest you ever came to even remotely feeling like I did was when you guys realized your bodies weren't compatible with Earth. But that didn't slow you down. No, you just used your alien tech and stole what you needed. And I guess I don't even have the right to complain since that same tech allowed me to experience freedom. And now...." No, I wasn't gonna lose it. "Now, when I finally, *finally*, get to live a normal life in a normal body, this happens. I wasn't asking to be rich, or famous, or athletic, or even beautiful. I just wanted to be like everybody else. I wanted to be normal."

"I think you're beautiful," he said, his words so quiet I could hardly hear them.

"What?"

He looked at me then. "I said, I think you're beautiful."

I heard him that time. No one had ever said that to me before. Well, except my dad, but technically, he didn't count. Was Jett aiming for a distraction? I knew how bad I looked, or I could at least imagine, so he was obviously blind or lying.

Before I could say anything, he halted. "Here, it's here."

I recognized the entrance, carved into a rockface covered over by brush.

"I'll hold her if you clear it."

I did as he bid, and once he had Tess inside, I recovered the entrance.

"My light." He gestured with his head and presented his back to me. I couldn't help but feel uncomfortable digging into his back pocket for it.

"Got it," I said, fiddling with the device until I got it to light up. I shone it into the tunnel, and we journeyed onward. In the end, we entered the huge cavern. Fortunately, it appeared unmolested by the enemy. I swiped my thumb over Jett's light, dimming it before slipping it back into his pocket. The area was more crowded than the last time I'd been there due to the numerous human pods. They appeared to be hooked up, which was good, considering I needed somewhere to store my body once I occupied Tess's.

Jett carried Tess over to the table near the Ghost Walk tech. He stared at her a moment, deep in thought.

"What's wrong? Are you worried about containing the ghost?" I asked. They had to have a force field device here somewhere. I glanced around, wondering if the ghosts of Tandem were lurking somewhere nearby.

"I was thinking once you're inside Tess, maybe you can trick that reptile into coming back here under his own power. It'd save us having to carry him." He stared at me a moment while I processed his words. "I'd be there too. Hidden, of course. Just don't get too close to it. Unless you're afraid. It's okay if you're too afraid."

"No. I mean, yeah, you're right, I'm afraid. But it may be easier — if I can pull it off, that is."

"It's not far. He won't understand your words. Maybe if you stay ahead of it and gesture for it to follow you? Hopefully, it'll think you've discovered where Kade and the others are hiding. We took all its weapons, and I didn't see any communication devices."

"Okay. Let's find a force field to contain that thing and swap it out before it wakes up," I urged, staring at Tess.

"There might be one in the weapons alcove. Watch her," he said, handing me his laser and marching off. He returned in short order, a device in his grip that I recalled seeing when Ben's ghost had been captured.

"Will that be okay to use? Don't you have to keep your finger on the switch or something?" I asked.

"No, I can set it to automatic. It's fine for containment of up to three ghosts. The devices you encountered inside the facility are for large areas or several ghosts," Jett informed me.

"Okay." He made sure Tess's body was arranged properly and then turned on the extraction tech. "Ready?" he asked. I nodded. He then positioned himself right outside the tube the alien's ghost would be transferred into once we removed it. "I'll be ready as soon as it comes out," he told me. "Then I can manually move it somewhere else."

He didn't need to explain that I'd be needing the tube next, once I was pulled from my body. Then hopefully, he could send me right into Tess's.

CHAPTER 25

The wires they'd hooked the six of us guinea pigs up to at the beginning of the project had been for show. It still galled me when I thought about how they'd played us when they knew all along Ghost Walk would work. The scam about the tethers test had fooled us as well. Little had we known it'd only been a ploy to fool the world and snatch a few extra bodies in the process. When Jett had put me back into my body, it'd taken him minutes, not the complicated process the scientists had made it out to be.

Tess lay prone while the wand ran down the length of her body, preparing to extract the occupant. As soon as the reptilian was pulled free and deposited into the tube, Jett was ready. Before it knew what was happening, he had it contained in an impenetrable force field.

And man, was it pissed.

Thankfully, the invisible barrier prevented the thing from getting at either of us, regardless of how much it wanted to. It hissed and thrashed about, its jagged, ghostly fangs and claws clamoring for leverage. Both of us visibly shook despite the fact it could do us no harm, or anyone else for that matter. But it could screech and howl and draw attention if it were to escape.

"How are we supposed to fool the other one into coming in here with all that racket going on?" I demanded, putting my hands over my ears.

"We'll have to stash it far from the entrance," Jett said. With grim determination, he worked the lasso-like forcefield, maneuvering the noisy beast to the farthest end of the cavern. I could still hear it, but not as much.

Jett returned, and I helped him to move Tess's body to another table before I took her place at the extraction device.

"Are you sure you want to do this?" he asked.

"It's the only way. I told you, I'm not leaving my little sister on that ship."

"There's no guarantee she's up there. And if she is, we may not find her before they figure out who we are."

"We'll just have to hope we find her in time. It's not like we could have questioned that thing for details when it was in her. I doubt it would have given anything up, and I wasn't about to torture my own sister for information," I said.

"Okay, just relax then. You know how this works," he said.

I laid back and took deep, calming breaths as the machine hummed, beginning a scan of my body. I had no misgivings about what I planned to do. There was no time to think anyway. This was the only feasible action I could formulate to get to Tess. If my reasoning was flawed, I guess I'd soon realize it. Less than two minutes later, I felt the weightless sensation of leaving my body. I blinked my ghostly eyes a few times before focusing on the glass transfer tube I now stood in. My gaze darted immediately to my body, now an empty shell. Strangely, in the past, I'd felt such relief in leaving it behind. Now it was cured, and all I wanted was to become reacquainted.

"Ready for phase two?" Jett asked.

I nodded, trying not to think about my state of being. Being light as air was intoxicating. I recalled how in the beginning, it'd felt like such a rush. Even now, I felt the allure.

Jett opened the lid of a human pod and lifted my body to carry me over. The way he cradled me in his arms as though reluctant to let me go caused a strange fluttering in my ghostly belly. Gently he placed me inside, a look of sadness crossing his face as he sealed it up. He'd said I was beautiful. What did he mean by those words? Was he merely making an observation of the human body in general, or did he mean something more? He couldn't possibly find my physical appearance appealing, not considering we were two completely different species. Maybe if I'd been a feeble, pale waif, I might look better to him. But then, what about me? I had to admit that despite what I'd seen in that alien pod, despite what Jett really was, I felt drawn to him in a way I'd never been drawn to the real Ben. It was all very puzzling.

Finished with my body, Jett replaced Tess's body on the table. He gazed at me before he pulled the switch. I nodded, and he returned the gesture. Then I was whirling through space, billions of scrambled atoms, before being deposited into my sister's body. It wasn't similar to when I'd returned to my own. Jett had warned me there'd be a period of adjustment. Feeling weird was an understatement—as though I wore someone else's clothes that felt too tight, including the underwear. I sat up gasping, clutching at my chest. Jett was beside me in an instant, wrapping a strong arm around my shoulders, pulling me against his chest.

"Just breathe, Casa. It'll be okay," he reassured me.

I did as he said, pulling deep, rapid breaths into my lungs. My head felt unsteady—too big for my body. My hands and feet as well. I bent my knees up and leaned my head against them.

Jett continued to hold me until my breathing slowed.

"I feel strange." The voice wasn't my own. It took me a moment to realize it was Tess I heard. Surprised and elated, I looked around for her...then remembered.

As though sensing my loss, Jett held me tighter. "Take a minute to get your bearings, don't rush," he instructed.

Squeezing my eyes tight, I clenched my fists and pulled from his arms. "No. We need to do this. That thing out there won't be surprised if I'm acting off. If anything, it'll make my performance more believable."

Grudgingly, Jett agreed.

We armed ourselves to the teeth and headed back out. When we got close to the reptile ship and our hostage, Jett hid a distance away. We stared hard at each other before he disappeared from my view.

Then I stalked towards the alien.

To my relief and dismay, it was moving. I waited several feet back while it gave its great ugly head a shake and shifted to a sitting position. The tail swished back and forth momentarily, mesmerizing me. Remembering the plan, I gestured at it wildly. I turned my back, took several steps, and turned back around.

"Come on," I snapped with frustration I didn't have to fake. Recalling the name the other alien had used for Kade, I shouted that at it as well.

Catching my meaning, the thing lumbered to its feet and started following me.

I kept well enough ahead and took full advantage of its dazed state, leading it to the entrance. Jett was smart enough to keep downwind of us.

When I, at last, made it to the opening, I tossed aside the concealing brush that we'd replaced earlier. Now came the moment of truth. I entered the dark tunnel and tugged a palm light Jett had given me from my back pocket. Despite my head start, I could hear the reptile's deep wheezing breaths and low growls close behind. My skin crawled and gave a tremor of revulsion and fear, knowing that thing was so close. I could only imagine the fear Tess was feeling being held captive by them. When I reached the cavern, I moved well away from the tunnel entrance and turned to face the beast. I pulled my laser weapon from its holster on my hip, and when the alien emerged, it stared around in what I assumed was awe and satisfaction. It turned its sights on me and gave a nod in what I assumed was approval.

Then it noticed the weapon I had trained on it.

Realization of my duplicity dawned, and it gave a mighty roar that almost made me pee my pants. In vain, it felt about its body, searching for weapons, but of course, there were none to be found. Before it could take three steps towards me, Jett appeared at the tunnel entrance and fired.

The reptile had been in motion and simultaneously must have sensed the trap. Its body had turned slightly just as Jett fired, causing him to miss his mark. Instead of a blow that would have brought the beast down, it glanced off its shoulder and only succeeded in pissing it off. In seconds, it had turned and was on Jett before he had a chance to fire again. The pair grappled, moving like a conjoined distorted animal. I held my weapon steady, watching intently, waiting for an opening to shoot the lizard.

"Fire, Casa! Fire!" Jett hollered.

Belatedly, I remembered my weapon was set to stun. I fired at will, trying desperately to hit my target. If both were rendered unconscious, our plan would be delayed. Even if I could work the ghosting tech controls, there was no way I could lift Jett and put him on the table by myself, never mind that hulking beast.

With a thud, the alien hit the floor, taking Jett with it. I inched closer to inspect them. They were mangled together in a heap of arms and legs. Beneath the shoulder of the reptile, I made out Jett's face. His eyes were open.

"Get it off," he gasped.

Both of us worked to untangle and free him from the great weight crushing the breath out of him. Once Jett was free, he leaned on me and took several gulps of air.

"Are you okay?" I asked, looking for any signs of damage to Ben's body.

He bobbed his head. "Give me a moment." After several moments, he, at last, appeared to be okay. He stared at me hard. "That was only one. You want to get on a ship full of those things," he reminded me.

I recalled what a chicken shit he was. Though I guess that stemmed from having a tiny body with more brains than brawn.

"You will be one of them, remember? Besides, there's no other way. If you're having second thoughts on helping me, then fine, I'll wear him."

He glared at me. "I'll go along with your plan. We're probably all dead anyway. Help me move him."

Ignoring his negativity, I grabbed the beast's heavy clawed feet and tried not to inhale. After crossing the floor with major effort and many stops, we swung the thing to the table with a mighty heave and prepared it for extraction. Jett switched on the machine and stood ready to snag the ghost with another handheld force field device. Moments later, we had another thrashing, screaming reptilian ghost to contend with.

Jett lassoed it to the opposite side of the cavern from where he'd stashed the other one. "I don't want them communicating," he explained.

Once he returned, I helped him move the lizard's body onto another table. Thankfully it had wheels, and I'd be able to swap the tables once Ben's body was on the other one.

Jett took his position on the table, firing instructions at me all the while on how to work the tech, though I'd seen it done like a million times already.

"Okay, I got it. You're stalling," I scolded him.

"Do you blame me?" He gestured at the Srotagillas body. "You're about to put me into my mortal enemy."

I took a deep breath and let it out slowly. "I know. You're right. This is all going so fast. I'm sorry. I appreciate what you're doing. Really. I know what a sacrifice you're making."

"Platitudes," he snarked.

"It's all I got right now."

He gave the reptile another scowl, sighed, and laid back on the table. "Fine. Get it over with."

CHAPTER 26

The switch was complete. Jett's ghost now resided in the hulking lizard on the table. As its mighty chest rose and fell and its nostrils flared in agitation, I wondered if I should have set restraints in place before finishing the transfer.

"Jett? You in there?" I asked from a safe distance.

Beady reptilian eyes narrowed to slits, regarded me as I came closer.

"Just nod your head," I suggested.

The huge noggin bent down and up in the affirmative.

"Good," I said, releasing a breath in relief.

I waited impatiently while Jett got acquainted with his new form. My transfer had gone more smoothly since it had been into a human body and a blood relative. His—not so much. He stepped about tentatively, unused to the long heavy legs, scratching his clawed feet on the cavern floor, tripping several times. He swung his lengthy muscled arms about, hitting himself in the head a few times. He blinked a lot and cocked his head at a weird angle when he looked at me and listened to my words, getting used to his new senses.

"You can understand me?" I said slowly.

"Yessssh." His lipless mouth twitched, and his forked tongue darted out and poked against his sharp teeth. He tried to clench his meaty paws in frustration and scratched his palms with his talons. He hissed again in annoyance.

"Take it easy," I soothed. As much as I wanted to rush things along, we'd get nowhere fast if he couldn't pull this off. "Can you help me get Ben's body into a pod?" I couldn't lift him on my own.

Clumsily, and with my help, Jett was able to lift Ben and settle him into the waiting pod. I closed the lid and pressed the controls to begin the stasis process. For the hundredth time, I wondered what the hell Kade had done with the ghosts. The real Ben was somewhere—his body lived, therefore, so did he. I swore after I rescued my sister off that ship, I was going to settle things with Kade—one way or another.

We waited around for at least half an hour for Jett to establish a hold over himself. Just as we were about to head out, he hesitated.

"What?" I asked.

"I was jusss thinking. That firsss one we pulled out of Tesss; maybe I could communicate with it. You know, get sssome info on where they're keeping her on the ssship. It could sssave time, and I don't think it'd hurt anything."

I wished we could communicate without him talking. "Can you do that?" I almost added, "Without blowing it," but refrained. He was right anyway. What would it hurt?

He shrugged. Or attempted to. "I can accessss the language. I'll need a cover ssstory, though, or it'll wonder why I'm not freeing it."

"I dunno." I thought for a moment. "They're heartless

bastards, right?"

"Yesss," he confirmed.

I cringed, watching his big mouth trying to form words, and that tongue…. "Maybe tell it that it failed in its mission and deserves to rot. Or that you can't trust it to not screw things up for you. Say you know where Kade and the others are, and you're going to finish this. Tell it you'll consider coming back for it."

"Yeah, that could work. But how do I get it to tell me where Tess'ss ghoss is? Ssince it wass occupying her body, then itss body could be in the ssame place as Tess'ss ghoss, unlesss they moved Tesss. And what do I ssay if it assks where Tess'ss body iss?"

"Turn it back on it, maybe? Say, 'why you asking me?' Maybe tell it you're heading back to the main ship for backup, that your fighter was hit, and the communication controls are damaged. Say you can't risk taking it on board the mother ship in case you get in shit for it. Say you'll try and return with its body. Act like you have an attack of conscience. That you'll do your best to retrieve its body, but you need to know where it is."

"You'd think they'd have a lab onboard. It'ss a big sship. I doubt they have ssigns up. I'll have to make it believe I've never been in that area before."

"Well, just do your best. And hurry," I said.

He ambled away with a nod.

After a span of time, Jett finally appeared. I leapt up from the spot I'd been sitting, leaning against the wall.

"About time," I snapped, before noticing how terrible he looked — even more so than before.

He came over next to me and leaned against the wall for support.

"What is it? What's the matter?" I asked.

He closed his eyes for a moment and took a couple of breaths. "You're not gonna believe what I heard."

"Don't keep me in suspense. What? Did it say where Tess is?"

He stared at me blankly as though he'd forgotten the plan. "Tesss? Oh, yeah. I have a general idea of where to find her now. Better than before," he said distractedly.

"Okay, let's go then," I urged, heading towards the artillery alcove. The weapons from the two captured reptiles were onboard the fighter, but I figured he'd probably want to add to the arsenal. I turned around when I didn't hear him following me.

"Casa, I need to tell you what I learned."

I headed back over to him. At least his speech was less annoying. "Okay." I hoped my tone relayed my urge to hurry.

"It's about Kade. Why they're after him." He paused. "He's the target."

"Yeah, we knew that, though. He's the leader. Remember what I said about taking out the man in charge?" I reminded him.

"No. You don't understand. This entire thing is about Kade. Revenge on Kade. It's why they're here."

I processed that. "They're not here to invade Earth?"

"Most likely, that would be an afterthought. Their main goal is to eliminate Kade."

"What? Why? Why come all this way just for Kade?" Was he really that important? Or was he the only real obstacle standing in the way of a total invasion?

"This whole operation is led by one rogue Srotagillas with an axe to grind. A commander. The others are following orders — some reluctantly. It hinted that some of them believe it's futile and self-serving. It said there's other planets to conquer, and they've wasted too much time on this vendetta."

I guessed our scaly ghost captive was one of the reluctant ones. I watched Jett, waiting while he paused to put things together, as though trying to make sense of it all.

"Remember I told you about the invasion on Cambrius?" Jett continued. "It's where this all began. Kade launched a counterattack on the Srotagillas. Although it was ultimately unsuccessful, it did some damage. The enemy was hit hard with whatever we had. There were many casualties — on both sides. Several enemy fighter-crafts crashed near our location, and our side dragged out a few of the survivors and brought them to Kade."

By the look on his ugly reptilian face, I could see Jett's memory of the event remained etched in his mind, haunting him.

"Kade made an example out of them, hoping it would raise morale and spur our side to fight harder. And it did, for a while."

"He killed them?"

Jett nodded his great beastly head. "Eventually."

From the way he said it, I got the feeling that first, some terrible horrors were enacted.

"According to our little friend in there, one of them was the reptilian commander's son. Once he learned of it, the commander was so enraged he swore revenge on Kade."

"Hence, our current dilemma," I stated.

Jett's head dropped as though weighted down by this revelation. "We never should have come here."

I pondered him a moment. "Look, whether they came here by way of following you, seeking to invade Earth, or looking for revenge, it's happening. There's nothing we can do about it now except deal with it one step at a time. The first step — our disguises — is done. The next step is getting on that ship and getting Tess back."

"And the third step?" he asked, now looking me in the eyes. "Beat them any way we can."

CHAPTER 27

This time the ride in the fighter went smoother. Jett handled the craft like he was one with it, sending us shooting up in the sky towards the giant reptilian vessel. As we got closer, the ship appeared to fly itself, Jett no longer needing to man the controls.

"Auto-pilot landing," he informed me, flashing a lipless grin.

I nodded, not trusting myself to speak. Tess's body trembled despite the tight cradle of the seat, my fears taking root in her. I'd run through every possible scenario from every single alien movie I'd ever seen involving spaceships. Putting our faith in the disguised bodies we wore gave me some strength. Yet, it was this same body that gave me such fear. If I messed this up and Tess was shot and wounded, or God forbid, killed, I would be sucked back into my body, newly resting in stasis, whereas Tess would be gone, body and ghost, forever. I'd known the risk before we began. Now faced with the reality of it, I hesitated.

Steadily we were sucked forward into the waiting maw of the mother ship. Jett and I exchanged glances. Knowing him, I knew he was as nervous as me. Time slowed as we traveled the length of a wide, narrow passageway that would take us into the belly of the beast. When at last, we entered the landing bay, I was in awe over the sheer magnitude of it. Of course, I'd seen the size of the mother ship as we approached, but I was still unprepared for the vast expanse of the area before me. It appeared that hundreds of fighters were coming and going through the dozens of landing passages, much the same as a great hive of wasps. How could we ever hope to overcome such a force? This was only one ship. So many more were spread out over Earth.

The fighter slowed considerably and guided itself onto one of the landing docks. Once there, I detected movement outside the windshield that appeared to be a huge transparent bubble enclosing the craft.

"What's that?" I asked.

"It's a docking collar. We had something similar on our great ships. It's a thin membrane force field containing oxygen. Once we exit the fighter, we keep to the right on that walkway, that's also contained, and move inside the ship." Seeing my uncertainty, he said, "This area has artificial gravity to keep the fighters and pilots in place. Don't worry, you won't get sucked out."

Craning my head around, I could see other landing docks with Srotagillas disembarking their fighters and heading into the ship. No one seemed to be paying us any attention as they went about their business. Although, once I stepped out, things could change.

Jett took a deep breath. "Ready?"

I took one as well. "As I'll ever be."

We exited the fighter and began striding down the walkway.

"Don't stop, and don't look around. Act like we belong here," Jett cautioned.

Keeping my eyes set straight ahead, and my pace steady, I concentrated on the doorway ahead. Both of us sighed with relief once we reached it and passed through. We now stood in a dim corridor that stretched to the right and left. At the moment, it appeared vacant, but judging by the amount of activity going on, it would soon fill up. Strange symbols were etched on the wall in front of us. Jett moved closer to study them.

"This one," Jett said, reaching up to touch one. "I think it means lab. That lizard I questioned said something about the lab."

I noted the symbol of a small U, almost shaped like a beaker. "Is this an arrow?" A horizontal line with two dots on the top right of it was beside the U. Considering there were other symbols with corresponding lines and dots, either to the right or to the left, I assumed I was correct.

Jett bobbed his head. "Yeah. I think you're right. Let's go."

We headed off down the corridor to the right. When the passage split off into other directions, we continued to follow the U symbol and corresponding arrow, hoping we were correct. If I didn't know I was on an alien spaceship, I would have thought I was exploring the basement of a hospital, considering the stale air and bland walls.

The first pair of Srotagillas we passed didn't acknowledge us at all. However, both their heads had been lowered, eyes fixated on a flat tablet-like device one of them held in its hands. Their voices had been raised as though in an argument. I did note Jett's giant hand had gone to his side to rest upon the weapon he'd fastened there. He'd also brought along a black belt-bag that crossed over his shoulder and rested at his hip. I assumed it was a weapon of some sort, considering he was armed to the fangs.

Loud voices ahead made us aware we were about to pass another pair of reptiles. Instead of chancing it this time, Jett ducked to the right of the corridor as it branched off, pulling me along with him. He set me in front of him, hidden by his large body, making me virtually invisible from behind. Thankfully, the passageway in front of us was vacant. Once the reptiles passed, we backtracked to the main corridor and continued on.

Several twists and turns and tense minutes later, we, at last, came across a doorway marked with the U symbol. Jett and I stood outside and stared at the foreboding metal door. There was a small square button to the right of it, but we were both hesitant about entering. Who knew how many Srotagillas were beyond it? Would they confront us? See through our disguises? Would Tess be in there?

"It's now or never," Jett said, at the sound of approaching voices.

We both tensed as he hit the button and the door swished open. Ahead was a large room filled with what appeared to be medical and laboratory equipment. Across the space, at the back right-hand side, was a glass-encased room containing several tables, two vertical transfer devices, and half a dozen stasis pods.

Bingo.

I counted a total of four Srotagillas in the entire area. We moved ahead, waited for the door to swish shut behind us, and started towards the glassed-in room. One of the reptiles, holding a vial in each hand, slid into our path. It spoke to Jett in a series of gruff sentences accented by hisses. It was hard to be sure, but by the way it kept gesturing at me, I assumed it was annoyed by my presence. Of course, Tess's body was supposed to be harboring one of them, and it being here defeated the strategic purpose of infiltrate and destroy. The reptile, clearly frustrated by Jett's responses, turned to question me. I opened my mouth and hissed a couple of times, put a hand to my throat, and shook my head. Jett said a few words, relaying our agreed upon story that I'd lost my voice. The reptile shook its head angrily. Its loud voice had gained us the attention of the rest of the small crew who furtively watched us, inching closer to better hear the reprimand.

As soon as all of them were in range, quick as a flash, Jett whipped out his stunner and zapped them all in succession, knocking them to the ground. It helped that they appeared to be unarmed. He went back to the door and pressed a red button that I assumed locked it. Stepping over a body, he led the way towards the glass room.

When I entered within, the first thing I heard was muttered swearing.

"Slimy, body stealing sons-of-bitches!"

"Tess!" I squawked, staring around, desperate for the sight of her.

The left corner of the room had two privacy dividers set up. I stalked forward and pulled one aside, revealing my little sister — angry as a venomous snake — caught in a force field.

"Give me back my body, you scum-sucking lizard!" she spat.

She knew that in this state, she was invincible. Judging by the look of her, I had the feeling she hadn't been so brave before she'd been ghosted. Her transparent body looked haggard, hair standing on end, ghost clothing torn in places, a wild haunted look in her eyes.

"Tess, thank God," I said.

"You even sound like me!" she gasped indignantly. Her sights whipped to Jett next, and she scowled even harder.

I moved closer. "Tess, listen to me. I'm not one of them. It's me, Casa. We figured out what happened, and Jett and I ghosted the alien in your body and put me in here. We nabbed another one and swapped it out for Jett. We also stole its fighter." I motioned to Jett when I spoke, hoping she would believe me. "It's the only way we could get on this ship."

She stared at me in silence before she whispered, "Casa?"

I nodded. "It's me."

She moved back slightly and shook her head. "No. You're lying. You're trying to get more information out of me so you can take my place. Well, you're not getting it. I'm not an idiot."

This was going to be harder than I thought.

"Tess, it is me! I know you pick your nose when you're half asleep. I know you're a drooler too. You had a crush on Jimmy Kensik in grade three despite the fact he wore the same shirt to school every day. You used to hold your pet goldfish, insisting it liked it. The first time you shaved your legs, you almost bled to death. You smoke like a chimney, and you're scared to death Mom and Dad will find out. Shall I continue?"

"No." She held up her hand and looked at Jett with embarrassment. "And I do not pick my nose."

"Whatever. Are you ready to leave now?" I asked.

"Damn right." I bent to move the force field, and she shifted clear of it. She looked at Jett and me and chuckled. "Wow, you two are something else. I admit I'm impressed."

"How were Mom and Dad when you left them? And how the hell did you get caught?" I had a feeling I already knew the answer to the second question.

She had the sense to look embarrassed. "Mom and Dad and the others were fine last time I saw them. They were headed deeper into the woods—there were no signs of lizards. For something so big, they're stealthy. Anyway, I said I needed to pee and went off on my own. That's when I got grabbed. I didn't make a fuss, really, 'cause there were two of them, and I was afraid Dad would come running, and they'd either take him too or kill him."

My hard stare made her squirm.

"All right, all right, I went off to have a smoke, okay? Do you have any idea what Mom's like when she's freaking out and doesn't have wine?"

I released a deep sigh.

"Can we go?" Jett snapped.

"It's so weird seeing my body from the outside. I guess this is how everyone else sees me. What do you think? How do I feel?"

"Jett's right, let's go," I said, ignoring her questions. "Keep close to us."

"Tess, you can move your ghost right into your body for camouflage. No one will notice you that way," Jett suggested.

"Won't that be kinda...weird?" she asked, eyeing me critically.

"Weird is better than dead," I snapped. "Just do it." I braced myself when she moved closer and then stepped inside me. Her body gave a tingle, as though in recognition. The sensation was similar to wearing a light bodysuit or shaking heavy powder all over your body.

"You need to relax, Tess. Give up all control. Casa is still in charge of your body. You may feel like you can do things but don't. It won't work. It'll only give you away. Not to mention frustrate the hell out of you."

"Give over complete control? Of my own body?"

"Unless you'd rather push through the wall of the ship and float to the surface." From her aghast look, I assumed she wouldn't. "And keep your trap closed. It'll look strange if you start talking, and my mouth isn't moving," I instructed.

"Don't you mean my mouth?" she responded.

"Oh for f—"

"Knock it off!" Jett yelled. "We need to leave—now." Shaking his huge head in frustration, he stalked towards the exit.

Tess relaxed, no longer fighting me, and I followed Jett. He glanced back to inspect us before hitting the release on the door and then the open button. The door swished aside, and he peered out.

"All clear." Hand resting on his weapon, he started off down the corridor with us in his wake.

I silently prayed we'd make it to the hanger unscathed. Tess's faint whispers echoed the sentiment.

CHAPTER 28

"Where we going?" Tess whispered.

"To the fighter," I hissed, trying not to move my lips.

Every time we heard the approach of the enemy, we ducked into another passageway, or Jett pretended to scold me about the mission. I, of course, kept my lips clamped shut and lowered my head as though suitably chastised. The symbol we followed this time looked like a little fighter, which seemed blatantly obvious to us both. It didn't take long before we stepped out into the hangar and moved down the walkway towards a craft. They all appeared identical. I didn't think it mattered which one we took, although ours most likely contained more weapons than most.

As soon as I climbed aboard, I moved over into the co-pilot seat. When Jett didn't immediately enter, I stared at him in exasperation. "Come on," I urged.

"Casa, don't freak out, but I'm not going back with you."

I felt Tess pull free and push herself into the back of the fighter. "What do you mean?" she demanded before I had the chance to.

He held up his hand to forestall an argument. "Sit here." He gestured to the pilot seat. "There isn't time to argue. Just do it."

I moved, glaring at him.

"Watch what I do." He flicked a few switches, and the fighter hummed. "These," he pointed at a pair of controls, "act as reverse and forward. You can also use the control arm, just like a video game joystick. Don't overthink it. The thing practically flies itself. As soon as you get close enough to the ground, use the autopilot to land."

I recalled how his first landing had been, and now he expected me to do this on my own? "You said the fighters on your planet were similar to these," I reminded him. "I've never even driven a car, for God's sakes!"

Tess leaned halfway into the seat beside me. "I have," she announced.

"There you go. The pair of you will figure it out," he assured me.

The fact that my underaged sister had driven a car was something I was going to have to let slide — for now. "Jett. Come on. It's not me I'm worried about. It's Tess. If her body falls apart in a crash, there's no coming back for her."

"Aww, you love me," Tess gushed.

"Shut it! I'm trying to save your life here," I snapped.

Jett attempted to casually peer around the hangar. I did as well and noticed a few reptiles were beginning to stare our way.

"This is the only chance I have to make a strategic move. If I can disable this ship, it'll be one less for Earth to deal with," Jett rationalized. He'd leaned in close to hiss his plan discreetly in my face. His breath was terrible.

"Disable? How?" I asked, trying not to inhale.

He leaned back and patted the belted pouch slung across his chest.

"Oh. But—"

"It won't take long. I promise. Then I'll be right behind you," he assured me.

"Why can't we wait then?" I argued.

"Please, just go. I promise I won't be long. Every second you delay takeoff makes them more suspicious. They won't think anything of me strolling around."

"He makes sense," Tess offered. "Come on, Casa, I want to get out of here. We can do this."

The stupid, stubborn look on Jett's reptilian face was what made up my mind. There was no way I was going to change his mind. "Fine," I snapped. "But if we crash, or you get caught, it's on you."

He cringed, my angry remarks stinging him. "It'll be fine. When you land, try and aim for as close to the cavern entrance as possible. Can you remember the location?" he asked.

"I think so," I guessed.

"Even if you have to hike around a bit, you should be safe enough in that body," he reminded me. "Sit tight and wait for me. I'll meet you there."

"You better," I threatened.

"Okay," he said, bending in again to show me a few more things. "Hit these buttons here. That will autopilot you out of here. All you need to do is take it down slowly, find your location, and land."

"Right." I nodded. He made it sound easy, but my hands were already shaking.

"Good luck," he said, making eye contact with Tess, then me.

"You too," we said.

"Hey, thanks for rescuing me," Tess called out. "And it was nice meeting you."

There was that lipless smile again. "You're welcome. Nice meeting you as well. Be safe."

Then he was gone, striding down the walkway, not looking back.

"Here goes nothing," I said, hitting the buttons Jett had indicated. The airlock collar retreated, and the fighter lifted and began backing up. It did a one-eighty and aimed its nose towards the exit. We edged forward till about halfway when it shifted automatically into overdrive and took off. Tess and I screamed. My seat hugged me tight as we blasted out of the mothership. I turned my head as much as I could, trying to catch a glimpse of my sister.

"Tess? You still here?" I shouted, grabbing hold of the joystick as autopilot disengaged.

Her head poked through to the copilot seat, and she heaved her way all the way forward. "Wow, that was intense. Almost lost me out the back." She gave me a strained grin. "Hey, how'd you guys team up? That was pretty ballsy, flying up there and springing me. I had no idea what a badass you are."

"Thanks. I think. Jett's been helping me out." Now wasn't the time to get into who and what Jett was. She still believed the person inside of Ben's body had been Ben. Time enough later for her to hear the truth. It'd be hard enough helping her get over the shock of seeing all those alien pods in the cavern...that was if I could find the entrance Jett and I had used.

"Ease up," Tess said, indicating my hands gripping the joystick, my knuckles turning white. I eased my grip and tried to get my bearings while lowering us gently towards the mountain.

After a few minutes, I began to get the hang of the easy gliding descent. "Hey, this isn't too bad."

Tess smiled. "There you go. See, you're a natural."

"Tell me that when I land us in one piece," I reminded her.

I made a sweep of the mountainside, hoping for something familiar. Then, "Hey! There. We need to go there." I recognized the spot where Jett and I had landed before.

"Okay, take us in," Tess urged. "Nice and slow. That's the way to do it. Nice and s—"

"Shut it!"

I inched lower, slightly angling to the right, then engaged the autopilot, hoping it would land us safely. We watched the ground get closer and closer, my eyes peeled for signs of life. Trees threatened to reach out and grab us, rock faces beckoned as we drew past. Amidst a tiny clearing, barely allowing us within, the fighter set down. A few deep breaths later, I released the door latch, and we exited the craft.

Instantly on alert, my eyes and ears strained for any movement or voices. "I don't hear anything, do you?"

Tess shook her see-through head. "Negative."

"Let's head out, but remain cautious. I'm pretty sure I know the direction of the cavern—hopefully, we won't run into the enemy."

"If we do, I'll sink into a tree to hide. You can just pretend you're still one of them."

"Pray it doesn't come to that. I don't think I could pull it off."

I stepped carefully through the terrain, Tess moving effortlessly beside me.

"Jett was convincing. I thought he was one of them," Tess remarked.

I grunted, not wanting to comment about how he should be a pro at acclimating to foreign bodies by now.

"This is all so messed up," she said, aiming her sights upward at the hulking alien ship.

"More than you realize," I stated.

She gave me a puzzled look, intrigued at the innuendo. "What do y—?"

A massive explosion suddenly erupted overhead, shaking the mountaintop. I dropped immediately to the ground, as did Tess from reflex. Head buried in my arms, I chanced a look at our surroundings. Falling chunks of flaming debris were landing everywhere like volcanic ash. I pushed myself up and gained my feet under me, coming to a wobbly stand.

"Are you okay?" Tess demanded, eyeing her body critically.

My ears rang. "What the hell?" My gaze searched the blazing sky, registering that the hulking goliath resting above only moments before was no longer.

"God, Casa! The ship. It's gone. Jett's done it," Tess cried.

Fury swelled up in me, and something else. Fear? Regret? Loss?

Jett!

"He said he was going to disable it. Not blow it the hell up!" Dizziness overcame me, causing me to barely register Tess's voice, telling me to move to avoid some fiery ash.

"Casa! Snap out of it," she called, her voice sounding far away.

"Jett. He was up there." How could she be so calm? Why wasn't she falling apart the way I was about to?

She came up close to me and reached out, ghostly hands passing through my arms.

"He's not up there, dolt! He was in one of their bodies. Pull it together!"

I shook my head, desperately trying to focus on the meaning of her words.

"You—you're right! Shit, I forgot. His body is in the cavern.

His real body." Relief washed over me.

"Let's get there then," Tess said matter-of-factly.

"Right. Okay, yeah. Let's go," I agreed, my brain suddenly working overtime. Jett was in there all right. In the cavern. Not resting in a human pod, as Tess believed. But in one of the alien ones. In his alien body.

CHAPTER 29

"Tess." I hesitated inside the entrance of the cavern to which I'd just recovered with brush.

She paused. "Yeah?"

"There's some things I need to get straight with you before we go in there." I indicated the long tunnel ahead.

"You're not gonna lay into me for leaving Mom and Dad to smoke, are you?"

"No. It's about what you're going to see in there. I want to prepare you."

"You got those bastards trapped, right? The ones you ghosted?" She appeared to ponder a moment. "Oh, though I guess they're gone now, right? Both their bodies just blew up with the ship."

I nodded. "Yeah, their ghosts will be gone too." We obviously assumed that Jett blew up with the mother ship. It hardly seemed likely he'd bother to steal a fighter and fly off before the explosion.

She studied me with a narrow gaze. "Why are you so mopey? This was a win. A big one, thanks to Jett. Really, I can't wait to meet him — well, again — and shake his hand, as soon as I'm back in my own body. Will you be able to remove him from stasis yourself? Then we can get me and you back where we belong."

"That's the thing I want to talk to you about," I informed her.

"Hey, what happened to Ben? Last I saw you, you two were together. Is he okay?"

How was I going to explain this? "Ben is fine," I assured her. "I think maybe the best thing to do is just show you."

She shrugged. "Okay."

I gestured ahead, and we started through the tunnel. She stopped so suddenly at the end that I walked right through her.

"Shit. Is this what you were talking about? Look at them. All of them." She meant the pods, row upon row.

"These are the alien pods they've been hiding away. And yeah, before you look, they're full. Their bodies are different than ours. Little, fragile. They can only last so long in Earth's gravity before it eventually crushes them internally."

"How terrible. So this is what all the fuss was about. The whole grand scheme with Ghost Walk. All so they could take our bodies. I know they'll never admit to it, but I think they're the ones who caused the plague in Tuck."

"None of that matters now," I reminded her. "The greatest threat is the Srotagillas."

"And now there's less of them," she remarked with a smug smile.

She strode ahead and began stalking past the alien pods towards the human ones placed along the far side. I knew what she was doing. She was trying to figure out which one Jett was in. "Tess."

"What?" She stopped suddenly. "Hey. Ben is in here!" She stood at the first pod, the one Jett and I had moved aside. "Why is Ben here? What happened?"

I came up beside her and stared down at my friend, feeling so many emotions. "I haven't been entirely truthful." A small tremor passed through Tess's body, and I wondered if it was going through nicotine withdrawal.

She stared at me, her eyes drawn to my clenched fists.

"When you saw me with Ben, it wasn't exactly him," I began.

"What do you mean?"

"I mean, it was Ben's body, but it wasn't Ben's ghost. It was Jett's." I watched her as she pondered my words.

"Okay. So where is Ben?"

"That's the thing. I don't know. All these aliens here are inhabiting human bodies. Where the ghosts are is anyone's guess. Kade hasn't said."

"But Kade said it was only him and Anna who were residing in hosts," Tess reminded me.

A lie. One of many. "Lies, Tess. Kade told many of them in order to get the world on board with an allegiance against the reptiles."

"You're saying all of them are walking around in human form right now, but no one knows where the human ghosts are?" she asked, gesturing at the alien pods.

"Kade knows. He's not fessing up, though."

"Holy shit."

"Yeah, holy shit," I agreed. "There's more."

She visibly gathered herself, digesting what she'd learned. "Okay. Lay it on me."

"Jett is also an alien. Now, before you go off, I want you to know he's been helping us since the beginning. He's against what Kade and the others are doing. He took Ben's body, but he broke Ben's ghost out of Tandem, where they were holding him. I met up with them when I came up here the second time."

"Ben knows Jett's in his body? Is he pissed?" she asked, eyes bulging.

I shook my head. "No, he was okay with it. He told me that before he was recaptured by Tandem. He knew Jett was helping us. Before the Srotagillas arrived, Jett showed me this place. He and I made a video and broadcast it to the world, warning everyone about Tandem being run by aliens and their intention to use our bodies. That Ghost Walk was a sham. Jett did that, despite the risk, despite him being one of them."

"Okay," Tess said, appearing slightly appeased.

"Anyway, it doesn't matter right now—one problem at a time. The biggest problem is saving Earth from the reptiles. At least Kade came clean—sort of. Now the world knows about him and the others and we're working together. It's in both our interests." I didn't want to tell her about the million more of them due to arrive.

"How are we supposed to trust anything Kade says?"

"Good question. But we don't have much choice right now. They have the technology. They know the enemy better than we do. We need them." I also didn't want to reveal the reason we were being attacked in the first place was due to Kade.

Tess wandered over to one of the alien pods and glanced within. It took her a moment to comment. "You weren't kidding. They are fragile. I can practically see inside it. The skin is so transparent."

"When they crash landed here over a decade ago, they used salvaged tech to carve out the mountain for a base. The ones who did it wound up dying. They need our bodies to survive here."

"It doesn't justify stealing them. Despite the cures they offer, they should have come clean from the beginning," she insisted.

"Jett said the same thing. Speaking of Jett, let's wake him up.

The sooner we do, the sooner we can get you back in here."
indicated her body, and she nodded in agreement.

Jett had shown me which pod contained his alien body
Looking down on him, I could hardly quantify what I saw now
with the guy I'd come to know. Would my feelings change fo
him once I saw him walking around as who he truly was? Wer
my feelings for him only skin deep? I guess I'd soon find out
Carefully I lifted the lid of the pod. Tess came up beside me a
Jett slowly came around.

The wafer-thin eyelids jerked from side to side. Long narrow
fingers with tiny white nails wiggled around.

"Jett? Can you hear me?"

His eyes peeked open as though hesitant to awake from
slumber. His thin lips puckered.

Reaching in, I took his small cool hand in mine. "Jett?"
called softly.

The little mouth formed an O. "Casa," he faintly whispered

"I'm here," I assured him, watching him struggle to suck ai
into his chest cavity. I knew that feeling well. "I'm going to lif
you now."

Gently, I got one hand under his shoulders, the other hand
under his knees. Once he was cradled in my arms, I carried him
to the nearest free table. He trembled, so I hurried to the alcov
and grabbed a blanket to cover him. When I tucked it under hi
chin, I met his gaze.

"Thank you," he croaked.

I nodded, not trusting myself to speak. When I'd held him
he'd felt so light—like a child.

"You did a brave thing up there," I told him.

He looked away.

Tess came over and looked down at Jett. Her blank expression made it impossible to gauge her emotions.

"I want to put him back into Ben's body." Before she could argue, I justified my decision. "We still need his help, and I can't leave him like this. He'll die."

Tess rolled her eyes. "Fine."

"Are you strong enough for me to pull you out and put you into Ben?" I asked Jett.

His light bulb-shaped head bobbed once. I lifted him into my arms again and brought him over to the table before the transference case. It only took a few minutes before Jett's ghost was pulled free.

Our eyes met.

I'd seen him in his ghost form earlier when I'd pulled him out of Ben before putting him into the reptile. Freeing Tess had been so paramount in my mind that his alien form had hardly registered with me. I smiled at him now before turning my attention to his alien body. Gently I returned it to the pod and closed it up again. Then I wheeled a table to Ben's pod and lifted the lid.

As I contemplated the much larger, heavier body, Tess joined me.

"All you gotta do is get him on the table," she said.

"Yeah." Easier said than done.

I put my hands under his knees and bent them upward towards his body. Using his legs as leverage, I pulled hard and managed to get him half turned. After several minutes of shifting, grunting, tugging, and pushing, I eventually managed to get Ben out of the pod and onto the table. I wheeled him over before the transfer tech.

As I hit the switch, I heard Tess say, "See you soon, little dude."

Once the transfer was complete, Ben's body gave a little shake. I was standing there when he opened his eyes. This time he held my gaze.

"You okay?" I asked.

"Yeah," he whispered. "I'm sorry —"

I held up a hand. "Save it. I understand. I wish you'd have warned me first."

Tess came over and stared at Jett as he scrambled to pull himself into a sitting position.

"That was pretty bad, obliterating those scaly turds," she told him.

He smiled tightly.

"Now get your ass in gear. As fun as all this has been, I want my body back," she said.

CHAPTER 30

Tess and I were soon back where we belonged, our ghosts residing in their rightful bodies. The first thing Tess did was reach inside the pocket of her jacket and grab her pack of smokes and a lighter.

"Really?" I asked, watching her light one up and take a deep drag.

She blew out the smoke slowly, eyes closed, clearly savoring the experience. "What? I'm stressing out here. I need one—it's been like hours," she said defensively. "Anyway, what do you want to do now? Should we stay put? Find Mom and Dad and the others? Find Kade?" Her hard look at Ben's body warned me there would soon be a reckoning between them despite my insistence of his good intentions.

"We need to find Kade," Jett decided.

"I think he already knows what happened," I informed him.

"Unless he missed the giant overhead explosion," Tess said with sarcasm.

Jett ignored Tess's obvious disdain for him. "The ship may be gone, but there's still a bunch of fighters and reptiles on the ground. We're still in danger."

"Then maybe you should stay here. That's not a disposable body you're wearing now," Tess reminded him.

Jett drilled her with a glare. "Have you got something to say to me? After we risked a lot going up there to save you?"

His words failed to have the desired effect. "The only thing you risked was my own body, thank you very much. And it seems you had ulterior motives for being up there anyway," she snapped.

He shrugged. "I merely took advantage of the opportunity."

"I bet you do that a lot," she responded.

"Will you two knock it off?" I said. "Holy crap, enough already." When they quieted, I wondered what Jett hoped to gain in finding Kade. "Why do you want to risk heading out there now? You know the remaining reptiles will be pining for blood."

He stared at me and then at Tess, as though unsure about what to reveal. "To tell him, you know...."

"Tell him what?" Tess's eyes narrowed.

I sighed. "Might as well tell her." Not like it'd make her distrust him any less.

"Tell me what?" Tess demanded.

"That this whole invasion is aimed at Kade. A vendetta that began on my planet," Jett informed her.

Tess opened and closed her mouth a few times. "You're telling me those reptiles are here because of Kade?"

"Yes. It's obvious they stole the ghosting tech from our planet after we fled. We saw a few pods and transference chambers, but they must have more," Jett speculated.

"Why do you think that?" I asked.

"Because unless they rotated a lot, or bred vengeance into the next generation, they've been chasing us for fifty years," Jett replied.

"Fifty years! What the hell did Kade do to piss them off so much?" Tess demanded.

"Killed their commander's son," I revealed.

Tess pondered the revelation. "Your ship crashed here over ten years ago. Why now? How did they finally find you here?"

Here came the fun part.

Jett didn't look happy about what he was about to say. "Kade's been sending out a signal. The Srotagillas heard it."

"What kind of signal? To who?" Tess asked, narrowing her eyes.

He took a deep breath and plowed on. "We weren't the only ship to flee Cambrius. As far as we know, we are the only ones to find a hospitable planet. Kade had a duty to inform the others since returning home isn't an option."

"The Srotagillas destroyed Cambrius — the Teratilas' planet," I filled her in.

"And did your people receive the message?" Tess asked, her face grim.

"Eventually, yes," Jett responded. "Just recently."

"So more of you are coming here? Something else Kade failed to inform the higher-ups when he was begging for their help," Tess surmised.

Jett could only nod in agreement.

"Isn't that just great? Not only will we have the reptiles to deal with, but we'll also have an invasion of the body snatchers to boot."

"Tess." I put my hand on her shoulder.

She stiffened and pulled away. "You knew about this!" She glared her betrayal at me.

"One problem at a time," I reminded her. "If the Teratilas

arrive soon, they have the ability to deal with the Srotatillas."

"What a choice!" Tess snapped. "Earth invaded by two sets of aliens, and the winner takes all."

"At least the world knows about Kade's kind now. And they can offer cures for millions of terrible conditions," I said.

"All for the small price of unlimited Earthly bodies for their use," Tess retorted.

"It won't be like that," Jett said. "We can figure things out. But Casa is right. One problem at a time. Right now, we need to put our fears and differences aside and work together."

"Fine," Tess snarled. "I don't like it, but I'll do it. For now." She dropped her smoke on the ground, crushed it out with the heel of her boot, and promptly lit another.

"I still don't see why we need to risk our necks to find Kade. The reason for the reptiles being here isn't going to make any difference in how we deal with the matter," I said.

"You're probably right." He ran a hand over his face in agitation. His obvious exhaustion, no doubt, matched mine despite my body's recent nap.

"If your people aren't here by now, maybe they're not coming," Tess speculated.

"And now that Tandem is destroyed, the signal won't be sending, so they may not even know where to look, even if they are on their way." I supposed I should have felt somewhat bad for the Teratila race, floating around in outer space desperate for a home. But my fear of their arrival far outweighed my sympathy for them. It didn't seem likely that they'd show up "guns blazing," as Jett had warned. Most likely, they'd see the lizard ships and pass right on by. Maybe they'd already done so. I hardly imagined them fighting alongside humans to liberate us.

"No. The signal was sent from our ship that crashed in the

mountain. The deck was still in pretty good shape. And I have no doubt that Kade has it shielded, as well as this place," Jett informed us.

I thought for a moment. "The ship. I wonder if that's where Kade stashed all the ghosts."

Jett's eyes opened wide in awareness. "Damn. I bet you're right. Hardly anyone goes there but Kade. It'd be the perfect location. It's certainly big enough. Not that you need a ton of room to store ghosts."

"Can we get to it from here?" I asked.

Jett shrugged. "Probably. I haven't been there in years. If the tunnels aren't destroyed, we may be able to find it."

"Kade can't keep covering them up if they're out in the open," Tess said. "It'd give us an advantage if we could set them free. That is if we can win the fight against the reptiles. Otherwise, I guess it doesn't really matter."

From the rebellious look on Jett's face, I could see he struggled with the fact that his brother could still be up to no good. He couldn't hide from the fact that Kade hadn't been entirely forthcoming with the truth.

"Okay. Let's see if we can get there," he relented. He headed for the weapons alcove first and urged us to arm ourselves just in case.

"If we can make it to the ship, maybe we can get some idea of how things are going with the battle over the rest of the world," I speculated.

"Yes. We should be able to communicate with others from there," Jett agreed.

We headed out, moving stealthily down the snaking tunnels, forced to reroute many times when sections became impassable. It was a long while before Jett finally announced we were close.

He stopped suddenly, and I walked into his back.

"Hey! What is it?" I asked. The tunnel we followed abruptly opened up into another cavern, not as large as the others, and having the appearance of being carved out haphazardly, in a rush. A huge mass of metal, half-buried in rock and dirt, rested ahead. I assumed it was the ship.

"There's light ahead," Tess said, pointing to it with her cigarette.

And indeed, there was. "Is it from the ship?" But then I saw it moving around from behind what appeared to be small glass windows.

"Someone's inside," Jett said.

"Who though?" Tess demanded.

Jett began moving forward at a more sedate pace. "I've no idea."

We came up before a large hatch that was obviously a main door into the ship. The control panel beside it had a bunch of strange symbols on a keypad. Jett punched in a code, and the door creaked upward. We stepped inside what I guessed to be an airlock chamber, the door closing behind us with a loud clang. I figured this was where people would get on and off the ship if it landed, maybe allowing decontamination judging by the sterility and the several small nozzles placed on the walls and overhead. It probably also functioned as a security feature, having to pass through another door with a large thick window, allowing the crew to make sure any unwanted guests didn't breach the ship. Again, Jett used a keypad to enter a code to open the door. We went through that one as well, it clanging down behind us, echoing around the vast space. From where we stood, the only lights I saw now were the wall sconces placed along the three corridors branching off from our area.

"Which way to the main deck?" I whispered.

Jett indicated the direction. Tess and I flanked him as he started off. He'd drawn his weapon before we even entered the ship. Now, I drew a hand laser from my belt, and from the corner of my eye, I saw Tess pull out something as well. I hoped it wasn't another smoke.

We soon stood before the door leading to the bridge.

Jett had to enter another code into the side panel to open the door. As soon as it swished up, we saw the source of the moving light we'd seen earlier. Anna stood before a command center of high-tech instruments, a palm light in her hand. Beside her stood Kade.

CHAPTER 31

"Kade?" Jett began.

Both heads swiveled in our direction, each sporting a look of annoyance and surprise.

Anna had levelled her weapon at us but lowered it once recognition registered.

"Looks like you had the same idea as us," Kade said, a tight smile on his lips.

Jett moved closer to get a look at the overhead monitors that were set up similarly to the command center in Tandem. There were five of them, each showing a major city on Earth. It took a moment to dawn on me what was different about them.

"The ships," I said, confused. "The other ships. They're gone." Had they gotten word, the one over Tuck had exploded, and they were rushing here now in retribution? The screens flashed, showing other cities, all with the same scene—empty skies. I focused on the screen showing the sky over Tuck now—blissfully empty, except for the scores of motherless fighters circling around in confusion. There was no way I was going to hope that the others had fled back into space.

"What's going on?" Jett asked. Tess just stood there with her mouth gaping.

Kade beamed. "Don't be afraid. At first, I didn't understand it either. But then I realized what I was seeing. The other ships, they weren't real. Only the one over Tuck was."

"Wait. What?" I asked; sure, there was no way we were gonna be that lucky. "What about the power? It was out all over the world."

Kade nodded. "One ship has the ability to cause a major power disruption. I believe it won't be long until power is restored."

"But why? Why the grand hoax?" Jett asked. "Did they really think we wouldn't figure it out?"

Kade looked pensive for a moment. "Knocking out the power prevented us from seeing what was happening elsewhere — for the most part. It caused a huge panic. Each city wound up focusing on their immediate safety and not rushing to where the real threat was."

"Pretty clever," Jett said.

"Yes," Kade agreed. "It did the trick." He frowned for a moment. "The thing I can't figure out is why? Why here? Although, it stands to reason they followed the signal from this ship. Maybe they figured we were the biggest threat they faced." He looked at me. "No offense to Earth."

I nodded, waiting for Jett to burst his bubble.

"Um, Kade. We've been through some stuff," Jett began.

Kade and Anna both stared at him curiously. "What stuff?" Kade asked.

"It was my fault," Tess blurted. "I snuck off for a smoke, and I got taken by a lizard."

"No!" Kade and Anna exclaimed.

Tess nodded and lit another smoke.

"They brought her to the mothership and ghosted her. Replaced her with one of them so she could infiltrate our group. They were—" Jett stared at Kade uncertainly.

Kade stared back, waiting for him to continue.

Jett exhaled loudly. "They wanted you," he said.

"Me?" Kade responded. "Why?"

"Because this whole invasion was about you!" I couldn't help my outburst. Deep down, I knew it wasn't Kade's fault—at least not intentionally. But so many lives had been lost. Even though the arrival of the Srotagillas had made Kade fess up to the world about the Teratilas' existence, it had come at a great cost.

"I don't understand," Kade said, staring hard at me, then Jett.

Jett looked embarrassed. "We ran into Tess at the bottom of the mountain. But it wasn't Tess. She was disoriented and said your real name. That was a dead giveaway. She was a lizard parading as Tess. We put it together. They had Ghosting tech. They must have stolen it when they invaded us decades ago. Anyway, another fighter landed, and we were able to knock him out and take him and his ship and Tess back up the mountain. We got Tess into the pod cavern. After we pulled the Srotagillas out of her, we trapped it in a force field and stashed it. Then we put Casa into Tess's body. She was able to lure the other lizard from the fighter into the cavern, him thinking Tess was still occupied by one of them. Once there, we knocked him out again and ghosted him. I was put into his body."

"You went into him?" Kade asked incredulously.

"There was no other way to get on the ship," Jett said defensively.

"Get on their ship!" Kade exploded.

"Cool your jets," Tess said, actually defending Jett.

"Once I was in the reptile, I had a conversation with the

other one, who thought I was one of them. He revealed in anger that this whole invasion was a vendetta against you," Jett said. "Remember when we were first invaded on Cambrius? We launched that counterattack, and we took prisoners."

Kade had the sense to look ashamed.

"Well," Jett continued. "One of the reptiles you had tortured and killed was a commander's son. He is the one who's been roaming the skies with our Ghost tech searching for you for payback."

"Are you kidding me?" Anna finally spoke.

"I wish I was," Jett told her.

Kade sat down heavily on one of the flight seats. "I can't believe it. All this time."

"They've been looking for you for fifty years," I said. From the look on his face, I detected genuine regret. At least I hoped that's what it was.

"They picked up the signal you sent out to our ships. Followed it here," Jett said.

"This is all my fault," Kade said, his voice almost a whisper.

Could it be he was kicking himself for not seeing through the ruse? For coming clean with humans and exposing his own perfidy?

"Kade, I have something to ask you," I said.

He stared at me blankly, still too focused on what Jett revealed.

"Where are the ghosts? All of them? Are they on this ship?" I watched him carefully. "I know you didn't reveal that part of your story to the world leaders, and I understood it at the time. But now, it's time to let them go."

"They— Yes. They're here. I was going to let them go. I swear it, Casa. As soon as we won. I couldn't take the risk until that time."

"Well, no time like the present," Tess snarked.

"Wait." He stared at Jett. "You were the one! You blew them up."

Jett grinned. "Yessir."

Kade got to his feet, went over, and pulled Jett in for a tight hug, slapping him on the back a couple of times. He stood back and looked at each of us. "Thank you. All of you."

Tess blushed.

"Casa. If you want to come with me, I'll take you to the others," he said.

I watched him closely for any signs of deceit. There were none, so I smiled.

Just as we started off towards the door, the monitors started going mad, sounding an alarm. All our eyes darted back to the screens, scanning them for signs of danger.

"What's going on?" Tess demanded. "What's happening? Are we under attack?"

I couldn't detect anything wrong. The pictures appeared undisturbed except, of course, for the disoriented fighters over Tuck.

Anna fiddled with the controls at the helm, and the annoying beeping quieted. Then suddenly, another sound filled the room. Crackling at first, it took a second to register it was coming from the radio.

"Alto, mettleforitom dettno," came a voice.

"What the hell is that?" Tess asked.

Jett stared at me in shock, then looked at Kade and Anna before returning his gaze to me. "It's Teratillian," he informed me.

Kade looked me in the eyes, his face unreadable. "It means

'We have arrived.'"

Six Months Later...

It took two months for Kade to get the world on board with his grand plans.

Being that humanity was fully aware of the Teratilas' presence on Earth and the fact they had nowhere else to go, things had eventually been hatched out between the two species. A huge factor in the aliens' favor — one that couldn't be ignored — was the benefit of all the cures they offered.

It'd been far from smooth sailing.

There were a lot of feathers to unruffle, especially when Kade had followed through with his promise to me and freed the over one thousand ghosts he'd been hiding in the mountain. That had resulted in weeks of questioning and criticizing from the powers that be and much back-pedaling and apologies from Kade and his cronies. To his credit, Kade owned up to everything.

Well, almost.

We all agreed that any suspicion there'd been about him being responsible for the plague in Tuck would be forgotten. In the name of peace, I'd allowed him that concession.

The first thing that had to happen was for Kade to relinquish his body to the real Kade, along with all the aliens who were catching a free ride on the human-express. Lawsuits were discussed and neatly diverted with the offer to the victims to be first in line for free healings for life, not to mention unlimited free access to all the perks Ghost Walk tech offered for adventure-seekers and explorers. The deal included their families as an added incentive.

The idea of putting the tech to use with the incarcerated was surprisingly fully embraced by almost everyone, behind bars or not. The first to try out the jailhouse bodies were the Teratilas, considering their brains and technology were needed to pull all this off.

About three months ago, I'd been surprised and unexpectedly thrilled when Ben—the real one—paid me a visit. He'd had with him a quiet, unassuming young man, blond hair, six-foot, dazzling smile, sporting big muscles and some tattoos—Jett. I couldn't resist looking him up online on the "Newly Occupied" database that'd been set up, mainly to avoid people flooding police departments with calls about on-the-run convicts. The guy Jett wore was eighteen and serving time for small-time fraud. His three-year sentence would be reduced after one year if he allowed the occupation of his body. Of course, he'd taken the deal. It was the same with most of the others as well, allowing the swap out in exchange for reduced sentences. The main stipulation was that only the criminals serving time for minor offenses—not murder, rape, or violence—were considered for occupation. After Jett was evicted from his newest body, I assumed he'll take over another one.

The arrival of the Teritilas' ships had not been as bad as expected. And to his credit, Kade came clean about them as well. Only two ships with a total of two thousand more aliens arrived.

The new technology they offered to put aside any doubts Earth had about accommodating them. As far as the new arrivals knew, their other ships were still out searching the universe for a place to call home. If they ever happened to arrive on Earth, we'd have to deal with that situation when and if the time came.

Kade never revealed — as far I know — the real reason for the invasion of the Srotagillas. The only ones who knew had been in the control room of his buried ship; Anna, Jett, Tess, myself, and of course, Kade. All of us had agreed it would do no good to anyone to reveal this information.

Things in Tuck went back to normal. The army left, and construction was well underway to repair the damage to the town. One of the buildings that hadn't been hurt — to Tess's dismay — was the high school. I officially enrolled, and I've actually made a few friends. This small town isn't so bad. We've all grown to like it here. Tess and I are as close as we were before — hardly any trace of the weirdness between us lingers. I guess it helps I'm not a ghost anymore. I've connected with the others of our six from the program on social media and some in person. I had been especially glad to hear Mason's mom and Dad made up, and she moved back to Tuck. Mason enrolled in school here, sharing some of my classes and dodging Tess's unending attempts to get him to ask her out.

Jett still lives and works at Tandem, which was one of the first buildings to be repaired. We're dating, and I have to admit, I think I'm starting to fall for him. I know things will be strange for us, especially considering the body-surfing he'll be required to do if he wants to walk the Earth.

My mom put herself into rehab, finally admitting she had a problem with alcohol. She was gone for a couple of months, and since she's returned, I noticed she's trying hard to rebuild her relationships with all of us.

My dad is ever stoic, the one we all lean on when things get too dicey to muddle through alone. With two teenaged daughters, he has his share of drama.

The world is different now. No longer do we gaze up at the stars and wonder, "Are we alone?"

Now we know.

There's some scary shit out there. And some good stuff too. In the end, I think we're all the same. Just trying to survive.

I'm glad the Teratilas came, despite all the awful shit that went down.

My body is healthy. My family is mending. Relationships are being restored.

Who could ask for more?

About the Author

Julie is a long-time resident of Hamilton, Ontario, where she lives with her husband of 25 years. She has two grown sons who recently left the nest. Working in a library for several years inspired her to pursue her long-time love of writing. Please check out her website http://www.julieparker.net

Made in the USA
Middletown, DE
09 February 2021